Dear Mr. Redtree,

I know you write stories for the newspaper. I have something <u>VERY</u> <u>IMPORTANT</u> for you to write about. I think it would be good for you to write about the effects of divorce on kids and their dogs. My mom and dad are splitting up even though they are still in love, and I think that's really dumb. <u>Please help!!</u>

Victoria Sloane
(and her dog)

Dear Reader,

Sometimes your life can change in a heartbeat. For the residents of Grand Springs, Colorado, a blackout has set off a string of events that will alter people's lives forever....

Welcome to Silhouette's exciting new series, 36 HOURS, where each month, heroic characters face personal challenges—and find love against all odds. This month, Karen and Cassidy Sloane's marriage is on the rocks, and their young daughter may be the only person who can make them see that they are still very much in love....

Next month, amnesia victim "Martin Smith" finds love— and his true identity—thanks to beautiful librarian Juliet Crandall. And when "Martin's" memory finally returns, all of Grand Springs' secrets will be revealed! Don't miss the exciting conclusion of 36 HOURS, available only from Silhouette Books!

Sincerely,

The editors at Silhouette

36 HOURS

THE PARENT PLAN

PAULA DETMER RIGGS

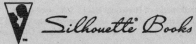

Silhouette Books

Published by Silhouette Books

America's Publisher of Contemporary Romance

Special thanks and acknowledgment are given to Paula Detmer Riggs for her contribution to the 36 HOURS series.

For Carrie Brock, Kris Denney, Judy and Ladene Culp. Friends and fellow writers. Thanks for the pleasure of your company.

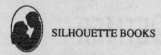 SILHOUETTE BOOKS

THE PARENT PLAN

Copyright © 1997 by Harlequin Books S.A.

ISBN 0-373-65016-7

PAULA DETMER RIGGS

discovers material for her writing in her varied life experiences. During her first five years of marriage to a naval officer, she lived in nineteen different locations on the West Coast, gaining familiarity with places as diverse as San Diego and Seattle. While working at an historical site in San Diego, she wrote, directed and narrated fashion shows and became fascinated with the early history of California.

She writes romances because "I think we all need an escape from the high-tech pressures that face us every day, and I believe in happy endings. Isn't that why we keep trying, in spite of all the roadblocks and disappointments along the way?"

Paula has won two Career Achievement Awards from *Romantic Times* and is a five-time RITA Award nominee. Her books have appeared on the *USA Today* list. In addition to her numerous Silhouette titles, she is also writing mainstream fiction for Ballantine.

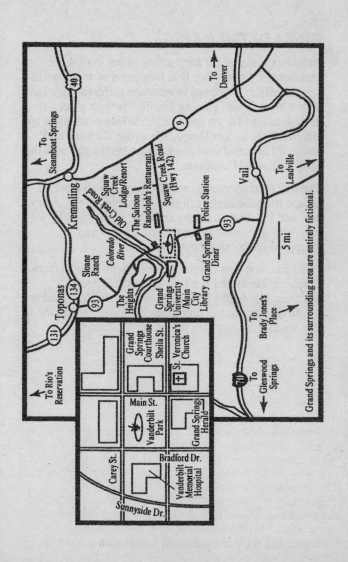

Grand Springs and its surrounding area are entirely fictional.

Prologue

Saturday, June 7
Lazy S Ranch.

Dr. Karen Sloane was used to working under pressure. In med school, she'd found out she was a wimp when it came to dealing with the suffering of others and she'd trained herself to remain absolutely steady, her mind clear, her reflexes lightning quick. But now, standing alone near the makeshift canteen just beyond the glaring spotlights that bathed the side of Devil Butte in brilliant light, she was close to shattering.

Silhouetted by the harsh glow, rescue workers in protective clothing and miners' helmets struggled to reach the spot below a thick slab of red rock where her eight-year-old daughter, Victoria, was trapped in the entrance of an unknown cave. Torrential rains had tumbled tons of rock and earth from the face of the butte, exposing the dark pit.

In the past ten hours since her arrival, she'd experienced shock, disbelief, terror, and finally a numb misery that increased minute by minute. Only one thing remained constant. Vicki was alone in that pit—and time was running out.

Karen had been on duty at Vanderbilt Memorial when Cassidy had called around ten that morning, and told her to come home. She could still hear the raw note in her husband's distinctively husky voice, the stark undertones of desperation. The unspoken plea for help.

Somehow she'd managed to get through the roadblocks and detours set up by the state police, and she'd reached the site to the west of the main house shortly after Lieutenant Brendan Gallagher and the fire department's mountain rescue unit had begun on the rescue shaft now angled down toward her little girl.

Cassidy had been like a crazy man, shouting at Bren to let him help, threatening his poker buddy with castration and worse if Bren didn't give him something to do. Something, anything. If he had to, he'd claw his way to his daughter with his bare hands.

Catching sight of Karen half running, half stumbling down the mud-scoured slope, Bren had silently pleaded with her for help. She'd put aside her questions long enough to coax Cassidy away from the knot of grim-faced, dedicated men. A shiver transited her spine at the wild suffering she saw in his eyes. And for an instant she wasn't sure he even knew who she was. And then his arms crushed her to him, his need a living thing.

Between hard shudders, he told her about Vicki's trip to the butte with her dog Rags and her regular baby-sitter, Wanda June, to watch the clouds. About the tons of mud that had torn down the hill. And told Karen of their little girl's sudden disappearance and Wanda's frantic search of the area before she'd run across the storm-ravaged pastures to find Cassidy.

It had been Rags who'd led him to the raw gash in the granite.

The torn flesh of Cassidy's face and hands bore testimony to his attempts to reach their child. But his shoulders had been too broad to allow him to reach into the black pit where Vicki had been trapped.

Knowing her husband's almost irrational fear for his daughter's safety, Karen had a good idea how terribly he'd been suffering when he'd all but ridden a gelding into the ground in order to call for help. She suspected, too, that leaving Vicki with only Wanda and Rags to guard the site had almost torn him apart.

But when Karen tried to comfort him, he suddenly stiffened, as though jerked out of a terrible nightmare. His face twisted, his head snapped up. The arms that had bruised her flesh, so tightly had they held her, relaxed.

Suddenly he was in control again, his gaze steely, his emotions shuttered safely, as he jerked his hat from his head, placed it on hers and ordered her into taking his slicker, all the while castigating her for not wearing a jacket, for driving too fast, for a half dozen things she no longer remembered.

It was Cassidy's way. Reaming her out while at the same time making her breakfast after she'd worked a late shift the night before. Growling orders at her as though she were one of his hands even as he put in endless hours helping her paint Vicki's room or till the garden plot.

Maybe he never said he loved her in so many words, but a woman knew when she was loved. For all his firmly rooted beliefs and sometimes inexplicable opinions on the way of things, Cassidy was a gentle man at heart.

Karen was sure of it.

With a sigh, she searched for her husband's tall form. But though she recognized friends and neighbors and the whey-faced paramedic she'd helped to patch up various minor injuries, Cassidy was nowhere in sight.

Had he gone back to the house for a moment? Or taken Wanda June home to be with her family on their neighboring ranch?

But no, Wanda was still huddled into a blanket in the first aid tent, looking scared and forlorn and far younger than her sixteen years. In the stark light, her normally vibrant face was pinched and drawn.

God, but it was a hellish night, Karen thought, swiping a tired hand over her face. Somewhere to the south, lightning rent the air like the vicious slice of a scalpel while thunder crashed and rolled in its wake. The trailing edge of the storm had finally moved out around six that evening, leaving chaos in its wake. Power in the Grand Springs area had been out since last evening, and according to the reports on the radio, many roads were closed and the emergency resources were stretched to breaking.

A sudden movement to the left caught Karen's gaze an instant before Rags stuck his cold nose against her thigh. Ignoring the mud, she dropped to her knees and threw her arms around the Australian shepherd's shaggy neck. Oddly, the warm, pungent odor of dog and dirt served to soothe her in ways that nothing else could manage. Perhaps because she'd so often smelled that same combination on her daughter's skin.

"Oh, Rags," she whispered. "She has to be all right. She just has to." His tail wagged once, but his heart wasn't in it.

"Everything will turn out just fine," she murmured, her voice hollow as she got to her feet again. As hollow as the comforting words she'd shouted down at Vicki only a few minutes ago. Words that echoed obscenely in the bottomless void where Vicki waited for someone to come for her.

As though sensing her thoughts, Rags licked the hand that had fallen to her side, then turned to jog to the spot in front of the jagged hole where he'd been almost constantly since Vicki disappeared.

Her eyes filled with tears at the sight of her daughter's beloved pet waiting patiently for his mistress's return. And heaven help anyone who tried to make him move.

Oh, baby, don't give up, Karen prayed as she pulled the slicker closer to her throat. *We're coming. Daddy and I are coming for you.*

She saw Cassidy then, standing alone at the edge of the light, an intensely physical man who expressed himself with actions and kept his own counsel, taller than most, his large, well-muscled body a match for any there.

She took a hasty step, then stopped, suddenly uneasy, as he tipped back his head and looked up at the sky. There was a look of stark anger about him that almost frightened her as she, too, stared upward.

The overcast sky seemed as solid as the hard red Colorado ground, yet she knew those murky, threatening clouds contained enough water to swamp the ravine and half the ranch with torrents of angry, swirling, liquid mud, tearing down trees, scouring away precious grass, filling every crevice.

"No," she whispered, staring helplessly at the black hole in the ground. "Please, God, don't let it rain again. Please, please, don't."

* * *

Standing alone at the edge of light, Cassidy Sloane fought down a fierce need to fall to his knees and beg whatever God might be listening to spare his daughter's life. Not that it would do any good, of course. God had abandoned him a long time ago—and with good reason.

Still, somewhere in his cynic's heart, buried among unspoken longings and shameful secrets, he still hoped for a miracle. A reprieve for an innocent little girl whose only "crime" had been a desire to see the top of a cloud from the edge of the butte.

The need to plead came again, stronger this time. Almost as strong as his need to lash out at that same God. Or fate. Or even the damned weathermen who hadn't foreseen the monsoonlike deluge.

As though issuing a parting insult, thunder rolled again, more distant this time, and off toward the eastern part of his land where the stream feeding his meadows hooked toward the south.

His tired gaze fixed in that direction, Cassidy was startled from his dark thoughts by the sound of a gruff voice calling his name. Heart thudding, he spun around to find a familiar bearlike man bearing down on him.

Lieutenant Brendan Gallagher of the Grand Springs Fire Department stood a good two inches taller than Cassidy's own six-one frame and still carried most of the muscle he'd developed while representing Burke Senior High at the state wrestling finals three years running.

"How much longer, Bren?" Cassidy demanded when the man was still a half dozen strides away.

Gallagher flexed his shoulders, then swept off his battered orange helmet and set it atop a cluster of oxygen cylinders.

"Two, three hours, if the rain holds off."

"That's what you told me two hours ago, Gallagher!" Cassidy realized he had raised his voice, drawing startled looks from some of the nearby volunteers dispensing coffee and sandwiches to the exhausted men. The Ladies Aid Society from one of the churches, someone had told him.

Gallagher moved a massive shoulder. "Maybe less. Hard to say exactly."

At the exchange of words, one of the volunteers stepped away from the fire department's mobile canteen and came toward the two men, holding out two large white foam cups filled with steaming liquid.

"Coffee, Lieutenant?"

"Thanks," Gallagher muttered before eagerly lifting the cup to his lips.

"Mr. Sloane?" The plain-faced woman in an army surplus poncho thrust a cup toward Cassidy. "Would you like some?"

"No." The clipped word had no sooner passed Cassidy's lips when he realized how ungrateful he'd sounded. "No, but thanks for offering," he said, tempering his response. Tact was Karen's forte. Not his. But that didn't excuse unprovoked rudeness.

"You're most welcome." The woman hesitated, then added in a kindly tone, "I just want you to know that we're all praying mighty hard for your little girl."

Cassidy's throat worked. Asking for help for his child had been easy. Accepting it for himself was all but impossible.

"I appreciate that, ma'am. Thank you."

The woman's eyes were shiny with unshed tears as she touched his arm, then turned away to return to the beat-up wagon.

Short of patience under the best of circumstances, Cassidy nevertheless forced himself to wait while the other man drank greedily. After brutally long hours of digging, with only occasional breaks, Brendan looked played out. But in spite of his leprechaun eyes and choirboy's smile, Bren Gallagher was tempered steel, with ice water in his veins, and, according to men who'd worked under him, one tough man to cross.

At the moment, Cassidy didn't care what kind of reputation Bren carried. Nor would he let himself think of Bren as a friend. No, pared to the basics, Brendan Gallagher was simply the man keeping Cassidy from his daughter. His feisty, bright-as-a-new-penny Victoria.

Vicki to her mom. Vick to him, more often than not. His little tomboy with angel eyes the same shade of dark brown as his own, though without the jaded remoteness he glimpsed in his shaving mirror on a daily basis.

Was it only this morning at the breakfast table when she'd flung her arms around his neck and begged him to let her ride out with him to check on the horses in the south pasture?

Afraid for her safety in the lousy weather, he refused and, instead, ordered her and Wanda June to stay within sight of the ranch house. For once Vick had done what he asked, wandering through the wet fields in a wide arc less than a mile from home.

The next time he heard her voice, it had come from far below the surface where she was wedged between slabs of icy granite like a cork in a bottle, and she'd been calling feebly for help. When he answered, he'd gotten no reply.

Since then, the only constructive thing he'd done had been calling the fire department and threatening the dispatcher with mayhem if the man didn't get a crew out to the Lazy S in record time.

"Beats me how something as vile as this could taste so good," Gallagher muttered when the cup was empty.

Too anxious to be polite, Cassidy released his pent-up frustration in a rush. "Dammit, Gallagher, I've had it with standing around with nothin' to do but watch other men work. That's my kid down there. They're doin' my job."

"Right now your job is taking care of your wife."

Though calm, Bren's voice carried a ragged edge of fatigue.

"Karen doesn't need me to hold her hand." It was foolish to wish she did, Cassidy thought, his gaze searching for her small, quick form all but swallowed up by his yellow slicker. He saw the slicker first, and his favorite Stetson covering that mass of curly brown hair that she kept short because it was easier to manage that way. It was soft, gold-spun hair he'd always longed to see brushing her shoulders—or his chest when they made love.

Outlined in the eerie blue glimmer of the propane lantern,

her face was wan but composed as she bent over the table, calmly applying a large gauze dressing to a stocky firefighter's forearm. Several other men slumped against nearby rocks or sprawled on the ground, waiting their turn to be patched up.

Chiseling away a mountain of granite chip by chip was tedious, spine-jolting work, but the crew didn't dare dynamite or even use hydraulic equipment for fear of injuring Vicki in the process. But using pickaxes and chisels in such close quarters had its risks, too, mostly to the men doing the work.

At least Karen was busy, while he had nothing to distract him from his dark thoughts. As though sensing his gaze, she turned her head to look his way. Though a good fifty feet stretched between them, he felt her compassion reach out to touch him, and he felt something give way inside, leaving him feeling more vulnerable than he could handle.

Sick inside, Cassidy shifted, swiped callused fingers through his hair and studied the worn toes of his working boots, all the while grimly working to drive his stampeding emotions back into the sturdy mental corral where they belonged.

Damn, but he was tired.

"Straight talk, Bren," he grated as the other man tossed his cup into a trash container near the canteen. "What are Vicki's chances of…" He had to take a moment to corral yet another unwelcome surge of emotion. "What are her chances?"

Gallagher flexed his shoulders as though resettling some heavy burden. "If another storm doesn't move in, floodin' us out, I'd say your daughter's chances are damned good."

"Keep me posted, okay?"

Bren grinned. "You got yourself a deal." With that, he snatched up his helmet and headed toward the tunnel.

A rustle of brush had Cassidy turning suddenly to find his wife hurrying toward him. "Cassidy, what did Brendan say?" she asked in the rushed, almost breathless tone she'd acquired over the years as her schedule had become more and more crowded. "Is Vicki all right? How much longer before they have her out of that horrible hole?"

Cassidy knew enough about the caprices of nature to realize just how much Bren *hadn't* said. At the moment, however, he didn't see any reason to share his private dread with Karen. It was bad enough for her as it was.

"Bren figures three hours, maybe less."

Karen stared at him in stark distress. Tiny droplets of the moisture-laden air clung to her hair, and wispy curls clung to her neck and cheeks. "Three hours?" she whispered in aching disbelief.

"Honey, they're working as fast as they can." That, at least, was the truth.

"It's going to be all right, isn't it?" she asked, lifting her gaze. Her lashes were long enough to cast dark shadows under her wounded eyes. She looked tired and worried and terribly fragile, but it was the misery in her eyes that ripped at him in ways she would never understand.

"These guys are the best, Kari," he hedged. "They know what they're doing."

"I've been talking to her every few minutes so she won't be scared, but I don't know if she... She doesn't answer." Her voice broke and she bit her lip.

He knew the words she wanted him to say, the promises she was desperate to hear, but he couldn't make himself lie. Instead, he started to reach for her, only to be interrupted by the approach of Vicki's sitter.

The fourth of six sisters, Wanda June Peavy lived on a nearby ranch with her parents and grandparents. She had been Vicki's companion and substitute mom for the past three years, ever since Karen had graduated from medical school and started at Vanderbilt Memorial, first as an intern, and now as a resident.

"Is...I mean, I saw Mr. Gallagher talking to you," the distraught girl said in a trembling voice when she reached them.

"He thinks it won't be long now," Karen hastened to reassure the girl whose face was now tear-stained and ashen.

"It's all my fault, Dr. Sloane. I told Vicki to stay back from the edge, but I was trying to see if the clouds were moving back toward us. I heard Vicki scream, and when I t-turned back to look, she was g-gone."

"Stop blaming yourself right this minute," Karen declared in a fierce tone as she took Wanda June's cold hand in hers. "I know how stubborn Vicki can be when she's got her mind set on something."

The teenager blinked hard. "I should have been watching her closer." She dropped her gaze and shifted her booted feet. "I keep thinking, if I close my eyes and wish hard enough, I could make this all into a dream and everything would be okay when I woke up. But…I can't ever make it go away." Casting an agonized look at Cassidy, she burst out, "You hate me, I know you do! And I don't blame you. I deserve to *die!*"

His face went stark white under the deeply layered tan. "Don't ever say that again. Don't even think it," he rasped, his voice rough. "Accidents happen."

"But—"

"Enough!" He reached out to enfold Wanda June in a clumsy bear hug, his big hand awkwardly patting her back as though she were six instead of sixteen. When he lifted his head to look at her, Wanda June offered him a watery smile.

"Okay now?" Cassidy asked when the sitter's breathing evened and the trembling eased off.

"Yes, I think so."

The girl lifted her head and took a step backward. Her eyes were still damp, but Karen was relieved to see that the haunted look was gone. "Honey, you need to rest," Karen told her gently. "Why don't you go on home?"

"I'd rather stay here until…you know."

Karen drew a breath. "Okay, but I want you to wait in the truck where it's dry."

Wanda June nodded. "Call me if…when…?"

"I will. I promise."

Karen watched until Wanda's slender silhouette blended

into the darkness, then shifted her gaze to Cassidy once more. "Thank you for that."

"For what?"

"For helping her to forgive herself."

"She's just a kid, doing the best she knows how. I knew better, and I let Vicki go out in this weather, anyway." His jaw took on forbidding lines, reminding her of a man at war with an enemy only he could see, and her heart ached for him.

"Cassidy, don't." Tears stung her eyes as she reached out to touch him. He jerked away, as though wasp-stung.

"Let it be, Karen."

"No, not this time." Karen took a deep breath and, at the same time, struggled to draw strength from her rapidly depleting reservoir. "You couldn't have known that cave was there. No one knew, not even the old-timers. And a mud slide can happen anytime, to anyone."

"But it happened here, Karen. On land I thought I knew as well as my hand."

"Cassidy, what happened was a freak occurrence, a one-in-a-million accident. If you need to blame someone, blame Mother Nature, because it's not your fault any more than it's Wanda June's."

His gaze pinned her with a ruthless intensity that was as much a part of him as the aura of command he projected, even when he was asleep. And yet, sometimes, when he was tired or stressed, she sensed a terrible torment beneath the hard-edged power of the man.

"You're dead wrong, Karen," he said in flat, even tones. "It's because of *my* mistake that our daughter is down in that cold hellhole, fighting to stay alive."

"How can you say that?" she protested with a fierce gentleness. "You were on the other side of the ranch when she fell."

Some powerful but unreadable emotion blazed in his eyes for one memorable instant before the fire was extinguished. "I can *say that* because I let you go back to your precious job when I knew you belonged at home with our daughter."

Karen felt the air leave her lungs in a harsh cry of pain. In response, his mouth twisted, then grew harder.

"I knew better," he went on mercilessly, his fists knotted and his eyes blazing, "but I kept thinking you'd come to your senses."

Karen couldn't breathe, so excruciating was the pain sweeping through her, and then her training and education kicked in. Cassidy wasn't himself, that was all. He was acting out of fear and desperation, lashing out at everyone and anyone. She'd just gotten in the way. Later, when their daughter was safe, he would take her into his arms and apologize.

"I...see," she murmured carefully. "Yes, I understand how you could come to blame yourself."

Karen was already turning away when she heard Cassidy's harsh intake of breath. She took two steps, then stumbled over some unseen obstacle. Cassidy was at her side instantly, his strong arm wrapping around her waist to keep her from falling.

"Kari, I didn't mean...I don't—"

"*Cassidy! Karen! Come quick!*" It was Gallagher's voice. And his tone was urgent—and exultant! Karen was already fighting tears of relief when he added excitedly, "*We have her! Hot damn, she's safe!*"

One

March 18

As Karen turned onto Gold Rush Street where she'd lived for most of her childhood, she couldn't help smiling to herself. In one of Grand Springs's oldest neighborhoods, the thoroughfare was wide enough for four cars and lined with huge, gnarled oaks and towering cottonwood trees that covered the generous front lawns with wisps of white every summer.

After parking the car in her mom's driveway, Karen propped her arms on the steering wheel for a moment and gazed through the sun-streaked windshield at her childhood home. Built in the twenties for a bank president, the house itself had an oddly disjointed style and a seemingly random mix of red brick and shiplap siding, which always reminded her of a slightly eccentric but sweet-tempered dowager taking her ease in the sunshine.

With a weary sigh, Karen closed her eyes for a second, wondering why on earth she'd come here. Although she'd told her mother she would be stopping by to drop off some steaks from a steer Cassidy had had butchered last week, that was only an excuse. The truth was that Karen had needed to come home, if only for a while, to lick her wounds and regroup.

Back to the womb, so to speak, though, technically, her first home had been a bleak apartment above a pizza parlor. It was all that her parents, Sylvia and Fred Moore, had been able to afford on his resident's salary.

After pulling the keys from the ignition, Karen glanced at

her watch. It was a few minutes past two. If running true to form, Sylvia would be waiting with a full pot of freshly ground French roast and a tray of pastries she'd picked up from the bakery, near the bank where she had worked her way up to the position of vice president. One of the perks of her job was being able to take off unannounced for a couple of hours to spend an afternoon with her daughter.

Karen slipped from the car and trotted up the shrubbery-lined walkway to the wide front porch, where she pressed the buzzer twice to herald her arrival, then let herself in. The silence of the huge old house settled over her like a soothing cloak as she slipped off her jacket and slung it over an arm of the antique coat tree.

"Mom?"

Sylvia pushed through the louvered double doors that led from the dining room into the large living area adjacent to the tiled entry. In her slender, well-tended hands, she balanced a silver tray, steam rising from the coffee urn to create smoky ribbons before her finely sculptured face.

"Hello, sweetheart," she called as she bent to set the tray on the coffee table. "A visit from you today is just what I needed."

Karen crossed the living room to give her mother the expected hug and peck on the cheek, her mind feeling strangely separate from Sylvia's cheerful chattering. Karen accepted a cup of coffee, which she cradled absently between her cold palms as she wandered aimlessly around the living room. Her mother, enthroned in her favorite damask-covered chair near the fireplace, watched her pace.

Very little had changed over the years, Karen realized as she stopped in front of the stone-and-oak fireplace and fixed her gaze on the photos on the mantelpiece. Pain shafted through her at the memory of those carefree days. With her life full to bursting these past few years, she'd pretty much lost touch with almost all of those friends. Even Eve Stuart, who used to be her "best friend in the whole wide world," had all but drifted out of her life before leaving Grand Springs for good six years ago. Though Eve was back now and living with her new husband, Rio Redtree, and their daughter, Molly, Karen never seemed to have a moment to spare for socializing with her.

She wanted to blame Cassidy for that, but her conscience wouldn't let her. She had been the one to refuse invitations for lunch or bridge and casual get-togethers, even though it had hurt her keenly.

"Is something wrong, darling? You look a touch sad this afternoon."

At the sound of concern in her mother's voice, Karen glanced over her shoulder and shook her head in what she hoped was a reassuring denial. "I'm just tired, that's all. One of the other residents is off sick, and I'm working part of his hours as well as my own."

Even as she lifted her bone-china cup to her mouth for a sip, Sylvia Moore pleated her patrician brow in a troubled look Karen knew foreshadowed a bout of maternal probing. "Winter's officially over in three days. Perhaps you've a touch of spring fever," Sylvia suggested with just a hint of a smile, her cup clinking softly as she returned it to the saucer on the piecrust table at her elbow.

Karen grinned, though she had little hope of sidetracking her mom. "I admit I've just about had it with fighting my way from the house to my car in knee-high snow more mornings than not."

She gave a dramatic shiver before turning back to continue her study of the framed photos. Since she'd been old enough to climb on a chair in front of the fireplace, she'd been fascinated by the people in those pictures, many of whom had faces very much like hers. Her father's, especially. Karen always felt a tingle of recognition when she studied his likeness, which reminded her so much of her own.

She'd been only three when he'd kissed her goodbye that fateful morning and driven off to work. Ten minutes later, his life had ended in a car crash. A broken neck, according to the reports she'd read. Just like that, and her mother had been a widow with a child to raise by herself.

Kari and I raised each other, Sylvia invariably declared

when anyone remarked on the unusually close relationship between mother and daughter.

Smiling to herself, Karen let her gaze move farther along the display of photographs. Her mother was there, too, as well as a steady progression of photos of Karen. As a bald baby. As a Brownie and then a Girl Scout, her sash covered with merit badges. As an honor student and valedictorian of her class at Colorado State.

There were other pictures, too. Silly ones. Special ones. Her first day of medical school with her arms full of bedding and her roommate mugging in the background. Posing in her brand-new uniform as an LPN at Vanderbilt Memorial, where she'd worked double shifts in order to earn the money for the next term. Sunbathing in the backyard with an old boyfriend, Squirrely Miller Greavy. Her entire life, encapsulated on glossy paper and framed with her mother's impeccable taste.

Her breath hitched as she finally allowed herself to look at the large, formal photo framed in silver that sat all alone on one end of the crowded mantelpiece. Her wedding picture.

She felt a tickle behind her eyes as she took it from its place of honor for a closer look. A fantasy done in the colors of the sun and swirls of fairy dust.

It had been Indian summer, and the sun had bathed the small chapel in gold. Cassidy had worn the rented tux with an authority that had taken her breath away. Not even her mother's friend and long-time beau, Frank Bidwell, in custom-tailored Armani had been as impressive.

Smiling, she traced the majestic line of those wide, wide shoulders with her blunt, unpainted nail. Clark Gable shoulders, she used to tease, just to watch him scowl. He'd been scowling when they'd met, too, between colorful curses that had questioned the paternity of the two ranch hands who had hauled him into the ER on a hot day in July.

"He's all yours, ma'am," one of the crusty hands had declared prophetically before hurrying to the safety of the waiting room.

"Best not try to take his pants," the younger cowpuncher had counseled, before he, too, had abandoned her.

A wild stallion Cassidy had been set on breaking had tried to return the favor, and Cassidy had ended up at the receiving end of the horse's flashing, steel-shod hooves. Still wearing his chaps over frayed jeans and dusty boots, he'd been all but out of his mind with pain from a gash in his forehead, a severe concussion and four broken ribs, one of which had been dangerously close to puncturing a lung.

While Karen helped the nurse with his vitals, he'd told them in no uncertain terms what they could do with their pain medication, threatened Karen with unspeakable horror if she so much as reached for the buttons on his fly and worked hard on turning the air blue in the small treatment cubicle, earning him a severe rebuke from a tough ex-army nurse by the name of Helga Tutt. He'd also gone down in history at Vanderbilt Memorial as holding the unofficial record for consecutive curses without a single repetition.

It had been love at first sight—on her part, at least. But when they started dating, Cassidy's motivation had been far more direct—he'd wanted to take her to bed. While she'd been weaving romantic dreams, he'd been skillfully knocking down her virginal defenses one by one. And yet, when she'd told him about the baby, he'd kissed her with great tenderness before informing her in his usual brusque manner that they would be getting married as soon as the law allowed.

"You were beautiful that day, Kari," her mother remarked quietly, drawing Karen's gaze. "Truly radiant."

"I was scared to death," she admitted, returning the photo to the mantel.

"So was Cassidy. I've never quite seen that shade of white in a man's face before."

Karen felt a lump forming in her throat as she recalled the possessive note in his voice as he'd repeated the vows. Her own voice had been barely audible and more than a little shaky. At one point, she'd stumbled over the words, and Cassidy had given her icy hand a reassuring squeeze that had calmed her.

She'd been giddy with happiness for a long time after that. Cassidy had made no secret of his determination to grant her every wish, and he had, she reminded herself as she returned to her chair and the coffee she'd left cooling on the silver tray—until she'd made the decision when Vicki was nearly three to return to medical school for her final two years.

He'd changed after that. Each day he'd seemed to draw more tightly into himself until she'd come to feel as though she was living with a taciturn, polite—and terribly remote—roommate instead of the man she adored.

Forcing a smile, she asked brightly, "So what did you decide to wear to the reception tomorrow night?"

Her mother tossed her a saucy grin that Karen envied. "What else? My little black dress and pearls."

"Of course." Karen recalled with fondness the hours of her youth that she and her mother had spent discussing fashion and style.

"I wish Olivia was going to be at the party," Sylvia murmured after a long moment of silence. "She and I used to tease each other about who wore pearls most often." Sylvia drew a sad breath. "I still can't believe she's gone."

Karen toyed with her coffee cup, centering it on her knee, tracing the handle, then repositioning it on the chair arm. Olivia Stuart and her mother had been friends for years—since the days when their girls had been in grade school together and almost as close as sisters.

Now pictures of Eve's mom flitted gently though her mind. For all her grace and innate charm, the mayor had been a strong advocate for the underdog. She'd also been a wonderful role model, especially for young women and girls, like Vicki and her own beloved granddaughter, Molly.

"It doesn't seem possible that a wonderful person like her should have been murdered."

Her eyes dulled by sadness, Sylvia shook her head. "I talked to Rio the other afternoon when he came in to make a payment on his truck loan. He said that the police have pretty much exhausted the leads in the case."

Karen heaved a weary sigh. As a doctor, she dealt with

death nearly every day, in one way or another, but that didn't make it any easier when the Grim Reaper struck so close to home.

"I'm sure Eve and Rio will be at the party. Maybe Rio's work at the *Grand Springs Herald* has turned up new information."

Sylvia let out a long breath. "If there *is* any new information. It seems to me things like this go on forever, and sometimes they're never really satisfactorily solved. That disturbs me almost as much as losing Olivia did." She shrugged a slender shoulder. "What a pathetic tribute to someone's life." She crooked her elegant fingers to indicate quotations marks. "'Case pending.' No sense of closure. No sense of justice being done. It makes a person wonder what it's all about. You know?"

Karen understood, perhaps better than her mother realized. What *was* it all about? She'd been asking herself that question a lot lately. She had no answers.

As if Sylvia sensed how gloomy her daughter was feeling, she declared firmly, "Enough depressing stuff. Tell me about your new dress. You never did tell me what you bought."

"Probably because there's nothing to tell. I don't have anything new."

Sylvia arched an eyebrow. "But I thought that's the reason you and Vicki made a special trip to the mall last month."

Karen grinned and rolled her eyes. "That was the plan, yes, but remember me, the mother of a precocious soon-to-be nine-year-old? I'd swear she was thirteen going on twenty-five, listening to her talk. Barbie dolls are definitely behind us, I'm afraid. Now she's lusting after makeup and panty hose with a gleam in her eye that will probably throw Cassidy into cardiac arrest when he realizes what's on her mind."

Sylvia chuckled. "She is shooting up fast, isn't she?"

"Yes, scary, isn't it? Anyway, by the time we settled on the *absolutely perfect* party dress, we'd run out of time to look for something for me."

This time Sylvia's cup clattered impatiently when she returned it to its saucer. "For heaven's sake, Karen, why didn't you tell me you were short on time? You know I leap at any opportunity to shop. I'm sure I could have found you something appropriate.''

''And expensive, no doubt,'' Karen returned with a rueful shake of her head.

Sylvia arched a graceful brow again as she said airily, ''Of course. After all, you're the wife of one of our area's most successful ranchers. You deserve the best, my sweet. Something with enough pizzazz to make that tall, dark and handsome husband of yours want to rip it right off you when he sees you wearing it.''

Karen nearly choked on her coffee. ''Mother!''

''Don't 'Mother' me, Karen McCormick Moore Sloane. As you just said, Vicki is going to be nine at the end of April. It's time she had a baby brother or sister to spoil. Otherwise, she might end up as set in her ways as you are.''

''If only it were that easy,'' Karen muttered, dropping her gaze. She would not cry. She *wouldn't*.

There was a weighty silence before her mother said softly, ''Darling, I was just joking. I didn't mean to offend you.''

''I'm not offended.'' Karen closed her eyes against the sudden sting of hot tears.

''Karen? What's wrong?''

Her mother's soft cry pierced Karen's brave front, and she had to swallow hard before she could speak. ''Oh, Mom, I'm so scared. I think my marriage is in terrible trouble, and I don't have a clue what to do to fix it.''

Sylvia uttered a soft sound of dismay. ''Oh, dear.''

Not entirely sure what had possessed her to confess such a thing, Karen lifted a hand to dash away the tears trembling on her lashes, then steeled herself to meet her mother's gaze.

''Cassidy blames me for Vicky's accident. He's been punishing me for it ever since.''

Sylvia's disbelief was almost palpable. ''You must be mistaken.''

''I wish I were,'' Karen declared with weary vehemence before repeating Cassidy's words to her on that awful night in June. "I thought it was just a form of shock, that he'd lashed out because he was hurting."

"Your father was like that," her mother stated firmly. "So was my father. I've often thought it must be some kind of a defense against feeling things too deeply."

"Oh, Cassidy feels things, all right. Resentment, anger, contempt." Karen wiped the tears from her cheeks with quick angry strokes of her cold fingertips. "These days he scowls more than he smiles, and the hands are threatening to force-feed him patience. As for me, I can't seem to do anything right anymore." She drew a breath. "And the only time he smiles is when he's talking to Vicki."

"Karen, Cassidy's never been a man to smile easily, which isn't surprising, given the fact that he's virtually been on his own since his father killed himself."

That was certainly true enough, Karen reflected with a frown. Cassidy had been barely seventeen and living in Santa Fe, New Mexico, when he'd come home from football practice to find his father dead by his own hand. Since his parents had been divorced for many years by then, the grim details of his father's burial had been left to him. As soon as he'd graduated, he'd sold the house and the few other possessions his father had left him, put the money and a small insurance settlement into a savings account, and enlisted in the army.

She knew very little of Cassidy's family history—only the names of his parents and a few sketchy details of his growing-up years. He'd had a brother who died before the age of five and a mother who'd left ten-year-old Cassidy and his father shortly thereafter. All of which had given him a deep-seated need to be in control of his own destiny. Very early in their relationship, she'd realized that she was wasting her time trying to pry open a door to his past that for reasons of his own, he'd locked and bolted tight.

"There are other changes, too. More...intimate ones."

Karen felt her face growing hot. Though she and her mother had always been close, they had only discussed sex in impersonal terms. To her credit, Sylvia had always been quite open about the joys of marital relations. Karen had been the one to shy away from the explicit details.

"In other words, you're not sleeping together?"

Karen hated the wave of weary bitterness that passed over her. It was becoming as much a part of her as the indecision about her marriage.

"Oh, yes, we're sleeping together," she admitted, watching a cloud drift across the frame formed by the living room's large bay window. "On our own separate sides of the bed."

Karen mentally cringed at the memory of the last time she'd tried to snuggle up to Cassidy while he'd been sleeping. He'd jerked away from her violently, as though she'd attacked him.

"Forgive me for asking, darling, but have you considered that the problem might be...physical?"

"If you're asking me if he's impotent, he's not." The idea was laughable. Cassidy was an intensely virile man with a strong sex drive. "We still have sex now and then, but it's mechanical. Nothing more than a physical relief."

"And you believe Cassidy is to blame for that?"

"He resents my career and I resent him for resenting it." She gave a short, bitter laugh. "How's that for complex?"

"But typical of you, my darling daughter. You always were able to see two or three layers deeper than anyone else. It's part of your physician's gift, I think."

"I'm beginning to think it's more like a curse." Karen lifted a hand to rub at the beginnings of a headache behind her eyes. "Tell me the truth, Mom. If you were in my place, would you give up medicine in order to save your marriage?"

Sylvia inhaled a quick, nervous breath. "Surely it hasn't come to that?"

"Not yet, but I have a terrible feeling that's where we're headed." Karen sat forward, her hands wrapped tightly around the heavy coffee mug. "You haven't given me your answer. Would you give up part of your soul to keep the man you love?"

"I don't know, Karen. Thank goodness that was one particular dilemma I never had to face. And before you tell me that's not an answer, I agree. Mostly because there *is* no one answer.''

Karen sighed. "Coward," she grumbled.

Laughing softly, Sylvia glanced down at the worn gold band she had never once removed since her nervous groom had slipped it onto her finger almost thirty-five years ago. "Darling, forgive me for saying so, but I really think you should be having this conversation with Cassidy, not me," she said gently.

"I've tried, Mother. But the moment I bring up a topic that remotely has to do with his feelings, he just ices over."

"Perhaps if you persisted. Gently, of course."

Karen sighed. "It's difficult to persist when the person you're talking with gets up and leaves the room."

"And you let him get away with that? Tsk, tsk, Karen, I'm surprised at you. You never used to be so tractable."

"Mother, there's no 'letting' Cassidy do anything. Once he's gotten it in his head to do something, nothing will stop him.''

"Do what, exactly?"

"Put me through hell until I agree to give up medicine." Her eyes flashed. "But I won't be blackmailed like that, Mother. I love him with my whole heart and soul, but a part of me is so angry, so...so disappointed that he's behaving like some kind of feudal throwback."

"Hmm, lord of the manor. Or in this case the ranch he loves so much. That does rather describe Cassidy, doesn't it?''

Karen nodded, her burst of temper ebbing as quickly as it had come. She drained her cup, then put it aside. These days she always seemed to be running behind. As for catching up, forget it.

"I have to go," she said, flexing her shoulders.

"I'll see you Saturday night, then," her mother said, rising. "If you need anything before then, just call."

"I will," Karen promised, giving her mother a hug. "And I apologize for unloading my problems on you. I know I have to find a way to solve them myself."

Her mother's still-pretty face took on stern lines. "Karen, asking for help isn't a sign of weakness, just the opposite."

To placate her mother, Karen smiled. "Don't worry. If I need you, I'll holler."

"Sure you will," her mother said with a little shake of her head as they walked out to the car together. "Mind how you go," she said as Karen climbed into the driver's seat.

"I will," Karen said before reaching for her seat belt. As she drove off, she prepared herself mentally for the hours ahead. At the end of this shift, she would be one day closer to the end of her residency. Eight more months of brutal hours and unending stress before she could take a few months off to rest, and maybe make a start on another baby, then ease into a private practice where her time would be her own. Things between her and Cassidy would be better then.

They had to be.

TWO

Cassidy had started his day in a decent enough mood, mostly because the tattered feed-store calendar hanging inside the barn doors said it was the first day of spring and there was a hint of warmth in the morning air. The land was coming alive again.

By the end of the day, his good mood had soured. Early spring thaws had left his beautiful ranch a sloppy, ugly mess, and everywhere he'd ridden, he'd seen wind-toppled scrub oaks torn from the ravaged earth as though by some angry hand. With a resignation born of ten winters in this part of the west, he calculated he had miles of fence to repair.

Worse, the melting snow had turned the pretty little creek meandering across the north pasture into a frothing torrent of muddy water. At last count the Lazy S had lost six prime heifers to the flood, with the tally far from finished. And if the fat black clouds hugging the treetops let go, it was bound to be a rotten night to be on the road. But in a couple of hours that's exactly where he and his ladies would be, heading for the fairgrounds on the far side of Grand Springs where tonight's so-called celebration would be held.

Much as he hated the thought of hauling out his party manners and shining the almost new boots that still pinched his toes, it suited his sense of irony that the party to celebrate the town's recovery from the June blackout was occurring on a night when the weather was nearly as brutal.

He'd been saddle sore and weary when he rode in from the pasture, a long list of urgent jobs for his men already taking shape in his head. As he hurried toward the house, he'd been desperate for a hot shower, a gallon of steaming coffee and, maybe, just maybe, a quick bout of loving from his wife. Tired as he'd been, he'd gotten hard at the thought. He and Karen hadn't had sex for weeks, and he was about as frustrated as the wild stallion he'd glimpsed racing the wind on the horizon a few hours earlier.

But, when he reached the house, he found Vicki in tears, Wanda June at her wit's end and Karen late getting home again. It had nearly torn him apart to see the disappointment in his little girl's big brown eyes when she came racing out of her bedroom at the sound of the back door closing, only to find him standing there instead of her mom. According to Wanda June, Vicki had been waiting for the better part of an hour for her mother to get home.

It had taken him five harrowing minutes to narrow the problem to a hem that needed to be pinned up and sewed in place. Wanda June had offered to help, but Vicki had wanted her mom to do it. Like they'd planned, she kept telling him, her eyes flashing with impatience at his failure to understand.

He'd wanted to smash a fist into the nearest wall. Instead, he swallowed the anger that flared inside him like a familiar stab of pain and offered himself as a substitute. Which was why he was presently standing like an awkward, barefoot idiot in his own dining room, one hand clamped on a patch of flimsy cotton skirt, the other awkwardly trying to retrieve yet another tiny dressmaker's pin from the small plastic box on the table. He'd rather eat dust and wrestle fifty terrified calves on branding day than pin up a damned skirt hem.

"Darn it, Vick, hold still."

Vicki was standing ramrod stiff on the tabletop, her small pixie face screwed into a knot of worry. He winced as she let out yet another long-suffering sigh. "How much longer till you're done, Daddy?"

"Couple of minutes," he mumbled, all thumbs and masculine frustration.

"You keep saying that."

He drew a steadying breath. "Cut me some slack here, peanut. I'm doing the best I can."

One pin later she was scowling at him again. "Your hands are too big."

"Luck of the draw, peanut." Damn pins were slippery, too.

"My hands are puny, like Mommy's." She lifted her hands and glared at them. "I can't throw a rope worth spit."

"Little girls aren't supposed to throw a rope worth spit— or otherwise."

Looking down, Vicki traced an imaginary pattern on the shiny tabletop. "Did your daddy teach you how to rope?"

"No, and hold still."

"If your daddy didn't teach you, who did?"

"I taught myself." Cassidy felt sweat sliding between his shoulder blades, and his head hurt from squinting at the striped fabric. "Son of a—buck," he all but shouted when the wickedly sharp sliver of steel pierced the ball of his thumb.

"*Daddy, be careful!* You'll bleed on my beautiful dress and ruin it."

His thumb stuck in his mouth, Cassidy regarded his daughter over the tops of his callused knuckles. "I'm bleeding to death, and all you care about is your dress?" he muttered.

Vicki's dark eyes danced with mischief. "You're not very good at this, are you?" She reached up to catch hold of his hand. After giving his injured thumb a quick appraisal, she wrinkled her nose. "It's only a little prick."

Cassidy turned his thumb to assess the damage. "That is *not* a prick. That's a *wound*. Probably get infected and ruin *my* roping for a solid month."

He stuck the smarting digit into his mouth again to stop the bleeding, his indignant gaze locked with his daughter's laughing one. At least she was no longer worrying that her pretty new dress might not be finished in time for the party tonight, he congratulated himself.

Maybe he wasn't much of a seamstress, but he could still tease a smile out of his little girl, even if she did seem more grown-up and femininely unpredictable with each passing day.

"After you pin it, you have to sew it by hand," she informed him, her small mouth twitching suspiciously at the corners. "With a needle and thread, and you have to make sure the stitches are real little so's no one can see them. Mommy said."

"So you've told me about a dozen times already."

Vicki nudged her chin down far enough to direct an imperious little-girl frown his way. "Just so you know."

"I know. Believe me, I know."

Cassidy gripped the blasted hem and braced himself for another attempt. At the same time, he cast another hopeful glance at the window. At the sight of the hovering clouds, which appeared to grow more threatening minute by minute, a nagging unease gripped him.

Karen had a reliable four-by-four Blazer and a cellular phone with extra batteries, and each fall, he made sure she had new tires. Nevertheless, he hated the idea of her driving back and forth to town alone at night or when the weather was bad. One more reason to hate that precious job of hers.

"Make sure it's pinned real even, okay?" Vicki ordered with a worried frown as he tightened his hold on the material. "I don't want to look like a dork in front of my friends."

Eyeing the scrape on his daughter's right knee, Cassidy bit off a sigh of his own. Yesterday, she'd been happily running wild on the ranch in dusty jeans and a cowboy hat. Tonight she was as haughty and poised as a princess about to depart for a fancy ball. Was this yo-yoing back and forth normal for little girls? Or was he just inept at parenting? Either way, he was as worried as a greenhorn facing his first branding.

"Look, I have an idea," he said with a forced heartiness. "Why don't you wear your jeans and a nice shirt tonight? Maybe that blue one with the fancy buttons you wore to church last Sunday?"

Vicki managed to look both offended and impatient. "Because tonight is *special*, Daddy. All my friends are going to be there. And some important people from town are going to give Mommy a certificate. I can't go wearing an icky old pair of jeans."

It was special, all right, he thought sourly. Half the town

would be showing up to honor the folks who'd helped out in last June's blackout—rescue workers, firefighters and hospital staff. Grand Springs's own heroes and heroines. Since the invitation had arrived last month, Vicki had talked about little else. Her mom was a genuine *heroine,* just like in the movies or on TV.

A man had to be blind not to notice how proud Vick was. The more she talked, the more Cassidy bit his tongue. Okay, so Kari was good at her job. He respected that. But dammit, her patients weren't the only ones who needed her care and compassion and love. What about a little girl who spent more time with a sitter or hanging around the corral talking to the hands than she spent with her mom? Or a husband who was beginning to wonder if his wife would even miss him if he suddenly up and disappeared?

"Stop fidgeting, Vick," he muttered, his temper almost as frayed as the ragged edge of the pink-and-white material he was trying to hide under a little fold.

"I wish I was as pretty as Mommy," Vicki murmured with a wistful sigh.

Seeing her shoulders slump dejectedly, Cassidy felt something tear inside. Before he could shore up his defenses, he was all but overcome by an urge to wrap her up in silk and sunshine and keep her safe from all the hurts he knew waited for her. But even as he fought it off, he knew he would always feel protective toward this marvelous little miracle in pink and white.

"Trust me on this, peanut," he drawled past the lump in his throat. "You're as beautiful as the dark-haired princess in that book you read under the covers when you think Mom and I are asleep."

Vicki wrinkled her nose. "I'm way too skinny."

"No way! I'm already dreading the day when the boys start lining up outside that door there." Summoning a decent enough grin, he playfully tugged on one of her long fat braids, hoping to win a smile. When he saw a frown instead, he bit off a sigh.

"You're willowy," he assured her. "Just like those ladies in the magazines."

Vicki looked unconvinced. "Brooks Gallagher says I'm as flat as one of his skis."

"Forget Brooks Gallagher," he said as he concentrated on the last few inches of unpinned hem.

"He's always hanging around Maria Del Rio, 'cause she wears lipstick." Vicki sniffed. "And a bra."

Good Lord. A third-grader, wearing a bra? Cassidy felt a flare of helpless panic. "Don't even think about it."

"I'm only talking about lipstick."

"No."

"Oh, please, Daddy! Just for tonight."

"No!" He fought down the urge to tuck her away in her room for the next twenty years. "You're too young."

"I'll be nine in six weeks."

Had it really been nine years since he first laid eyes on the doll-sized, red-faced, squalling scrap of femininity cradled in her mama's arms? Lord, but he'd been punch-drunk with happiness that morning. And proud enough to shout his wife's praises in the streets. He'd wanted another baby as soon as it was safe for Karen to get pregnant. She'd talked him into waiting. He was still waiting. But the so-called "right time" seemed about as far away as ever, and, at thirty-five, he didn't have a lot of years to wait. Not if he wanted to be around long enough to make sure his kids had everything he'd missed—like a mom they saw for more than a few minutes every morning...and if they got lucky, a few minutes before bedtime.

"No bra and no lipstick. That's final."

"You're just mad 'cause Mommy's late," Vicki accused, more perceptive than she should be.

"I'm not mad." Cassidy felt a sudden heat spread over his face at the blatant lie. "More like...impatient."

"You are too mad. I can tell, 'cause your face gets all hard and your eyes have a funny look."

Cassidy made a mental note to exert more control on his

thoughts. "Turn a little more to your right," he muttered, squinting at the target he'd selected for the next pin.

"Daddy, how come boys don't like girls who are smarter than they are?"

Cassidy blinked. "What makes you ask that?" he hedged.

"Wanda June said I wouldn't be popular if I keep on making straight A's in school."

Wanda June should learn to keep her mouth shut. "Honey, a girl as sweet and special as you isn't going to have any trouble attracting boyfriends." He had a mental image of pimply-faced punks trying to hustle his innocent daughter out of her virginity and felt his gut twist. "When the time comes," he added with more force than necessary.

"What if it doesn't? What if no one wants to marry me?"

Cassidy took a deep breath. He didn't have a clue how to proceed. This kind of thing was Karen's responsibility. "Someone will."

"Mommy said it's never too early to start thinking about the future."

Cassidy stabbed another pin into the material. "Mommy was talking about your education, specifically about why you need to take arithmetic."

Vicki huffed her disgust. "That's only important if I want to go to college."

Cassidy was beginning to think females were born with an innate ability to drive a man beyond his reason. "You're going to college."

"You didn't."

Cassidy felt an old ache flare to life. Every time he was around Karen and her doctor friends he was reminded of his poor education. Hell, he'd had to jump through hoops just to get through high school—and even then he'd had to take extra courses during summer school before the army would take him on.

"I wanted to. But I couldn't afford college and the ranch, too."

Vicki's expression turned cunning, and Cassidy nearly groaned aloud. "It probably cost a lot more now, and Billy says you're putting all your money into that new bull you're fixing to get in California real soon.''

"Billy needs a lesson in watching his mouth." Cassidy made a mental note to do some straight talking with his blabbermouth ramrod ASAP.

"Billy's my friend. He thinks it's great I'm going to run the Lazy S someday."

"Get this straight, Victoria. You will go to college. I don't care which one you pick or how much it costs, but you will get an education. Got that?"

"No. I'm going to help you run the Lazy S, and when you get too old, I'm going to take over as the boss."

"Vicki, we've had this discussion too many times already, and—"

"That sounds like Mommy's car!" Vicki cried, whirling around.

Even as relief flooded through him, Cassidy had the presence of mind to grab for the small box of pins just as Vicki's foot sent it flying off the table. Pins showered the carpet like silver hail. Before he could stop himself, Cassidy blistered the air with curses.

"Daddy! You're not supposed to say words like that when I'm around! Mommy said."

He felt his face flaming as Karen walked in, looking harried and tired, her eyes shadowed. She'd lost weight in the past few months, and her small body looked whisper-thin in the rumpled surgical scrubs. Even when she wasn't working, exhaustion seemed to roll off her in waves. And no wonder. She'd worked three-to-eleven for two months straight, getting home at midnight most nights. And then, this morning, she'd had to get up before dawn in order to work the seven-to-three shift for somebody else.

Anger seared through him. She was wearing herself out at that damn place. And for what? Money? Hell, he wasn't a rich man, but they weren't starving, were they? Prestige? A membership in the country club when neither of them played golf? The chance to be "Woman of the Year?"

He scowled, fighting off black memories, the dangerous,

ugly kind that would torture him for days if he let them take hold.

"Did you get my hair ribbons?" Vicki demanded before her mother had a chance to open her mouth.

"Of course."

"Got 'em in Denver, did you?" The sarcastic words were out before Cassidy could stop them.

Karen cast him a reproving glance. "No, at Farley's. Right after I picked up your suit from the cleaners and the colic medicine you wanted from the vet's."

It was then that he noticed the clear plastic cleaner's bag dangling from her hand. He felt a momentary jolt of guilt before habit had him twisting it into anger, one of the few emotions he tolerated in himself.

"If you didn't have time to stop tonight, you should have told me."

The shadows in her eyes turned to sparks, and her chin seemed to jerk upward. "And then what? Listen to a lecture about how you don't have time to run into town for every little thing?"

"Karen—"

"Not now, Cassidy," she said, pointedly directing her attention—and his—to their daughter. By tacit agreement, they had tried to keep their problems from hurting Vicki. Problems that seemed to grow worse daily.

"Sweetheart, you look just as adorable in that dress as I thought you would. Lilac is definitely your color."

Vicki glanced from one to the other, her brow knitted. "I wanted to wait to do the hem, but it was getting awfully late and Daddy said you wouldn't mind if he helped out."

Karen heard the apologetic note in her child's voice and fought back a twinge of guilt. Three-quarters of a year more and things will calm down, she promised silently as she crossed to the table.

"Of course I don't mind."

She draped Cassidy's suit over the back of one of the chairs and dropped her purse onto the table. Something crunched under her sneakers and she glanced down. Pins littered the carpet like shards of silver ice.

"Oops."

Vicki giggled. "Daddy dropped the pin box."

"I think Daddy has done a terrific job," she said, meeting Cassidy's gaze. "I'm sorry I'm late, but Noah asked me to consult on a patient he'd just admitted. It was an emergency. I couldn't very well say no."

"It's not hard, Karen. You've been saying it a lot to me lately." One side of his mouth slanted. "It's getting late. I'd best take a shower while you finish up." He grabbed his suit and headed for the back of the house.

Cassidy stepped buck naked from the shower, his skin tingling from the icy water. Scowling, he snagged a towel from the rack with one long arm and swiped away most of the drops clinging to his body before knotting the towel around his waist.

As he crossed to the sink, the sound of Vicki's laughter floated through the closed door dividing the bathroom from the master bedroom. Apparently she and Karen were now involved in the more delicate work of sewing those baby stitches Vick had warned him about.

With a jerk of one powerful hand he opened the hot water tap, then reached for the ivory-and-steel straight-edged razor given to him during the last year of his hitch by a crusty sergeant who was retiring to Tahiti.

Damn the jackass who invented birth control, he thought as he slapped lather on a day's worth of stubble. A woman with a houseful of kids wouldn't have time to traipse off to work every morning.

A scowl tightened his face, and he paused with razor in hand to stare at the angry man in the mirror. Hell, he knew better than most how much it hurt to wait in line for a mother's attention. He knew what it felt like to lie in bed at night and listen to his father beg his mother not to leave him. To beg God to help him control his temper and make good grades and remember to clean his room so they'd love him enough to stay together.

In the end, it hadn't mattered. Johnny had died, and his mother had left.

Cassidy's eyes burned with the sudden tears he'd refused to shed for a lot of years. His baby brother had been half Vicki's age when he'd bled his life out in the middle of a Santa Fe street, his terror-filled eyes begging Cassidy for help. And God help him, there hadn't been a day since that he hadn't hated his mother for leaving her children alone that day.

There hadn't been a day since that he hadn't hated himself more, he thought with bitter anger as he swiped the wickedly sharp razor with long, sure strokes over his face. A sudden pain seared his jaw, and he bit off a curse. Blood dripped from the nick to drop on the sink, forming a shimmering spot of scarlet.

Shock jolted through him, and his breathing changed. He felt hot, then cold, and his stomach churned. Alone, where no one could see, he leaned over the toilet and was thoroughly, violently sick.

Three

Though the thunder rumbled steadily as Cassidy drove his family into town on Saturday night, the rain itself held off. Even the wind had abated, as though Mother Nature had decided to join in the spirit of the town's celebration.

"Are we there yet, Daddy?" Vicki implored from the back seat of the truck's extended cab. Cassidy glanced over his shoulder and grinned. Lights from a passing pickup revealed the starry-eyed excitement on her small face, and he felt a hard knot form in his chest.

"Five more minutes, peanut," he told her, returning his gaze to the road ahead.

Vicki was silent for less than a mile before erupting again. "Drive faster, Daddy. We don't want to miss any of the fun."

Cassidy obediently nudged the speed up to the limit, though he would just as soon be heading the other way. Parties had never been his thing. The last one he'd willingly attended was his wedding reception. Even then, however, he'd been ready to leave as soon as they'd cut the cake and done the other folderol that Karen had set her heart on.

Just a few more minutes, she'd whispered, her face glowing. Those few minutes had stretched to the better part of three hours. Hours they could have spent alone, making love.

His loins ached at the memory of his restraint during the rest of that party. Karen had looked tired, but ecstatic, when he'd hustled her home to the ranch. The bed he'd bought especially for his new bride was waiting, made up with crisp new sheets that he'd picked out after a lot of second-guessing and embarrassment. Damn things had pink roses on them, the fluffy kind she'd talked about planting by the front door. He'd expected to feel like a sissy sleeping on flowers for the first time in his life. Instead, he'd lost himself so completely in Karen's soft, lush body that he'd vowed never to sleep on anything else.

Their wedding sheets were worn thin now, but Cassidy had balked at letting Karen rip them into rags. Embarrassed to tell her the truth, he'd settled on the need to economize as the reason.

His face suddenly too warm and his collar too tight, Cassidy found himself sneaking a glance at his wife. Karen hadn't said more than a few words since their talk in the dining room. He hated the tension between them, like a thorn buried too deep in his flesh to be easily removed.

Since this was her night, her party, he supposed he ought to apologize for being such a surly cuss. And then what? he asked himself sourly. End up like his father, a half-baked excuse for a man with no self-esteem and a spine about as stiff as a worn-out rope?

A familiar stab of disgust hit him squarely in his midsection an instant before the truck rounded a curve, bringing the bright yellow lights of the fairground parking lot into view. Resolutely, he shut the door on his past and turned his attention to the evening to come. Two hours, three at the most, and he could hustle his ladies home, where they belonged.

"Turn here, Daddy," Vicki ordered, beating him on the shoulder from her place behind him.

"Yes, ma'am," he said, his mouth twitching.

Vicki might look as delicate as a spring flower in her new party dress, but inside, she was determined to have her way.

"I told you, everybody's already here," Vicki wailed as Cassidy drove past row after row of mud-encrusted, well-used vehicles.

"Not everyone, darling," Karen teased with a grin. "Otherwise, we'd be inside instead of out here, looking for a parking place."

"Oh, Mommy," Vicki protested, her tone long-suffering.

By the time Cassidy nosed his rig into a slot at the end of

the second-to-last row, Vicki had snapped off her seat belt and was perched impatiently on the edge of her seat.

"You two stay put till I can help you out," he ordered as he killed the engine and tossed the key into the empty ashtray.

"Oh, Daddy, Mommy and me aren't helpless," Vicki said in an outraged tone that had him grinning.

"I know that, sweetheart," he said as he opened his door. "But you both look so pretty, I feel like playin' gentleman, okay?"

Vicki beamed. "Way cool, isn't it, Mommy?"

"I should say it is," Karen replied, glancing his way. In the dim illumination of the interior light, her eyes seemed to glow, and her smile was soft, reminding him of the kind young woman who'd bewitched him one hellish afternoon in a cold emergency room cubicle.

Cassidy suddenly felt fifteen and tongue-tied. "Anything for my girls," he said, and then winced. "Sorry. I realize that's not politically correct these days."

"We don't mind, do we, Mommy?" Vicki piped up, glancing anxiously at her mother.

"If it were anyone else but your daddy, I would mind," Karen disagreed gently. "But I know your dad doesn't mean to be condescending."

Vicki frowned. "Con-dee-sending? What's that?"

Karen glanced his way. "It means that some men think women should be pampered and coddled instead of treated like equals. But Daddy knows better. When we first met, he thought it was great that I wanted to be a doctor." Her eyes pleaded with him. But for what? Understanding? Approval?

An apology for wanting her to stay home with her child?

Something stirred inside him, part longing and part grief, two emotions he hated. Before either or both could take hold, he slammed the door and walked around the pickup's long bed.

The air was still winter crisp, with the last of the storm still lingering like a heavy mist. He grabbed a lungful of fresh air and let it out slowly as he opened the passenger door.

"Thanks," Karen said, putting her hand into his. As he

assisted her down, he felt the suppleness of her wrist, the strength in her graceful fingers. The warmth of her touch. His jaw hardened at the memory of the incredible massages she used to give him in the early days. No matter how tired he'd been when she'd started or how chastely she touched him, he'd invariably ended up hard and throbbing.

It had been his turn then to slide his palms over the tantalizing curves of her breasts and hips, to trace the soft mounds of her bottom, to test the texture of her skin with his fingertips. When, at last, he'd turned his attention to the warm, moist secrets between her lush thighs, she'd all but exploded in pleasure.

Tonight she was wearing his favorite dress. It was pale blue with a high neck and long sleeves, and it had a way of clinging to her breasts that made a man think he was seeing more than he really was.

He wanted his mouth on her, her body warm and supple beneath his. He wanted to stroke every inch of that curvy little body until she was wet and wild and trembling. And then he would sink into her, his engorged body filling the hot, smooth space that seemed fashioned just for him.

Thinking about those things now was a mistake, he realized as he felt his body harden instantly and painfully. Biting off a groan, he widened his stance, grateful that he was wearing loose-fitting trousers instead of his customary jeans.

"Mind the puddles," he all but growled in his frustration. No matter how hot it was inside, he had a feeling he'd be wearing his suit coat most of the night.

"Hurry up, Daddy."

Stifling a sigh, he released Karen's hand in order to open the cab's rear door. "There you go, Vick. Hop out."

"No, Daddy, hold out your hand like you did with Mommy," Vicki said with a pout.

"I beg your pardon, Miss Sloane." He bowed slightly, sending Vicki into a gurgle of laughter. "May I?" he added, extending his hand.

As regal as any princess, Vicki allowed him to help her

down from the high frame and his heart swelled at her innate grace and femininity. Just like her mama, he thought.

"Down, Rags!" Vicki ordered as she lowered the tailgate. The Australian shepherd bounded to the ground and immediately licked Vicki's hand. "Stop wiggling so I can put on your new leash," she ordered, tugging on his collar.

"Make sure you keep a tight hold on him," Cassidy reminded her with a pointed look at the fifty-pound dog now straining at the end of the braided chartreuse strap. The Australian shepherd's freshly shampooed black-and-tan coat glistened, and his ears were cocked forward, a sure sign he was eager to explore.

"Daddy!" Vicki said in a scolding voice as she scratched her adored pet's ears. "Rags knows how to behave. Besides, he's a *hero!* If it hadn't been for him, you might never have found me stuck down there in that gross hole."

Beside him, Cassidy heard Karen draw a quick breath and move closer to his side. Replying to her unspoken plea, he slipped a comforting arm over her slender shoulders. Maybe she did need him some, after all. His spirits edged up a couple of notches, inspiring him to tighten his hold.

"Of course Rags will be good, sweetheart," Karen said with a smile, the soft one that begged for a kiss. "Daddy was just teasing you. He doesn't like to think about how close we came to losing you, that's all."

"But you didn't, 'cause I'm as tough as Daddy, right?"

"Right."

Vicki tossed one of her beribboned braids over her shoulder before heading toward the brightly lit entrance. According to the child psychologist they'd taken her to for six months after the accident, she'd handled her ordeal with a surprisingly mature aplomb. In fact, she was quite pleased with herself for being such a brave little girl.

"Watch your step," Karen called after her.

"Save your breath," Cassidy muttered, winning him a pert grin that had him going soft inside. Until she shivered.

With a scowl, he dropped his arm in order to help her drape her lacy shawl over her shoulders. "Dammit, Karen, I told you to wear a coat," he grumbled, wishing not for the first time that he had the money to wrap her in expensive furs.

"Maybe I just wanted an excuse to cuddle up next to my husband," she said, slipping her arm through his. His already hard body began to throb.

"Are you flirting with me, Mrs. Sloane?" he demanded through the sudden thickness in his throat.

"Absolutely, Mr. Sloane." This time the grin she gave him was ripe with seductive promise. His heart speeded as he imagined undressing her with slow and careful deliberation.

"I can see lots of decorations," Vicki called from a spot just outside the door to the exhibition hall.

"Coming, sweetheart," Karen called back, tightening her grip on his arm.

"Brace yourself for a long evening," he muttered, eyeing the large concrete-and-steel structure with the same wariness he accorded to a suspicious pile of rocks in snake country.

Karen slowed, her gaze searching his face. "Cassidy, about the things I said earlier, I hope you know I don't mind running errands for you or Vicki."

Cassidy sensed her need to smooth over the rift between them, and his conscience walloped him a good one. "You're working too many hours. You're wearing yourself out."

Her lips curved, and the dimple in one smooth cheek flirted with him. "I'm fine, Cassidy. Really, but it's lovely to know you're worried about me."

He shoved his hands in his pockets to keep from getting them both in a tangle. "That's my job."

"Yes, I know. You take care of everyone around you, but when someone tries to take care of you, you buck like that beautiful white stallion you couldn't bear to see broken."

"I can take care of myself," he said, embarrassed now, and wondering how this conversation got started.

Her hand touched his arm, gentling him to a stop. "I love the way you blush when someone dares to pay you a compliment."

"The hell I do."

"And I love you."

"Do you?" The words were out before he realized he'd opened his mouth.

She nodded. "If you let me, when we get home I'll show you just how much."

Tension stretched across his shoulders and throbbed at the base of his neck. Need surged into him so fiercely he curled both hands into fists inside his pockets.

"Vicki's waiting," he reminded her, but she was already stepping into his arms, her face upturned, her lips parted.

"A quick lesson in patience won't hurt her." Palms down, she slid her hands over his lapels to his neck. Her fingers were warm against his neck as the tips threaded into his hair.

His little innocent-at-heart temptress, he thought, his mind beginning to cloud over. "Kari—"

"Shh."

He recognized the lazy droop to her thick lashes, even as she pressed closer. With a defeated groan, he dragged his hands free and reached for her. His emotions tangled as he lowered his head and covered her mouth with his for what he told himself was a quick husbandly kiss. Her lips parted—not in protest, but urgency—and shock jolted through him, as strong as the first time he'd tasted her incredible mouth.

The beguiling scent of her perfume swirled around him, and he drew it in, along with the pungent aroma of rain and earth and wet pavement. He let his tongue tease hers, absorbing the feminine taste of her mouth. The flavor of her was as arousing as it was sweet, and he felt the hunger in his gut grow stronger. His already throbbing body stretched to the edge of pain. In spite of his good intentions, he settled one hand on her bottom and pulled her closer in an effort to ease his pulsating discomfort.

This time the groan was hers, and he felt his control slipping. For one wild, illogical moment, he considered scooping her into his arms and returning to the truck. It was then that he heard the familiar sound of impatient barking.

Drawing on what little strength of character remained to him, he eased backward, supporting her only with his hands on her arms. Slowly, her eyes still dazed and her breathing far too rapid, she lowered her spiked heels to the pavement and rested her head on his chest.

"Aren't you two done yet?" Vicki called with audible impatience.

Cassidy raked one hand through his hair and straightened his spine. Though he tried, he couldn't seem to get enough air in his lungs, and his body was still rock hard.

"Talk about rotten timing," he said in a rasping voice.

"I'll say." Lifting her head, Karen smiled up at him, her eyes still passion-glazed and her lips rosy.

Feeling as though he had his boots on solid ground for the first time in months, he slipped his arm around her waist and guided her toward the entrance. Later, he promised himself as they reached the open door. As soon as Vicki was tucked safely into bed, he would close their bedroom door, lose the suit and make slow love to his wife.

They crossed the threshold into the cavernous hall and walked into a wall of noise and a blur of colors. From the look of things, Cassidy figured it had taken an army of eager volunteers to string thousands of tiny twinkle lights from the rafters, giving the place the effect of a star-studded summer night. According to the signs displayed prominently on sandwich boards near the entrance, local florists had donated enough flowers to turn the drab and drafty building into a perfumed garden, a perfect setting for a good old-fashioned Western fandango.

"Wow!" Vicki exclaimed, her face upturned to the fairy-tale sky overhead. Her mouth hung open and her brown eyes shone with a wonder he hoped would never desert her.

As he shepherded his ladies and Rags through the outer edges of the crowd, Cassidy glanced around, looking for a telephone booth. Later, when things calmed down, he'd give Billy Russell a quick call.

It wasn't that he was worried, he told himself. Vicki's mare, Golden Girl, wasn't due to deliver for another few days. Still, this was the dainty palomino's first foal and he'd felt uneasy enough to stop by the Russells' trailer in order to ask Billy to check on her a time or two during the evening.

"I'm gonna go find Elizabeth, okay?" Vicki murmured as they elbowed their way through the exuberant celebrants.

Cassidy surveyed the mingling throng, then nodded. "Just be sure to check in with your mom or me once in a while."

"Okay."

"Wait, sweetie, let me fix your sash." Karen bent to give the wide purple ribbon a quick tug. "There. Now you're perfect," she whispered. "And you look gorgeous."

Vicki's cheeks turned as delicately pink as a ripe peach. "Really and truly?"

"Really and truly," Karen said, straightening. "If you don't believe me, ask Daddy."

Obediently, Vicki swung her gaze upward to Cassidy's face. "Really, Daddy?"

His heart hammered at the absolute trust he saw shimmering in her big brown eyes. Karen's eyes had had that same beautiful sheen when she'd repeated her wedding vows.

"Trust me, sweetheart, you're a knockout," he said when he had control of his voice again.

"Even without lipstick and stuff?"

"Especially without stuff." He had to work hard to keep a straight face. "You and your mom are the two prettiest ladies in the place."

Still beaming, Vicki wrapped another length of leash around her wrist and turned away. "Let's go, Rags. Find Elizabeth for me."

With an exuberant "woof" that drew a variety of stares their way, Rags charged into the crowd, pulling Vicki along behind.

"It's a disgrace, bringing a filthy, slobbering animal into a public gathering," a woman's shrill voice declared loudly.

Instantly on alert, Cassidy whipped his head around to discover a prune-faced matron eyeing his daughter with obvious disapproval.

"Don't you dare," Karen muttered in a low voice while at the same time tightening her grip on his arm.

"Whose idea was it to bring the dog, anyway?" he asked, watching the crowd swallow the woman whole.

Karen bit the corner of her mouth in the cute way she had whenever she wanted to laugh but didn't dare. "His name was on the invitation," she said. "The woman I called to RSVP said that Rags is getting a certificate of appreciation along with the rest of us. For leading you to the cave."

"Guess that makes sense," he conceded, shoving down the memories that tore at him whenever he was reminded of those interminable hours in June.

Karen slipped her shawl from her shoulders and folded it over her arm. Her face was flushed, and her eyes were the color of shiny pewter, reminding him of the first time they'd made love.

"Come with me, Kari. Let me finish what we started outside." The words were out before he could call them back.

Karen slanted him a startled look before glancing around at the hustle and bustle of the people bent on enjoying themselves. "Come with you where?" she asked when her gaze returned to his face.

Cassidy shot a fast look at the oversized man in an undersized suit bearing down on them through the crowd, a purposeful glint in his heavy-lidded eyes. Though he didn't recall the man's name, he recognized him as a member of the city council. Part of the official welcoming committee, he guessed, his jaw tightening.

"Let's get out of here," he urged, slipping a hand under her elbow to turn her away from the councilman.

"But the ceremony—"

"Forget the ceremony. We'll have our own celebration, just you and me, naked on clean sheets."

A tiny shiver ran through her, and he felt his expectations soar. Moving closer, he let her feel the hard evidence of his almost violent need jutting against her thigh.

"Oh, Cassidy," she exclaimed softly. "You're shameless."

"No, I'm horny for my wife."

The quick nervous swipe of her tongue over her bottom lip

had his body throbbing. For good measure he moved to shield her and at the same time rubbed against her.

"Find your mom and tell her to take Vicki home for the night. We'll drive over to that little inn in Toponas and get a room with a fireplace and one of those canopied beds you like so much."

The sudden delight in her eyes made his heart leap. He had a notion to kiss her again, right then and there, before she could think of a reason to turn him down. Just as he'd resolved to do just that, however, he caught a movement from the corner of his eye and straightened.

"There you are, Dr. Sloane." The councilman had reached them, his hand extended and his florid face wreathed in smiles. "Name's Friendly, Bill Friendly. 'Friendly's my name, friendly's my aim.'"

Karen blinked up at him, an uncertain smile on her face. "I...see."

Friendly chuckled, the braying sound all but lost in the noise from the other people around them. "I represent the part of town where Vanderbilt Memorial is located, which makes you one of my constituents—part-time, anyway."

"Hell," Cassidy muttered under his breath as he dropped Karen's arm an instant before her hand was clasped between the councilman's sausage fingers.

Karen nearly groaned aloud as she acknowledged the man's greeting. "Mr. Friendly, I wonder if—"

"Call me Bill," he boomed over the drone of surrounding conversations.

"Bill, we, my husband and I, were—"

"No need to introduce your husband, Doctor," Friendly barreled on, his grin at the ready. "I recognized both of you from the picture in the *Herald* after those gallant boys from the fire department hauled your daughter outta that pit. Nearly tore this old man's heart out, thinkin' about what you two nice people went through."

Cassidy's jaw couldn't be any harder if it had been chiseled from that same cave granite, Karen realized with a sinking heart as the two men shook hands.

"Glad to meet you, Mr. Sloane," Friendly declared with all the gusto of a practiced politician. Karen stifled a sigh as a muscle jerked along Cassidy's jaw. Several inches now separated them, and she missed the heat of his body through the soft gray wool of his suit coat.

"Friendly." The pronounced drawl in his tone was a bad sign. Cassidy usually kept a tight rein on his temper, but now and then those reins slipped a little. The result was generally explosive.

"I guess I don't have to tell you how proud we all are of your wife," Friendly went on, apparently oblivious to the chill that had settled over their little corner of the huge structure.

Cassidy cocked a thick black brow. "You don't? Why not?"

Friendly's mouth opened and closed, reminding Karen of a particularly unattractive bass. She bit her lip to keep the giggle bubbling in her throat from escaping.

"Well, I, that is, *of course* we're proud of her," he said, making a fast recovery. "Why, it gives the strongest man pause to think of her working so diligently in the emergency room, not even knowing her own little girl was trapped underground." Friendly chuckled. "I reckon you know how lucky you are to have her."

Cassidy's jaw grew even harder. "Is there a point to this, Friendly?"

Before the councilman could blunder on, she leaned closer to Cassidy's side to whisper urgently, "We'll leave early, I promise."

"*Now*, Kari," he demanded, pinning her with a challenging gaze so full of promise her breath caught.

"But, Cassidy, we can't just walk out."

"Sure we can."

She glanced around, seeing the faces of friends and co-workers. The award she was to receive was for them as much as it was for herself. How could she live with herself if she simply walked out, as though it meant nothing? As though *their* hard work and sacrifice meant nothing? And yet, Cassidy had made it plain that he needed her now. Not an hour from now, but this moment. And, if she were honest, she wanted more than anything to take his arm and walk proudly to the door.

An anguished frustration thrummed through her, making her frown. Once again, she felt torn between her duty and the man she loved. But perhaps there was a third option. A compromise.

"Cassidy, listen to me, please," she pleaded, her gaze searching his. "More than anything, I want to be with you. But it wouldn't be fair to the committee and everyone who's worked so hard—"

"Forget it, Karen. I got the message." His face closed up. Just like that, he was once again the cold, angry man standing in the glare of rescue lights, his eyes rejecting her. But this time there was another emotion buried within those intimidating onyx depths, something that suggested an emotion far more complex than anger. It was a look she'd seen before, in patients suffering intractable pain.

Her heart contracted, and she felt the sudden, inexplicable press of tears against the backs of her eyes. Somehow she had to reach him, to make him understand.

"Cassidy, please don't *do* this," she whispered.

"Do what?" he challenged, making no effort to lower his voice. "Deny that I resent the demands other people make on my wife? Or the fact that you let them?"

Her body humming in ways she hadn't felt for months, she leaned closer, deliberately brushing his arm with her breast. "Cassidy, it won't be all that long before I've fulfilled my obligations and then we can leave."

"Don't kid yourself. We'll be lucky if we get out of here before eleven."

Conscious of the councilman's curious gaze shifting from one to the other, she turned slightly to hide her face and whispered, "I want to make love to you, Cassidy, but—"

Brow arched, he deliberately took a step away from her. "I've heard that before, Kari, and ended up sleeping alone while you're off on some emergency or other."

Karen heard the resentment buried in his caustic words and felt her stomach constrict. Take a chance, Kari, she thought. Grab that thick, strong wrist of his and make a beeline for the truck. Maybe they couldn't spend the entire night at the Fireside Inn, but—

"Great party, isn't it?" Friendly declared as he caught her eye again. Like all true politicians, it seemed, he couldn't stand a lull in the conversation.

"Excuse me, I'm goin' to find the bar," Cassidy drawled. With that, he nodded to the councilman, then turned away to be swallowed up by the shifting currents of humanity.

"Did I say something wrong?" Friendly asked, his brow furrowed over troubled eyes that suddenly seemed more perceptive than she'd thought at first glance.

Reminding herself that Bill Friendly was her host, Karen summoned a social smile. "It's not your fault. My husband hates to talk about Vicki's accident, that's all."

"Understandably." He cleared his throat. "Why don't I get you something cold to drink, and then I can fill you in on the presentation ceremony."

Karen bit off a groan. "Ceremony?" she asked warily.

Friendly held up a hand. "Nothing fancy, I promise. The VFW will present the colors, of course, and the American Legion marching band will play the 'Star-Spangled Banner,' then Hal Stuart will say a few words." He sighed, then glanced around quickly before adding in a low voice, "Don't get me wrong, Dr. Sloane, but I sure do miss Hal's mama coming into City Hall every morning with that sunny smile of hers."

Karen welcomed the distraction. Her cheeks were still hot as the result of the longing Cassidy had aroused in her. "Have the detectives handling the case uncovered any more leads?"

Friendly shook his head. "Not that I know of, but that young detective, Richardson, plays his cards pretty close to his vest."

"I suppose that's best." Karen glanced around. At six-three in his boots, Cassidy had the advantage of height on most of the males in the room. Her spirits drooped even lower when she realized he wasn't in sight.

"Shall we?" Friendly asked, offering his arm.

As Karen slipped her hand into the crook of the councilman's elbow and allowed him to lead her through the throng, she couldn't help thinking about the early days of her marriage when nothing short of a cataclysm would have pried Cassidy from her side.

Four

By eight-thirty, the formalities had been concluded, which for most of the attendees meant that the real party could start.

Slim-Boy Brown and the Old Time Fiddlers tuned their instruments and a couple of slicked-up, freshly barbered and cologned cowboys eager to dance with the pretty ladies cleared a space near the bandstand.

With a whoop of excitement, one of Cassidy's hired hands led a shy, freckled teenager onto the floor, and Slim-Boy shouted for the dancing to commence. Like a restless herd surging toward an open gate, couples spilled into the cleared area, some in jeans and boots, others in suits and sleek cocktail dresses, while friends and strangers alike cheered them on.

Across the cavernous hall, barbecued ribs and chicken sizzled on the grill of a huge old-fashioned chuck wagon while the caterer and her staff of gingham-clad cowgirls ladled up coleslaw and potato salad by the gallon. Nearby, bartenders in flannel shirts and derby hats served beer and wine to thirsty customers. As the bottles and kegs emptied, the noise level rose.

In the midst of the gaiety, Cassidy stood alone near the open doors of the main entrance, the silk tie he'd carefully knotted two hours earlier now wrenched free of the stiff collar, his patience thinned to tissue paper.

"Somethin' tells me you'd rather be out chasing strays than proppin' up the wall," Travis Stockwell commented as he ambled Cassidy's way.

Cassidy straightened, and for good measure, gave the knot of his tie another jerk. "You got that right," he said as he

saluted the younger man with the can of soda he'd been nurs-
ing for the past hour.

"'Pears to me you'd do better to grab you one of these,"
Travis advised, indicating the long-necked beer bottle in his
big hand.

Cassidy gave it some thought. He hadn't been drunk since
the night of his father's funeral. Now, on the rare occasions
that he indulged, he limited himself to two beers. Eight years
of watching his old man dive deeper and deeper into a bottle
had made him cautious.

"Guess I'll stick with the soft stuff," he said, taking a
swig. "Got me a mare ready to foal any minute now." He'd
been right to call Russell. Golden Girl had gone into labor an
hour after they'd headed for town.

Travis nodded, one cowboy to another. "The bay?" he
asked after taking a long pull on the bottle.

"No, the palomino, Golden Girl out of Goldenrod."

"I'm guessin' she's a maiden, for all the worryin' you're
doin'."

"You guess right."

Travis acknowledged that with an understanding nod. "Is
that the mare you bred to that wild stallion I been hearing
about?"

"Yeah. Took me two years to finally get a rope on that
big white hellion. Bred him three times, last time to the Girl.
Damn near lost two men trying to control him."

Travis's brown eyes gleamed. "Heard you set him free
after he covered your mares."

Cassidy nodded. He'd seen the stallion a time or two since,
racing the wind across the wildest part of the Lazy S. As free
as God made him.

"Word is you had a couple of sweet offers to take him off
your hands, provided, of course, he was green broke."

"One or two."

"You figure he couldn't be broke?"

Cassidy shrugged. "Didn't seem right to try."

Travis digested that in silence, then nodded. "You thinkin'
to sell the palomino's foal?"

"Not unless I care to spend the rest of my life explainin' my reasons to my daughter."

Travis snorted over the sound of nearby laughter. "Yeah, I know what you mean. My sweet Virginia's only a little past nine months and already she's got me bustin' my buns to make her happy. Peggy says I'm spoiling both my kids."

Cassidy heard the note of self-conscious contentment in Travis's voice and felt a sharp pang of envy. From rodeo gypsy to family man in the wink of an eye. A hell of a transition, he decided, but it seemed to suit Travis damned well. *At least he had had a choice about becoming a father,* Cassidy thought, then felt like an idiot. Karen hadn't gotten herself pregnant all by her lonesome.

"You still intending to take your family with you when the tour starts up again?" he asked during a lull in the music.

"Yep. Got me a honey of an RV and Peggy loves it. She's got it all decorated real pretty, even has a corner fixed up like a nursery for the babies. Says it's like taking her nest with her wherever she goes."

Cassidy took a long breath. He and Karen had worked for days on the baby's room, racing to get it done before Karen's due date. Damn, if they hadn't had fun, too. His heart ached at the memory of his new bride's laughing eyes when he'd swung her off the ladder and kissed her senseless. They'd ended up making love on the floor amid paint cans and roller pans. He shifted, frowned. The hardness that had subsided started to throb again and he cursed the idiots who'd come up with the idea for this bash in the first place.

"Sounds like Peggy's not planning on going back to work anytime soon," he drawled, then winced at the bitterness in his voice.

Travis shook his head. "No way! She's got all she can handle with me and the twins."

Cassidy hid his jealousy behind a grin. "Guess it's a toss-up who demands the most TLC, you or the babies."

Travis chuckled. "You could say that, yeah. Course, me being the easygoing sort, I don't take a lot of care. Mostly just the tender lovin' part."

After giving an obligatory chuckle, Cassidy took another sip of soda pop and let his gaze wander over the crowd. The dancing had started again, and he let his attention linger for a moment on one of the couples, friends of Karen's from the hospital. Noah Howell and his wife Amanda. Both doctors.

The last time he'd done time in this suit and tie, he'd been attending their wedding. From the way they were squeezing up to each other tonight, their thighs rubbing in time with the waltz, he figured the honeymoon was far from over.

Give 'em another few years and the groom would be leaning against a wall and wishing he could go home while the happy bride was off on her own, gossiping with her friends. Like Karen, he thought as he shifted his gaze to the cluster of tables to his left where she was laughing with a sleek blonde in a filmy dress the color of wood smoke. It took him a moment to place the face. Olivia's daughter, Eve, had come home for the funeral, and a few weeks later she'd up and married one of his poker-playing buddies, Rio Redtree.

Weddings and babies. Hell, it was an epidemic.

Karen said it was all due to the blackout, and that a sociologist from Denver was doing a study to see if the increase in life-altering changes was the result of heightened emotions.

Emotions. Hell, he thought. It was sex that produced weddings, just like it produced babies. The hot, steamy kind of sex that took a man by storm and messed up all his well-ordered plans.

His body stirring once more, he watched Karen laughing at something Eve had just said and brooded on the long restless nights he'd spent lately staring at the ceiling, his body hard and aching to be buried in his wife's soft warmth.

Before he'd met Karen, he hadn't known he had any real tenderness in him. The women he'd cared enough about to take to bed had excited other things in him. Hot, turbulent needs that settled as quickly as they rose. Dark, angry emotions that set his teeth on edge, even as he exerted a will of iron to keep his hands from bruising and his need from galloping out of control.

But somehow, with Karen, the ferocity of his needs was

tempered by the greatest contentment he'd ever known. Somehow, when he was holding her in his arms, his sated body still sheathed by hers, the accusing voice inside his head was silent, allowing him peace.

He'd been shaken right down to his boots to realize he'd wanted her love desperately, wanted something he'd stopped believing in on his tenth birthday. Wanted what he, himself, was no longer able to offer a woman.

He drew a breath and watched her lift her wineglass to her lips. He longed to feel that lush, sweet mouth on his, opening eagerly, her hands clutching at his shoulders as she made soft pleading noises in her throat.

Even now, when a part of him hated her for being so stubborn, he wanted her more than any other woman he'd ever known. His sweet wife, the mother of his child. The sexiest lady in the room, bar none.

A need to hold her tore through him, as raw as a bloody gash left by a brush from a rusty barb. It wasn't safe to let himself think about loving her. It would never be safe. The closest he came was a fierce desire to protect her and spoil her and make love to her so thoroughly she would forget to notice he'd never said those three little words that came so easily to her lips.

Lost in his brooding thoughts, it took him a moment to realize Travis had asked him a question. "Sorry, run that by me one more time?" he said as he shifted his gaze Travis's way.

A strange look came and went in the other man's eyes before Travis's mouth sidled up into a smug half smile. "I was just asking if things are any better between you and Karen, but from the droolin' you been doin' just watching her across the room, I gotta figure they are."

Cassidy scowled. "If it's all the same to you, I'd just as soon you keep your figurin' to yourself."

Travis lifted the bottle for one long, last swallow before wiping his mouth with the back of his hand. "Take the advice of an old married guy like me, Cass. Point those shiny Sunday boots of yours toward that pretty lady in blue yonder and ask her to dance." He chuckled. "Better yet, hustle her on home so you can finish the evening off right, just the two of you."

Cassidy restricted his response to a shrug. "Can't leave until the kid with the camera takes our picture for the *Herald*. Hell, he even wanted Rags in the shot. Vicki's got him all prettied up and smelling like a whorehouse pet for the occasion."

"Hell of a note, ain't it. A man's got his mind set on a soft bed and an even softer woman, and some darn photographer wants to snap his picture."

Travis slapped Cassidy on the back before shoving his hat back another fraction of an inch. "Time for this old boy to snag himself another cold one. You sure I can't bring you one?"

Because he was suddenly tempted, Cassidy shook his head. "I'll stick with colored water for a while longer."

Travis nodded. "Tell you what. If I see that photographer, I'll head him your way."

Cassidy grunted something noncommittal and Travis shrugged before slipping back into the crowd, leaving Cassidy alone with his thoughts—and regrets.

Across the room, Karen finished her second glass of white wine, then sat playing with the empty goblet, her foot tapping in time to the fiddle music. A smile played across her lips as she remembered her stint in dancing school. She'd had two left feet and a determination to lead, which had added a certain element of conflict to the traditional box step.

With Cassidy, however, there'd been no contest. No chance to exert her own will. Even if she'd tried, he wouldn't have allowed it. Cassidy danced as he made love, demanding her submission even as he made her tremble with longing for more.

How long had it been since he'd pulled her into his arms and swept her into a whirl of pleasure? Months? Years?

A wave of pure jealousy swept over her as she watched Noah and Amanda cuddle in time to the music. It was obvious that Noah adored his new wife. Karen already knew how

Amanda felt about her husband. No one who'd spent any time at the hospital these past months could fail to know.

The woman was over-the-moon in love.

"I don't know about you, but I'm crazy about happy endings," Eve murmured as she, too, watched the Howells swaying in time to the music.

Karen nodded, her smile tinged with an envy she was too weary to hide. "Speaking of happy endings, I would say that yours is right up there with the best of them."

"Definitely at the top of the list," Eve replied with a grin. "I still wake up every morning and pinch myself to make sure I'm not trapped in my own personal fantasy."

"If you are, Rio and Molly seem to be pretty content to be trapped in there with you."

"Thank goodness."

Eve took a sip of her wine, then cast a hopeful look at the nearby faces. Looking for the man she loved, Karen suspected, just as she'd searched earlier for a glimpse of Cassidy.

"If you're craning your neck in order to find that handsome husband of yours, I saw him over by the speaker's dais about twenty minutes ago," Karen teased before she, too, let her gaze wander. A smile curved her lips as she caught a glimpse of Vicki and Rags talking with Elizabeth Lindstrom Bennett before the crowd shifted, blocking her view.

"Poor Rio," Eve said with a sigh, claiming Karen's attention once more. "While everyone else is playing, he's working."

"Covering the reception for the *Herald*?"

Eve nodded. "And he is *not* happy about it. He told the editor he's an investigative reporter, not a social columnist."

Karen laughed at the image of hard-bitten Rio Redtree waxing lyrical over Edna Friendly's hot pink cocktail frock.

"Don't laugh," Eve muttered, her blue eyes dancing. "Molly and I threatened to brain him with his own laptop if he didn't stop grousing."

"Sounds totally reasonable." Karen drew a breath, then leaned forward slightly. "Speaking of investigations, has Rio come up with anything new about your mother's murder?"

Eve's blue eyes clouded. "Nothing he's willing to make public."

"What about the police?"

"They're still trying to find Dean Springer. Rio's pretty sure he's out of the country by now, especially since he must have read about the Jackson case in the paper. As a matter of procedure, though, the police have people checking the airports and the borders."

Karen nodded. "Who *is* this Joanna Jackson?"

Eve shrugged. "No one really knows. And that might not even be her real name."

"It doesn't seem right that the district attorney would let a woman like that make a deal."

"I agree. I was beside myself when I first heard about it." Her eyes grew sad. "No matter what they do to her, though, it won't bring Mother back."

"My mother misses yours terribly. We all do."

"Molly still talks a lot about her Gramma." Eve squared her shoulders and lifted her chin. "But at least she has another grandmother now. And *I* have a mother-in-law."

"How's that going?"

"Up and down, like most things."

Karen commiserated with a glance. "That's one problem I never had."

"Cassidy's mother is dead?"

"No, missing."

Eve blinked. "Pardon?"

"She left Cassidy and his father on Cassidy's tenth birthday."

"Good heavens. How terrible for Cassidy!"

Karen's gaze was caught by a tall man with black hair standing near the bar, and she started to smile, only to be disappointed when the man turned his head, showing a profile that was far less noble than Cassidy's and a chin that was decidedly weak.

"A great example of motherly love, isn't it?" Karen muttered before shifting her gaze to the man in bartender's garb standing a few feet away, waiting to be noticed.

Although Martin Smith was Noah's patient, Karen had been present during some of his examinations. Blond and blue-eyed, he was as fair as Cassidy was dark, but there was something about the angle of his jaw and the set of those big shoulders that reminded her of her husband.

Alpha males, one of her psychology professors had called men like them. Assertive, protective and powerful. Superior specimens.

Did Martin have a wife waiting for him somewhere? Wondering and worrying? Grieving? Did he have children praying every night for their daddy's safe return? It broke her heart to imagine how Vicki would feel if her father should suddenly disappear from her life.

"How are you feeling?" she asked Martin when the three of them had exchanged greetings.

"Antsy to find out the name of the guy behind this face." His grin, like everything else about him, was controlled. Though she had no hard facts to back her up, she would bet a year's salary the man didn't earn his living behind a desk.

"It will all come back to you, Martin," she reassured him. "You just have to be patient until it does."

He nodded, but she sensed the weight of the despair he must be feeling. "The caterer asked me to play waiter for a while." His startlingly blue eyes flickered to Karen's empty wineglass. "Care for another?"

Karen started to refuse with thanks, then changed her mind. "Sure, why not?" Drowning her sorrows in Chardonnay might be tacky, but at the moment, she didn't care. Besides, she had tomorrow off. A perk of being one of the town's honored guests tonight.

"Make that two," Eve said with an airy grin. "Rio is the designated driver for this evening."

Karen drew a breath. "I never thought to check with Cassidy." Why should she when she'd never once known him to have more than a beer or two, and that rarely.

"Where is Cassidy, anyway?" Eve asked, her gaze idly roaming from group to group. "I haven't seen him all evening."

"Oh, he's around someplace."

Her fingers toyed with the napkin beneath her empty wine-glass, and the tiny diamond in her engagement ring caught the light, flashing blue fire. Pain lanced through her, as acute as a severe laceration.

Eve leaned closer, her blue eyes filled with sympathy. "Does he still want you to leave medicine and be a full-time housewife?"

Had everyone in town heard about the things he'd flung at her last June? she wondered. Or simply a select few who'd gleaned the knowledge from one of the ladies providing the coffee? Either way, it didn't please her one whit to know she was the object of gossip. Or, worse, pity.

"He wants me to postpone private practice until Vicki's through school," she admitted while making a valiant stab at nonchalance. "Although tonight, I thought he'd—"

Karen was interrupted by Martin's return. "Your wine, ladies," he said, setting each one down in turn. "Enjoy."

He accepted their thanks with a slow grin that had Karen frowning at his back as he headed toward the bar.

"Something wrong?" Eve asked, brow wrinkling.

"Not really. It's just that Martin reminds me of someone and I don't know who," she murmured, watching his broad back as he threaded his way through the milling crowd.

Eve lifted her glass and took a sip, then whirled in surprise as a pair of strong hands came down lightly on her shoulders.

"Hello, wife," Rio Redtree said with a crooked grin that showcased his blindingly white teeth. "Miss me?"

"Terribly," Eve murmured, her face lighting.

Averting her gaze from the exchange of heated glances, Karen reached for her wine. In spite of his eager words earlier, Cassidy hadn't sought her out once tonight, she thought, taking a sip.

What's wrong with you, Karen Sloane? a voice taunted. You're an equal partner in this marriage, aren't you? You don't have to wait for your husband to do the asking. Muscles braced, she started to rise, only to be interrupted by a vaguely familiar baritone.

"Dr. Sloane?"

Startled, Karen glanced up to find one of the new interns smiling down at her. Though he'd only been at Vanderbilt six weeks or so, Chuck Zendajas had fully half of the eligible women on staff under the age of forty drooling over his astounding good looks.

"I didn't expect to see you here," she said after exchanging remarks about the size of the crowd and the level of gaiety.

"Actually, I had the night off and everyone I knew was heading out this way, so I just followed the crowd." His puppy brown eyes smiled down at her as he leaned closer. "Tell me, is it permissible for a lowly intern to ask a senior resident to dance, or am I risking my entire career by being so forward?"

Karen laughed. For all his wolfish behavior around the ladies, Zendajas was harmless. Still, it was Cassidy she longed to feel holding her in his arms.

"I'm sorry, Chuck. I was just going to find my husband."

"In this madhouse?" He swept the crowd with a well-shaped, well-kept hand.

"It's not so bad—"

"Tell you what. Dance with me just this once, and while we're on the floor, you can keep a lookout for your husband."

Why not? she reasoned. Besides, it was just a dance.

"Okay, but just one…"

Of course, Zendajas turned out to be a marvelous dancer, whirling her into a two-step with a devastatingly sexy charm.

"Better get an unlisted number, or you'll never get any sleep when you're off duty," she told him as they moved to the throbbing rhythm.

"Why's that?" he asked, grinning down at her.

"Because I have a feeling you're about to become Vanderbilt's designated 'most eligible bachelor.'"

He laughed and bent lower to whisper something in her ear. Whatever he said, however, was lost in the shock coursing through her as she caught sight of Cassidy standing at the edge of the crowd, watching her. Though surrounded by smiling, laughing people having fun, he seemed utterly alone, his expression stony, his eyes bleak.

Before she could break free and go to him, however, he turned and disappeared into the crowd, his broad back like an unbreachable barrier between them.

Cassidy was just congratulating himself on finding a quiet corner when he felt a rustling at his elbow. "You look like a man who needs a hug," Sylvia Moore declared, grinning up at him with an older version of Karen's smile. In spite of his sour mood, he found himself grinning back.

"Is that a fact?"

"Yep. It's also a fact that *I*, myself, am in desperate need of one, so how about getting with it?"

"Yes ma'am," he said as he leaned down to give her a hard squeeze. He'd always liked Karen's mother. She had a resilience and strength about her that he admired. And at fifty-six Sylvia was still an extremely vibrant, interesting woman with the figure of a runway model and an innate sense of style that Karen had always envied.

Karen had been six weeks pregnant when he'd met Sylvia for the first time. He'd been tied in knots the night he'd stood at Karen's side in her mother's stylish living room, braced for the lash of a mother's tongue.

Sylvia had simply sat there for a while, lost in thought. And then she'd left her chair and come to them. He'd willed himself to meet her gaze, grimly aware that he deserved whatever abuse she chose to dish out.

Instead, she'd framed his face in hands very like her daughter's and solemnly welcomed him to the family. Just like that, he'd been accepted. She'd never once blamed him for his past sins.

It had taken him a few years to learn to trust that easy acceptance.

"Nice dress. Sexy," he said, lifting a suggestive brow.

"Behave yourself," she retorted with a laugh. "I'm too old to be sexy."

"Guess that's why Frank Bidwell's been hanging around you like a lovesick puppy for the past couple of years."

Sylvia's face turned a pretty shade of pink, even as she offered him a reproving look. "Frank is too conscious of his dignity to be lovesick."

Cassidy snorted. At last count, Franklin Bidwell owned half the county. As tough as an old boot, the man had clawed his way up from nothing. Along the way he'd left a trail of beautiful but disappointed girlfriends. According to the buzz Cassidy had heard here and there, Sylvia was the first woman his own age Bidwell had dated since he'd been in junior high school.

"I understand you've been keeping secrets, Mr. Sloane."

He felt a clammy hand seize his heart. "Care to be more specific?" he hedged, careful to keep his voice even.

"Vicki tells me you're a whiz at dressmaking."

The sick pressure in his chest eased off. "I stuck more pins in my thumb than the darn hem."

Sylvia laughed. "She looks adorable, doesn't she?"

Cassidy nodded. "She tried to talk me into letting her wear lipstick."

"Aha. Well, it is a tad early."

"Try ten years early," he grated, watching one of his hands whirling Wanda June into a two-step. Randall Whitehorse was a decent enough kid, even though he'd flirted with a bad crowd for a while, but just to make sure the kid had his priorities straight, Cassidy made it a point to catch his eye. He grunted in satisfaction as the young cowpuncher turned red and widened the distance between himself and Wanda June.

"Frank said you had a reputation as a hard-ass," Sylvia said, watching the young couple spin into the crush of dancers. "I refused to believe it until now."

"Watch your tongue, Grandma, or I'll show you what I really am."

Sylvia grinned, and the diamond studs in her ears flashed. "You don't scare me, Cassidy Sloane. You talk tough, but you're really a very sweet man inside."

"Don't count on it." He scowled and thought about fighting his way to the bar for a cold one.

"Karen never would have fallen in love with a man who was cruel or thoughtless," Sylvia said, suddenly serious. "Which is why I'm breaking one of my own rules to ask you to try a little harder to understand who she really is behind that confident front she's so busy showing everyone."

"I know exactly who she is, Sylvia. Vicki's mom and my wife."

She pursed her lips, then exhaled slowly, as though preparing herself to do battle. "Karen loves being a wife and mother, make no mistake about that, but she's also a doctor, and a good one."

Cassidy heard someone call his name and looked up to see one of his fellow ranchers dancing past. "Lookin' good, Rafe," he called with a nod. He shifted, then reluctantly returned his gaze to his mother-in-law's now somber face.

"Might as well get it all out, Sylvia, while you've got me trapped."

Her mouth softened, but her brown eyes remained troubled. "I bought Karen dolls to dress, and she pretended they were patients. When she wasn't tearing up my best sheets to use as bandages, she was dulling my kitchen knives on pretend operations." Her lips curved into a fond smile that had Cassidy sucking in. "She gave up a lot for that dream, Cassidy. While her friends were spending hours on the phone with one another, Karen was in her room studying. She refused dates in order to study, lost boyfriends when she wouldn't put herself at their beck and call. All because she was determined to be a doctor."

Cassidy shifted and wished he could simply walk away. "I respect that, Sylvia, and I'm not saying she should give up the practice of medicine—just postpone it until Vick doesn't need her so much."

"Has it ever occurred to you that if she does, she might never go back to it? Or that even if she tries, she might be so rusty no one will invite her to join a practice?"

"So she can start her own."

"It doesn't work that way." Sylvia's voice came out sharp and impatient. "Cassidy, I'm begging you, don't make Karen choose between her love for you and her love of medicine. Otherwise, she just might end up hating you." Sylvia inhaled, then released the breath slowly. "You could lose her, Cassidy. And once she's gone, I'm very much afraid you'd never get her back. My little girl can be stubborn, too, you know. Especially when she's been hurt."

"Either way, I'll survive." He bent to brush a kiss over Sylvia's cheekbone before excusing himself.

Five minutes later he was standing outside, staring at the threatening clouds, his gut knotted. Sylvia had been right. His marriage was crumbling all around him, tearing chunks out of both he and Karen. Soon Vicki would be affected.

Why couldn't Karen see that as clearly as he could? Why couldn't she understand that he was fighting to keep them together the only way he knew how—the same way he'd fought for the ranch and the respect of his peers—by pushing and clawing and never backing down?

For the past few months he'd spent a lot of time trying not to think or feel or care. Karen had tried to talk to him a time or two. She'd come close to begging him to open up. To confront their problems head-on.

As far as he was concerned there wasn't all that much that needed saying. Unless she came to her senses and made her family her first priority, things were just naturally going to get worse between them.

Karen had never been drunk in her life. Tipsy, sure—a time or two—but never "hammered flat and left out to rot" as Cassidy had called it once when one of the men had come home reeling and stinking of booze. The way he'd said it had made Karen shake her head and wonder what possessed a person to medicate himself with mind-numbing poison.

Now she knew.

Sometimes it was just too painful to be awake and aware.

Like now, she thought as she and Vicki stood in a small alcove off the main hall, waiting for the bearded kid from the

Herald to finish adjusting the intricate dials on his camera long enough to take their picture. Using the blank white wall as a backdrop, he'd set up extra lights, reflective umbrellas and a tripod, then one after another, gathered the guests-of-honor together with some of those who'd received aid and comfort during the crisis.

Now it was Vicki's turn to be in the spotlight. Pleased as punch, she clung tightly to Rags's leash and watched the photographer with big eyes. Her friend, Elizabeth, hovered nearby, alternately making faces to make Vicki laugh or rolling her eyes.

"Hold still, Rags," Karen muttered when the excited pooch all but knocked her over in his eagerness to explore his new surroundings.

"I got him, Mommy," Vicki promised, tugging on her pet's tail.

Rags immediately sat down on Vicki's shiny black Mary Janes while at the same time letting out another exuberant bark, drawing laughter and good-natured wisecracks from Brendan Gallagher and the other men who'd been herded into the alcove with her.

As soon as the dance with the intern had ended, she'd found Cassidy and asked him to dance. He'd pleaded fatigue and suggested she ask someone else. Wounded, she'd done just that. But she'd been careful to pick someone safe, and so had chosen Frank Bidwell. Silver-haired, charismatic and charming, Frank had taken pains to make her feel like the belle of the ball.

It hadn't helped. It had been Cassidy's arms she'd wanted to hold her, Cassidy's warmth she'd wanted to feel enveloping her, Cassidy's deep voice murmuring to her above the sound of the music.

Damn the man, she thought, hugging herself in spite of the heat of humanity and the cloying smell of clashing aftershaves surrounding her. Now that she was nearly finished with her responsibilities to everyone else, he seemed to have forgotten he'd ever tried to hustle her away.

"Look, Grandma, we're going to be in the paper again!"

Vicki called when she spotted her grandmother entering the room on Frank's arm.

From her vantage point just inside the door, Sylvia grinned. "I see, sweet soul," she called in answer to her granddaughter's greeting.

"A little farther to the left, Dr. Sloane, if you please," the photographer called as he lifted his gaze from the viewfinder. "Yeah, that's good. Next to your daughter and the dog. Okay, that'll do. Now, if you guys in the back would just squeeze together a little more...yeah, like that. Great!"

"All right, everyone look this way." The harried young man frowned into the viewfinder, then lifted his head. "Something's wrong."

Looking upset, Vicki glanced around anxiously. "Daddy's not here."

"Sure he is, Vicki," Brendan Gallagher boomed. "Right over there holding up that there wall."

Vicki swiveled her head in the direction of Brendan's pointing finger. "Daddy, why are you over there?"

Grinning, Gallagher beckoned to his poker buddy, "Hey, Cassidy, you think you could get a little closer to your wife and daughter?"

Her heart pounding, Karen watched Cassidy straighten from his spot against the wall and amble toward the group. When had he come in? she wondered, watching him approach. Not even the expert tailoring of the suit could disguise the hard, well-muscled contours of his sinewy body. As for his shoulders, they seemed impossibly wide, sheathed in the dark material. In spite of the tension of the evening, she couldn't help feeling a purely womanly thrill that he was her husband.

"Stand next to Mommy, okay?" Vicki ordered with an impatient scowl. "Put your arm around her, like you did in the parking lot."

Karen felt a ripple of uneasiness that turned quickly to shock as Cassidy went instead to stand behind his daughter. He stared straight ahead until the photographer finished taking pictures, then walked out of the room. Not once had Cassidy even looked at her.

Five

By the time they left the exhibition hall an hour later, the night air had taken on the chill of a knife blade in winter. The rain that had threatened all day finally began shortly before they reached the edge of town. Within minutes, the winter-rutted road was treacherously slick, and visibility had narrowed to the limit of the truck's headlights. Even with the heater turned to high, Karen couldn't seem to get warm inside.

Huddled into the suit coat Cassidy had insisted she wear, she rested her aching head against the seat and watched the fence posts whizzing past in the rain-drenched night. Behind her in the truck's extended cab, Vicki and Rags were curled up together on the seat, asleep.

Next to her in the driver's seat, Cassidy drove with his usual efficiency—and in a stony silence that tore at her. Never all that talkative under the best of circumstances, he'd said very little beyond the usual words of a man settling his family into the truck for the long drive home. Once, he would have cuddled her close on the bench seat, his hard thigh pressing hers, his arm a comforting weight on her shoulders.

How many times in recent months had the two of them ridden home in silence, resentment and hurt stretching between them? Too many, she decided, opening her eyes and directing her gaze his way.

From the first moment she'd seen him stretched out on the stark white sheets in an ER cubicle, his hard jaw clenched and his skin stark white under the tan and stubble, she'd been fascinated by his face. Not because it was smooth and handsome or even noble, but because it seemed to reflect a life lived on its own terms.

Cassidy wasn't always a likable man—his manner was too abrupt and his sarcasm too cutting. But in all the years she'd known him, he'd never shaded the truth or broken a promise. As her mother had once told her, integrity went a long way toward smoothing a few rough edges in a man.

She still loved his face, she realized after a moment's reflection—the angular slopes and chiseled lines, the blatantly masculine set to his chin, the determination untouched by the harsh ravages of wind and cold and a blistering sun.

And yet, there had been times when she'd sensed an occasional easing of the tight rein he kept on his feelings, a momentary lapse in the iron discipline that ruled him. At those times, she'd almost held her breath in an agony of yearning, hoping deep in her heart that he might actually begin to trust her with his feelings as well as his thoughts. But no, he'd always drawn back at the last second, almost as if he were afraid to make himself vulnerable to her.

In the early years, she'd tried desperately to understand his need to keep an emotional barrier between them. When she'd failed, she'd made excuses for his remote ways, assuring herself there had to be a logical reason for his reluctance to trust her.

As a doctor, she'd taken enough psychology classes to know that people could sustain all kinds of injuries, not all of them physical, and she'd suspected that Cassidy had been dealt a nearly mortal wound to the soul.

She sighed—silently, she thought—until he turned his head to look her way. "Something wrong?" he demanded, his southwestern drawl unusually strong.

"What you said about the trip to Toponas, the inn with the canopied bed and you and I naked on the sheet—"

"Forget it, Karen." She could swear he was blushing as he returned his gaze to the road ahead.

"It was a lovely idea."

"It was a *dumb* idea, but I was desperate, and desperate men do desperate things."

She made herself ignore the edge to his voice. "We could still go. I'm sure Mother's home now, and we could leave Vicki and Rags at her place on the way. I have to work tomorrow afternoon, but we could spend Sunday morning in bed, the way we used to."

His gaze flickered her way once more, compelling even in the dimly lit cab. "I'm shorthanded on Sunday, remember?"

Karen refused to give up. She pulled one hand from his jacket pocket and let her fingers curl over his hard quadriceps. He stiffened, but kept his gaze fixed on the road ahead.

"Did I ever tell you how much I love the feel of your body in mine, Cassidy?" she murmured, careful to keep her voice low. "The hard, smooth power of you. The scent of sexual musk, the ripple of your back muscles as you make yourself go slowly with me."

His chest rose and fell in a jerky movement that gave her heart. Her own breathing was none too steady, either. "Stop it, Kari," he demanded, his voice as strained as his breathing.

Emboldened by the hard bulge behind the fly of his trousers, she slid her fingers a few inches closer to that impressive ridge, only to have him clamp his hard fingers over hers, trapping her. "Golden Girl's in foal," he said in a rough whisper.

She tensed, picturing the pretty mare writhing in agony. "How do you know?"

"Called Billy a coupla times."

She felt a pang of disappointment. "Is she doing okay?"

"Last I heard."

Karen heard the low rasp of impatience in his voice and frowned. "You're worried?"

"Some, yeah." With a sigh she slipped her hand free and settled back against the hard seat.

"Is that why you looked as though you wanted to rip my head off when I asked you to dance with me?" she asked a few moments later.

He spared her a look that did little to warm her. "Dancing's your thing, not mine."

"That's not true. I love the way you dance."

One side of his surprisingly sensitive mouth eased into a cynical slant. "Sure you do. That's why you looked like a cat lappin' up cream while you were dancin' with that hospital Romeo."

Karen blinked. "How did you know Chuck worked at the hospital?"

"Asked around."

A smile broke over her chilled face. "Why?"

"So I'd know whose jaw I was breakin' if he moved his hand one inch lower."

Karen laughed softly and hugged the knowledge of his jealousy to her like a cozy blanket on a frigid day. If he could feel one emotion, he could feel others.

"Chuck's harmless," she said with a shrug. "Besides, it was just a dance."

Cassidy took a tighter grip on the wheel. The last thing he needed now was a reminder of the sight of another man all but making love to his wife on the dance floor. Especially when his body was engorged and hurting. "Don't kid yourself, Kari. Good old harmless Chuck was angling for more than a two-step."

Her laughter was as soft as an early morning breeze. He felt the need for her all the way to the quick, where it twisted and burned like forge-heated steel.

"Oh, Cassidy, I do love you," she murmured, gazing at him with her heart—and expectation—in her eyes.

Those damn words again, he thought with a bitter weariness. Like they solved everything.

"Rain's lettin' up."

"Please, Cassidy, don't shut me out," she pleaded with soft urgency. "I hate this tension between us."

"Kari, I'm doing the best I can here."

"I'm trying to understand, but you're making it difficult." She leaned closer and her scent tantalized his senses. "All I'm asking is that you meet me halfway."

"There's no halfway in marriage, Karen. Either your family comes first or it doesn't."

"You're determined to make me feel guilty for wanting to heal people who are sick, aren't you."

She could have sworn he flinched, then decided it had been a trick of the light. "No, I'm trying to make you see how much you're hurting your child by insisting on having your own way."

He heard a rustling as she settled back against the seat. The soft sigh reaching him moments later tore at him. He'd hurt her—again. It seemed as though he was always hurting her these days. But damn, he just wanted what was best for the child they'd brought into the world. He'd tried in every way he knew how to bend.

They rode in silence for several minutes before the turn to the ranch came into view. Karen felt a change in the monotonous rhythm as the truck slowed and swayed, then rumbled over the cattle guard beneath the rough-hewn logs forming an entrance arch. Beyond the heavy timbers signifying the beginning of Lazy S land, the road turned to gravel, still heavily rutted by the winter thaw.

As they rounded that first slow curve before the track wended its serpentine way up the rise toward the house, she waited for the warm rush of anticipation and relief she invariably felt caressing her tired muscles whenever home was near.

Instead, she felt her muscles slowly, inexorably tightening in that same painful way that preceded her into the ICU where a terminally ill patient waited.

Yard lights splashed over her closed lids, rousing her. Above her head, the rain beat with a muffled fury on the steel roof, easing off only when Cassidy pulled into the covered shed where a half-dozen Lazy S vehicles were lined up in a tidy row.

"There's an umbrella in the Blazer," she murmured, sitting up.

Cassidy nodded as he killed the engine. His jaw was tight, his posture stiff. "Sit still. I'll get it."

With one fluid movement, he freed himself from the seat belt and opened the door. Cold air rushed into the cab, accompanied by the familiar scents of sodden earth and horse dung. Behind her, she heard a muffled murmur of protest, followed by sounds of stirring.

"Are we home, Mommy?"

Karen was already smiling as she turned her face toward the back seat where Vicki was struggling with her seat belt. "Home safe and sound, sweet stuff."

Vicki gave herself over to a huge yawn, then blinked. "Where's Daddy?"

"Right here, peanut."

At the sound of Cassidy's voice, Rags scrambled to his feet, his wide hindquarters wagging along with his tail as he jumped from the truck's narrow passenger area. Stifling another yawn, Vicki started to follow, only to have Cassidy stop her.

"Hang on a minute. It's nasty out there."

Along with the umbrella, he'd fetched the old woolen lap rug Karen kept for emergencies. He gave the umbrella to Vicki and put the rug on top of the truck.

"Here, use this. Don't want to ruin that new party dress, now, do we?"

"What about Rags?" she asked when the rambunctious dog took to running circles around her.

"Rags has his own coat," Cassidy said as he opened the passenger's door.

As Karen put her hand in his, a longing to rekindle their earlier brief moment of rare playfulness ran through her. Later, she told herself, when he's not worried about the mare.

"Look, Daddy!" Vicki exclaimed, pointing toward the long, low building made of rock and situated a good twenty yards from the shed. "The lights are on in the foaling barn. Goldie must be having her baby. Hurry, Daddy, before we're too late."

"Now, Vick, it's been a long day for you and—"

"You promised!"

Karen felt the sigh rumble through his chest and hid a smile. For all his steely control and unquestioned command over his men—and himself—he invariably melted when Vicki worked her feminine wiles.

"Okay, but just for a few minutes."

"I can get myself out," Karen assured them both. "You two go ahead to the barn and hold Goldie's hoof."

"Oh Mommy," Vicki muttered, rolling her eyes.

"Hang on, Vick," her father ordered. "Give me a minute to help your mom before you go running off."

"But, Daddy, Goldie *needs me,*" Vicki protested, struggling to open the umbrella.

"She'll still be needing you two minutes from now."

"I'm fine, Cassidy," Karen assured him, her hand still in his.

Pointedly, he dropped his gaze to the thin pumps she'd bought on a whim. In retrospect, it seemed foolish to have worn them on such a night, but—

"Ooph." Sensation jolted through her as he suddenly scooped her into his arms. She quickly circled his neck with her arms and held on tight.

"Best run before that big black cloud lets go, peanut."

"C'mon, Rags," she shouted before charging full tilt toward the shed, Rags barking excitedly as he raced ahead.

"Here, put this over your head," he ordered as he reached out one hand to grab the tattered blanket from the top of the cab.

"Don't let her see something that will hurt her," Karen said, wrinkling her nose at the woolen cloth's musty smell. "She loves Golden Girl very much."

He said nothing as he carried her through the now-driving rain to the back porch. After climbing the steps, he set her down carefully, then stepped back. "Don't wait up. I figure to spend most of the night getting this little one born."

Karen mourned the loss of his body against hers almost as much as she missed the easy warmth that had flowed for a few precious moments outside the exhibition hall.

"Why don't I make a pot of coffee and bring it out to you," she said quickly before he could turn away.

Something flickered in his eyes, but they were too dark to read. "Don't bother. We have our own pot out there."

The rain pounded mercilessly against the porch roof, showing little sign of stopping, as he turned and headed back the way he'd come.

Karen had just finished removing her makeup and was drying her face when she heard Vicki calling her. "In the bathroom, sweetie," she called back.

After folding the towel, she hung it on the rack, then switched off the light and returned to her bedroom a moment before Vicki came rushing in, her small chest heaving violently. Karen started to smile, then realized that Vicki's face was gray and her eyes bright with anguish.

"Sweetheart, what's wrong?" she cried anxiously. "Has something happened to Golden Girl?"

"Oh, Mommy, I'm so afraid." Vicki ran into her mother's arms, her face pressed to Karen's midriff. Raindrops glistened like tears on the little girl's shaking shoulders and the hem of her new dress was torn and muddy.

"Shh, it's okay," she murmured, hugging her daughter close. "Take a deep breath and calm down."

Vicki's small body trembled violently, and her thin arms tightened around Karen's waist like a small vise. Bits of straw clung to her braids and she smelled of horses.

Karen pictured her child trying to get her small arms around her horse's strong neck in an instinctive gesture of love and comfort. From her infancy on, Vicki had been a hugger, like her mom.

"She's dying." Vicki choked on the words and had to take a breath.

"How do you know?" Karen prodded gently. "Perhaps it just looks that way."

Vicki shook her head, spattering Karen's robe with raindrops. "I heard Daddy talking to the vet on the phone in the barn, and he told him to hurry or we might lose the foal, too."

"Oh, no," Karen murmured, tears springing to her eyes.

Golden Girl was a beautiful animal, but more important, she had a loving heart and a sweet disposition. Karen never worried about Vicki's safety when she was astride her beloved Goldie.

"Sweetheart, maybe it's not as bad as you think," she soothed, praying she was telling the truth. "Doc Caine is a wonderful vet. Remember, he saved Rags when he was bitten by a rattler."

Vicki's head moved in a weak nod. "Daddy made me come inside," she cried, her voice muffled by the thick material of Karen's robe. "He said Goldie was hurting too bad for me to watch."

If it would hurt Vicki, it would hurt Cassidy more, Karen realized sadly. Not only because he hated to see an animal suffer, but also because he'd allowed Vicki to help him raise the mare from a filly. She'd been there when he'd soothed and petted the skittish two-year-old into letting him slip a saddle onto her back. And she'd been there when Cassidy had ridden Golden Girl for the first time.

Vicki had never lost a pet before. Cassidy's animals tended to thrive, especially the horses. Even the ones that had suffered serious injury received such diligent care that they invariably survived.

Once Cassidy had given his protection, it became a sacred trust. A point of honor. Her instincts told her that he would die rather than betray that trust. It frightened her sometimes, even as it did give her a sense of absolute security.

"Honey, I know this is rough for you to handle," she said in the quiet way she often used with the distraught relatives of dying patients, "but I think the best thing you could do now is go on to bed and get a good night's sleep. If Doc Caine does save Goldie and the foal, you'll need all your strength in order to help Billy take care of her."

"But I want to be with her!" Vicki cried, lifting her head and looking up. "I promised her I'd be with her when it was her time." She lifted a hand to dash away the tears streaming down her cheeks. "I *promised!* And Daddy says promises are sacred."

Karen took a careful breath. Why did children always think in black and white when so much of life was played out in shades of gray?

"Daddy's right about promises being sacred, sweetie, but this is a special case."

"No, it's not! Goldie expects me to be with her."

Karen led the little girl to the bed and sat down, facing her. "Vicki, I remember when I was in labor with you. Grandma had promised to be with me then, just the way you promised Goldie. But when the time came, I was so busy doing what I needed to do to get you born I didn't have time to pay attention to anything else. It's like that with Goldie now."

Vicki bit her lip, her face so pale the freckles dotting her nose stood out like bright specks of gold dust. "If you promise me she won't die, then I'll go to bed."

Karen gently tidied Vicki's shiny bangs, allowing her hand to linger in a caress the way Cassidy sometimes did. "I can't make you a promise like that, sweetie. I wish I could."

Confusion settled in Vicki's innocent brown eyes. "You're a doctor. Maybe you could help Goldie with the birthing."

"I'm not that kind of a doctor. Besides, Doc Caine knows what he's doing."

As though summoned by her words, she heard the crunch of tires on gravel. "There he is now," she said. "Goldie's in good hands, the best."

"Doc Caine's?"

"And Daddy's. If anyone can keep Goldie alive and fighting, it's Daddy. Right?"

Vicki blinked, then nodded. Her absolute trust in her father was heartbreakingly touching. Karen felt a wave of anguish when she realized just how hard it would be for their child if she and Cassidy were ever to separate.

"If I go to bed, will you promise to call me when the foal is born?"

Karen smiled. "As soon as Daddy tells me, I'll tell you. That's a promise."

Vicki turned to look toward the window one last time, then

squared her small shoulders and nodded. "Okay. I'll go to bed."

"Good girl." Karen pulled her close for a long hug, then rose and walked with her to the cheery room at the end of the hall.

Six

Two hours later, Cassidy stood by the wide double doors of the foaling shed and watched the taillights of Paul Caine's pickup disappear into a wall of rain.

The pastures would be soup, he thought, turning toward the light and the chores that still needed doing. The sudden motion sent a wave of dizziness sweeping over him, and he staggered. Reaching out a hand, he steadied himself against the barn's rough exterior.

Pain shot up his shoulder, a reminder of the agonizing, long hours he'd spent fighting the dying mare's spasming muscles, trying to turn the foal before its delicate bones were crushed. In the end it hadn't mattered.

Golden Girl was gone. And so was her foal.

"Boss, you feelin' okay?" Billy and one of the younger hands who'd been helping stepped quickly to his side.

Cassidy offered his ramrod a curt nod. "Just catchin' my breath before I finish cleaning up."

"Why don't you go on in and let me'n Randall here do the cleanin'?" Billy suggested, pulling a cigar from the pocket of his filthy shirt.

It was tempting, but Cassidy made himself refuse. Instead, he stepped away from the wall and took a testing breath. The dizziness was gone. In its place was a heavy lethargy that was almost as bad.

"You go on home, the both of you. I already owe you enough overtime to damn near bust me."

"Hell, boss, I'm already into you for two months' advance," Billy drawled, striking a wooden match on the wall behind him. "Don't make me no never mind if you pay me extra for tonight, anyway," he said between puffs as he fired his smoke to life.

"Me, neither," Whitehorse added, sweeping off his Stetson with a weary hand. "Got me no place to spend my money anyhow."

Billy snorted. "The hell you say. I thought you had plans to escort Wanda June to some big dance at the high school next month."

"She got herself in a tangle over me wearing this fancy tuxedo." The young cowboy flexed his shoulders as though trying to shuck off the very idea. "When I told her I'd rather be shut up in a ten-foot corral with a Brahma stud than put on sissy duds, she up and told me to get lost."

Billy exchanged a wry look with Cassidy, who suspected his men were deliberately ragging each other in an attempt to take his mind off the mess inside. He ground his teeth. Even after years of trying, he'd never quite conquered the queasiness that invariably followed the sight of blood.

He did his best to hide it. Sometimes he succeeded. Mostly he failed. Tonight his men and Caine had had a ringside seat while he'd puked up his dinner. Though they'd pretended not to notice, he was still feeling raw.

"Dawn comes early," he said, his voice rasped by the memory of his earlier humiliation. "You guys can stand here and jaw all night if you want, but I'm fixin' to wind things up and try for a few hours' sleep."

"Sure thing, boss." From the corner of his eye, Cassidy saw Billy jerk his head at the kid who looked puzzled for an instant, then took his cue.

"Night, Billy, Mr. Sloane."

Cassidy nodded. "Appreciate your help tonight, Whitehorse. Thanks."

The kid's tired face creased into a wide grin. "Sure thing, boss. Sorry we couldn't save her. She was a sweet animal." Whitehorse turned and walked toward his truck. Seconds later, the engine roared to life and Randall headed home to his bed.

Ignoring a tug of envy, Cassidy squared his shoulders and

started to step across the threshold, only to have Billy stop him. "Let me do it, Cass," he said.

Cassidy had to unlock his jaw to answer gruffly, "You've done enough, but thanks for the offer."

"Cass, listen to me." His gaze bored into Cassidy's, full of a rough intensity. "So the sight of blood makes you sick. So what? There's no shame to it. Tonight, in there, when the doc…well, I was pretty queasy myself."

Cassidy fought down the nightmare image of Caine's scalpel flashing in the light. "Nice try, Billy, but I have to handle this my way."

The ramrod nodded slowly, demons of his own surfacing for a moment in his tired green eyes. "I'll leave you to it, then."

Cassidy watched the man he considered his best friend climb into his pickup and drive away, knowing even as he stood there with the rain sheeting past him that he was stalling. Anything to keep from going back inside, where the stench of blood still hung in the air like a curse.

By the time the sound of the truck faded, he was beginning to wish he'd shucked his pride and accepted Billy's offer. He searched for an appropriate phrase to describe his own stupidity, then realized he was too tired to swear.

"Just get it done, Sloane," he muttered as he made himself walk inside.

Even though he was prepared, the metallic odor that enveloped him had him gritting his teeth by the time he'd taken only a few steps. Get it done, he repeated silently, reaching for the pitchfork. He'd pile the blood-soaked straw out back, then scour the stall and the section of the cement floor he could reach with bleach and disinfectant. He'd have to wait for the animal disposal guys to move the corpses before he could finish the job. Still, he'd have the place clean enough so it was safe to let Vicki come in to say goodbye.

Willing his body to cooperate, he set to work. His muscles ached at the abuse, but the pain kept his mind from wandering. Overhead, the rain beat a steady rhythm, like the tick of the metronome Sylvia kept on the piano.

When Vicki had been four or five, it had been one of her favorite toys.

His hands tightened on the fork as he let himself think, finally, of the task that awaited him when this one was done. No matter how he circled the truth in his head tonight, he knew in his gut that telling Vicki was going to be pure hell.

Vicki and her Golden Girl had grown up together. Two frisky and willful youngsters galloping through the fields.

And now, because he'd wanted to breed Goldie's beauty and heart to the stallion's courage, Vicki was about to learn the pain of losing her best friend.

Karen started to turn over in bed, only to find herself teetering precariously on the edge of the mattress. Still half asleep, she pried her eyes open in order to check the time by the clock radio. It was then that she realized she had fallen asleep on Vicki's narrow bed while waiting for Vicki to drift off.

Next to her, Vicki was cuddled into a ball, her cheeks rosy from sleep, her breathing regular and deep. The room was dark with the exception of a square of muted light from the security lamp shining through the ruffled curtains. The house was quiet. No sound from outside penetrated the old house's thick walls.

Karen had no idea what time it might be, though she suspected it was a few hours before dawn. Her head ached from too much wine and too little sleep, and her back was stiff from her awkward position.

The last thing she remembered she'd been staring at the glow from the small lamp she'd left burning on the dresser, thinking about the first time Cassidy had made love to her.

It had been in the hayloft of the main barn, a huge old dinosaur of a structure, with a granite foundation and huge oak beams.

Cassidy had been bucking hay bales that day and the scent of fresh-mown alfalfa had filled the air with a delightful sweetness.

It had been close to a hundred degrees that Saturday afternoon, and he'd been working without a shirt. Incredibly strong, utterly beautiful, he'd handled the monstrously heavy bales with an economy of motion that had amazed her. Under a shimmering sheen of sweat, his body had been deeply tanned, a magnificent creation of fluid muscle and resilient sinew, furred across the chest with a soft pelt of black curls.

He'd said very little, but his deep-set dark brown eyes had been liquid with a longing so fierce she'd taken a step backward. But when he'd held out his hand and beckoned her to step from the ladder onto the dusty, hay-strewn floor, she'd obeyed without a second thought.

Even as he'd kissed her out of her shorts and top, she'd been aware of the incredible power of his body, the massively muscled chest, the steely strength in long legs capable of controlling a half-ton horse with ease.

He hadn't asked for her love, but it had been his from the first gentle, almost shy touch of his callused hand, the first slow smile that reached his eyes as well as his hard mouth.

In her heart they had been wed from the moment he'd slowly eased his body into hers, inexorably stretching her to accommodate his hard length, his muscled frame shuddering from the effort to be gentle. Though he'd said little, she'd felt the hunger in him. The wild, desperate need that seemed to burn through his skin. In return, he'd made her soar.

Vicki had been conceived that hot, dusty day; she was sure of it.

Cassidy had doted on his daughter from the first magical moment of her birth, so much so that he'd wanted more children as soon as Karen's doctor had given her the go-ahead.

She'd wanted more children, too. A houseful. But later, after she'd finished her education and established herself in a practice. At the time, Cassidy had appeared to understand.

With a sigh, she smoothed the covers closer to her daughter's stubborn little chin. As Karen started to ease from the bed, she realized that a blanket had been thrown over her as she'd slept. The light had been extinguished as well, she realized belatedly.

Cassidy must have come in to check on Vicki and found

her there, too. Had he kissed her when he'd covered her? she wondered, then rejected the notion. Even in her sleep, she would have responded to him.

Bracing herself against the cold, she got to her feet and tiptoed barefoot out of the room. The light was on in the master bedroom. Cassidy was awake, lying naked on his back, his powerful arms folded under his head. One thick forearm bore a long, angry-looking scrape, and on his right shoulder was a large bruise already purpling and puffy, both giving testimony to the battle he must have waged to bring a new foal into the world.

He'd obviously showered. His black hair was still damp and only haphazardly combed away from his lined forehead and he smelled faintly of soap. The covers lay in disarray, as though jerked free in anger, and only the sheet covered him.

At her entrance he turned his head and looked at her. Though his gaze was direct, his expression was shuttered. Oh, no, *no!* she thought, already preparing herself for the worst.

"Golden Girl?" she asked quietly as she closed the door behind her.

"Gone. The foal, too. Prettiest little filly you ever saw." His gaze flickered, then held steady again. She wondered again what had happened to him in the past to prompt him to guard his feelings so brutally.

"I'm sorry."

He acknowledged that with a curt nod. "Doc tried, I'll give him that. But it was a breech."

Karen saw in his eyes the things he'd omitted, and she wanted to weep.

Feeling as though she'd aged a hundred years in the span of one day, she removed her robe and tossed it toward the foot of the bed. Outside, the wind strained against the branches of the towering aspens, and the old house creaked in a familiar nightly ritual that had never failed to soothe her—until tonight.

"I told Vicki I would give her the news as soon as you told me, but I don't have the heart to wake her," she said as she slipped beneath the already tumbled covers.

"I'll tell her. It's my responsibility."

"But *not* your fault."

His control slipped long enough to reveal a muscle ticking along his jaw. His voice, too, held a harsh note of self-censure. "It was my call, my decision to breed the mare."

"Of course you bred her," she hastened to assure him. "Goldie was a beautiful animal with excellent bloodlines. There isn't a rancher in the state who wouldn't have bred her."

"Tell that to my daughter." He plowed a hand through his already rumpled hair.

"I will, even though I have a feeling she'll figure that out for herself. Vicki has your instincts, your love of animals. She'll make a marvelous rancher."

His eyes flashed. "The hell she will."

Karen drew a calming breath. "Please, let's not get into another argument about our conflicting views on gender-specific careers."

Cassidy felt rage tearing at the edges of his calm, the strangling, desperate kind that always came when his thoughts threatened to slide into a pit of icy blackness where some nameless, faceless terror was always waiting.

"If that means I don't intend to allow my daughter to burn herself out doing a man's job, then, yeah, there's no point in arguing, because it's a done deal," he said with more force than finesse.

"No," she said quietly, distinctly. "It isn't. Victoria will have the same unlimited choices I had growing up."

"Yeah, and we all know how well you turned out, don't we, Dr. Sloane?"

"Damn you," she whispered, her voice as raw as a blizzard wind. "I don't deserve that."

"No, you're a great doctor. Everyone says so."

She breathed in sharply, then let the air out in a slow stream. "What's happening to us, Cassidy?" she asked, looking at him beseechingly.

"We're worried about Vicki, that's what's happening."

She shook her head. "No, it's more than that," she said after a long moment of deliberation.

"You're just upset."

"Why are you shutting me out when we both need each other so much?"

Need wasn't an emotion he allowed. Not for a long, long time. "Karen, I'm not exactly in a mood for a deep philosophical discussion at the moment." His voice came out hard and clipped, and he couldn't make himself say the words to ease the hurt now shimmering in her eyes like unshed tears. But it was the tears quivering on the tips of her lashes that broke him.

"Damn." He was moving before he thought, rearing up to close the distance between them, reaching for her even as he crashed his mouth down on hers.

He absorbed her unique taste, part sweet, part tart, and felt her lips soften. In the back of his mind he knew what he was doing wouldn't solve a thing, but the need to try one more time to bind her to him was too strong. But even as he argued that he was fighting for what was his by law and by need, he struggled against a feeling of revulsion at his own behavior. With a groan, he dragged his mouth from hers.

"No, don't stop," she pleaded, her voice thick with tears.

"It tears me apart when I hurt you," he rasped, blood surging to his loins. "I just can't seem to stop doing it."

"I know." Reaching up, she traced the line of his mouth with her fingertip, and heat shot through him. "I wish I'd declined the invitation to that stupid party."

"Goldie would still be dead, party or no party."

"Yes, but the party reminded us both of the things we said to each other that night at the cave entrance."

"You mean the things I said, don't you?"

She nodded. "They hurt, Cassidy. I can't deny that."

He felt an odd twisting in his gut. "Would you rather I lied?"

She shook her head. "I can't go on feeling guilty forever."

"I want you home, Kari. That's not going to change."

He saw the play of emotions in her eyes, bled a little when the glow left.

"Where does that leave us now, at this moment?" she asked, her chin angling defiance and strength.

"The same place it always does in this room. I want you."

"All right."

"Just like that?"

Her smile was ragged, but it still had the power to draw him closer. "No, not just like that. I want you, too."

Worn out from so much talk, he captured her finger between his teeth and used his tongue to lave the tip. Gentleness was a skill he'd only marginally mastered, but he steeled himself to go slowly. For her sake, he told himself. Not because he was hoping against hope that this time his will would prevail against the pill keeping her safe from his seed.

Yet it felt as though all the demons of hell were riding him hard, urging him to love her so completely she wouldn't have the strength to leave him. Helpless against a building need, he found her mouth again, this time to plunder and possess. Instead of retreating, she rose to meet him, her hands linking behind his neck to tug him closer. His breath mingled with hers, great warm gasps of desperate need, and soft, eager cries poured from her throat, exciting him into a fever only she could break.

Shaken, he ended the kiss, only to have her begin her own seduction of his mouth. His control teetered on a hot, honed edge, then shattered at the first tentative touch of her tongue against his lips. With a sound that was both anger and surrender, he opened his mouth and welcomed her pillaging tongue.

When he couldn't stand the torment any longer, he dragged his mouth from hers in order to concentrate on the warm, sweet treasure at the base of her neck. She tasted of bath soap and smelled delicious, exactly as a woman should.

His woman, he wanted to shout as he felt her fingers skimming his shoulders. As she arched her neck and pressed her breasts against his chest, flames licked at him, hotter than the man-made hell where he'd spent most of his life. In her kiss was the promise of release he craved—not only from his physical torment, but also from the talons of guilt and regret that never stopped clawing at him, no matter how desperately he tried to make his life count for something.

Karen writhed under him, her hands seeking and desperate, her strangled cries escalating. Again and again he filled his mouth with her, then tried to slake his pain and anger and shame by worshiping her breasts. Warm, full breasts tipped with hard little nubs so eager to be suckled, so temptingly sweet, even through the silky flannel of her gown.

"Yes, oh *yes!*" she urged, her voice thick with a passion that spurred his own onto higher ground. "Faster. Go faster."

"Easy," he managed to say between burning kisses, his body riding a dangerous ridge between pain and pleasure while he groped with the hem of the nightie.

"No, I want to feel you inside me," she urged, twisting and bucking like a wild thing even as her fingers fumbled to push his T-shirt to his armpits.

"Oh, baby, you feel good," he murmured, pulling her down onto the bed. He leaned over her and brought their hips closer together. She gasped when his engorged body probed hers, and he felt her welcoming heat through a thin layer of fabric.

He groaned with impatience and triumph as his fingers found the warm, sleek skin beneath the flannel. "Help me," he grated, his voice sounding thick as molasses.

Between kisses, she helped him free her from her gown. With one snap of his powerful wrist, he sent the thin material whooshing halfway across the room. His other hand shook a little as he skimmed his palm over her rib cage, over her belly where a few silvery lines attesting to her pregnancy still remained, to the soft nest of springy curls between her thighs.

He palmed her first, and felt her shiver. Burying his face between her breasts, he slipped one finger past the swollen folds protecting the tiny nubbin nestled just inside. He massaged the hard kernel of acutely sensitive nerve endings and felt her shudder, then come alive, arching, tearing at his hair, bucking against his thigh.

"Soon," he whispered, trying to gentle her the way he gentled a skittish mare, but she wouldn't allow restraint. On a groan of surrender, he slipped two fingers into the warm, moist sheath and felt the tremors shaking her. She was so slick, so hot, her readiness like a rare and precious gift that he would treasure always, especially in the dark nights ahead.

Panting, her breath coming in little sobs of need, she moved against his fingers. Gritting his teeth, he forced his mind off the hot, throbbing pressure in his groin and concentrated on stroking her into readiness.

Inarticulate cries broke from her as she moved faster and faster, her hair a tumble on the pillow as she arched her head backward. Awash in the musky, womanly scent of her, driven nearly to breaking, he strained to feel the first tiny shivers deep inside her, where his body craved welcome.

When he felt the spasms take hold, he drew back, his knee nudging her thighs wider. Bracing himself, he plunged downward, filling her. She cried out, her eyes flying open and her hips thrusting upward to take him deeper. Moaning, her breath came in rasping gasps now. She gripped his buttocks with hard, desperate fingers and urged him to move with her.

Pain tore at him, mingling with a rising urgency until finally he felt the hot tension inside her give way, and she cried out. He thrust harder, seeking desperately to escape the black prison cell where his sins had confined him.

His heart thundered in his ears, mingling with the guttural cry of his own release. At the same time, he heard Kari call his name and wrap her arms and legs around him. Once, twice, he felt himself convulse into her, until he was at once depleted and sated.

Later, as she slept in his arms, he let his eyes drift closed and told himself they could work things out. He wasn't sure he could stand it if they didn't.

Seven

Waking to a predawn gloom, Karen found herself alone. A quick check of the clock told her that it was past the time Cassidy usually awoke. Even so, she felt a pang of disappointment that he hadn't lingered long enough to kiss her awake. Still, she took heart in the fact that he'd made love to her so thoroughly she felt utterly cherished. No matter how fierce his need to control his life might be, there was still a part of him that she could reach. It wasn't much, but it was a start.

Shivering in the morning chill, she hurried down the hall to Vicki's room where she discovered her daughter snuggled into her bright coverlet, her small heart-shaped face as peaceful as an angel's. Something poignant and sad passed through her as she bent to kiss her daughter's temple. Today Vicki would find out that life wasn't always warm puppies and frisky colts.

After slipping into the slippers she'd left by the bed earlier, Karen headed toward the kitchen and the aroma of fresh-perked coffee. Double-strength and black as the road to hell, she thought as she poured herself a cup. Moments later she was standing by the kitchen window, staring out at the still-darkened buildings, while she waited for the caffeine to wake up her tired brain.

There should be a light in the barn, she realized with a fuzzy frown. Although it was still too early for the hands to begin showing up, Cassidy had a rule about checking things out early. By the time Billy and the others arrived, he would have his gelding fed and saddled, and the day planned out for each man.

No doubt he was waiting to break the news to Vicki before he started his day, she decided, taking another greedy sip. It wouldn't be easy for either of them, but she trusted Cassidy to break the news gently. That realization made her sigh. The tenderness he showed their daughter never failed to move her. And dammit, it made her ache inside because she wanted some of that tenderness for herself.

A few seconds later, her cup gripped in one hand, she approached Cassidy's office. The polished pine door was ajar, and light from within spilled into the shadowed hall in a long, thin wedge. Like the man himself, the room was unpretentious and spare. Everything had a purpose—his accounting books, breeding logs, a top-of-the-line computer that he hated but used with precise skill.

The desk itself was a one-of-a-kind treasure, a massive slab of western pine fully eight feet long, crosscut by some gigantic saw blade long ago and darkened by age and hard wear. One corner, the right, bore countless scuffs where Cassidy invariably propped his boot heels when lost in thought. There were no keepsakes on the desk or the floor-to-ceiling bookcases other than the ones Vicki had made for him and no pictures on the wall except her crayon drawings and a recent watercolor of Goldie she'd done for a 4-H art project.

Cassidy sat in his big, worn chair behind the desk, his back to her, his bare feet propped atop a stack of computer printouts. His favorite coffee mug with the broken handle and chipped rim was close at hand, still half-full of the same black sludge steaming in her own mug.

His ebony hair spilled onto his forehead, and his jaw showed the dark shadow of unshaven whiskers. He was wearing jeans so old the hems had long since frayed away and a faded blue shirt, the sleeves of which had been carelessly rolled back to the elbows, revealing roped forearms.

A spreadsheet glowed on the computer screen in front of him, but instead of studying the figures in their neat columns, he was gazing down at something in his hand. A photograph, she realized after a moment's study. Of Vicki and Goldie, she suspected, from the sadness that seemed to grip him.

He suddenly lifted his head and shifted his gaze toward the door. At the same time he slipped the photo in his hand beneath the desk blotter.

"Come in," he said quietly.

There was a stillness about him that made her uneasy. It was as if he had pulled everything inside, where it could be protected as fiercely as he protected his daughter.

"Vicki's still sleeping," she told him as she entered. "I'm glad it's Sunday so she doesn't have to go to school."

"Might be better if she did." He let his head fall back against the age-dark leather of the chair. "I hate to have her watch while the meat wagon hauls Goldie off."

"If I know Vicki, she'll insist." Life goes on, she thought as she moved to the window. After opening the drapes, she leaned against the heavy material and stared out at the new day.

The rain had stopped, and the sun was nudging the horizon, the first fingers of daybreak already turning a brilliant orange-red. She stood silently, letting the splendor soothe her.

"It's almost dawn," she murmured, loving the look of the ranch bathed in early morning mist. Then, turning slowly, she offered him a smile. "I missed you when I woke up."

His mouth softened a little. "I'm not much for sleeping past dawn."

"I know. I guess I was hoping you'd make an exception." She let her smile take on wanton edges. "I wanted to make love with you again."

"Kari, after last night I'm thinking I'll be lucky if I can ever make love again." Though his voice was tinged with a laconic humor, a flush spread over his hard cheekbones and into the silver-flecked thickness at his temples.

She felt something loosen and curl inside her. Hope, she realized, taking a step forward. Glorious, miraculous hope.

"Cassidy, we can work this out," she said eagerly. "I know we can."

A muscle jerked along his jaw as he met her gaze with unreadable eyes. "I'm open to suggestions," he said, his voice surprisingly gentle.

"Once I'm settled in a practice, I'll be able to hire a full-time housekeeper and maybe a nanny for Vicki."

His jaw tightened, then relaxed as though the muscles were answering some inner command. And for a second she thought she saw disappointment shimmering in his eyes. "Trust me, Karen. It's not the same."

"How do you know?"

His eyes grew bleak, then steadied. "My brother and I were pretty much raised by a baby-sitter."

Karen blinked. "You never told me that."

His shoulders moved only a fraction. "Why should I? It had nothing to do with you and me."

"Your mother had to work?" she asked, an idea taking shape in her mind.

"I don't have a mother."

"But you said she left when you were ten. That you found her address after your father died and sent her a wire, but she never answered."

Pain he thought he'd conquered years ago tore through him. He fought it the only way that was safe—with a cold anger.

"Hire the housekeeper if you want. I never wanted you to wear yourself out scrubbing toilets."

"In other words, you'll give me anything I want—as long as I quit my job and stay home full-time."

"Is it so wrong to want a normal life?"

"Normal for you, but not for me."

"And what about Vicki?"

She had to take a breath. "Vicki is totally well-adjusted and happy, and before you start accusing me of neglecting her, most of the time when she's not in school, she's out with you or Billy or one of the other men. And when we're both busy, Wanda is here."

He rubbed his callused fingers over the worn padding on the chair seat. "A child needs her mother. She needs *you*, Kari."

"She *has* me, Cassidy. Just not every moment of my time or every ounce of my energy."

She saw his eyes narrow a split second before he lowered his gaze to the desk. "Did you ever stop to think what it feels like for a child to live on leftovers?" he asked with a deadly softness.

"What are you talking about?"

"Scraps, Kari. Of time and attention and...other things."

Kari couldn't breathe. Was that how Cassidy had grown up? Feeling like a stray dog hanging around waiting for bits of attention or pieces of love?

Her heart softened. "Vicki has always been my first priority. No matter what, I always make sure I spend quality time with her."

"And your husband, Kari? Was that what happened last night? More quality time from Dr. Sloane?"

"You know it wasn't," she whispered.

"No, Karen, I *don't* know."

Karen heard a truck pull in and doors slam. It wouldn't be long before Billy was knocking on the back door, eager for a cup of coffee and a little gossip with the boss before they started the day.

Cassidy's expression told her that he, too, had heard the men arrive. She waited, expecting him to go out to start them on their day. When he didn't, she told herself that was a good sign.

"You don't want a nanny and you don't want Wanda," she repeated calmly.

"Wanda's fine. When you're not here."

"Which is exactly my point, Cassidy. Vicki's needs are being well met."

A flush ran up the back of his neck. "Quit the damn job," he said in that same quiet tone. "Call the hospital administrator tomorrow and resign."

His face was stony, his eyes cold, no reason at all to suspect that he was pleading with her. And yet, she felt as though he were staking everything he held dear on this one demand. Some of her anger fell away.

"I tried it your way," she said, careful to keep her voice

calm and reasonable. "For three years. I nearly lost myself as a result. I can't take that chance again."

His jaw tensed. Karen studied the deeply chiseled lines of character and experience in his hard face and marveled that he really had no conception of the power he held in those big work-worn hands because she loved him.

"Cassidy, listen to me, please." She leaned closer and touched his arm. His muscles contracted, and she let her hand drop. "Part of me loved being a full-time mom, especially when Vicki was toddling around, discovering something new and wonderful practically every minute of every day. And I loved fixing up this funny old house. But another part of me was dying by inches. Inside, I felt ashamed because I was—"

"Just a poor, uneducated rancher's wife?" The raw bitterness shuddering through his harsh question slammed into her like a body blow.

"No, that's not it at all! I love being a rancher's wife. And you have more knowledge of animal husbandry and agronomy than most PhDs."

"You said you were ashamed," he snarled.

"I said I was ashamed because I'd broken a promise I'd made to myself and my father to become a doctor," she said in deliberately calm tones. "To carry on the work he intended to do."

He narrowed his eyes to slits of glittering onyx between jet-black lashes, but in some strange way, his anger seemed forced. To keep her from getting too close? she wondered, and made a mental note to think about that later, in private.

"Let me get this straight, Karen. You consider this promise to your father more important than the promises you made to your husband. Is that about the right of it?"

"Be fair, Cassidy. I promised to love and cherish you, not turn myself over to you body and soul and mind."

"In other words you're—what? *Your own person? No one's domestic slave?*" Something volatile flashed in his eyes. "Well, screw that politically correct garbage. I grew up with a mother like you and I can tell you it ain't fun!"

"Cassidy—"

"If you hated the idea of staying home so damn much, why didn't you abort Vicki and be done with the whole thing?" The venom in his voice stunned her.

"Is that...is that what you wanted?"

"No, damn it! You were beautiful with my child in your belly. Everything I'd always dreamed—" Cassidy broke off to rake his hands through his hair. He felt his last hope slipping away, like the end of a lifeline slithering down a cliff where he was trapped. The knot in his belly twisted harder.

"Why isn't it enough for you to be my wife and Vicki's mother?" The question broke from him against his will, shaming him. It shamed him worse to realize his entire image of himself depended on the answer.

"It just...isn't. I've tried to live up to your ideal of the perfect woman, but it's destroying me."

"I don't want perfect, dammit. I just want my wife to stay home and trust me to take care of her and our children."

Karen drew a breath. "Cassidy, you're the fairest man I know. One of the kindest and gentlest, when you think no one's watching."

He looked offended, and she wanted to hug him almost as much as she wanted to shake him. "What's the point of this?" he demanded.

"The point is, I'm asking you to work with me to find some kind of accommodation we can both live with."

"No."

"That's all you have to say, after nearly ten years? Just no, without one word of explanation?"

He stood up, a powerful, intimidating male presence. She refused to retreat. "Excuse me. I have something important to tend to."

"Don't you dare walk out of here before we hash this out!"

Something dangerous bled into his eyes. "Don't give me orders, Karen."

"Why not? You just gave me one. Quit my job or lose my husband? Isn't that your final offer?"

Color slashed his cheekbones. "You're determined to take this to the wall, aren't you."

Her shoulders heaved as she ran an agitated hand through her tumbled hair. "I can't live this way, Cassidy. One minute you're making love to me like you really mean it and the next you're acting like you actually hate me."

"Not yet, but it's heading that way."

She turned pale, even as her chin came up. "Why? Because I refuse to bend to your will?"

His dark eyes smoldered between narrowed lashes. "Okay, you asked for it, Karen." He drew in a harsh, angry breath, and let it out fast. "My mother was a 'liberated' woman, just like you. She was also a cold, ambitious, self-centered bitch. Her career was everything to her. *Everything!* She destroyed my father and she did her best to destroy me. I swore, if I ever got married, it would be to a woman as different from her as I could find."

Karen felt her hands trembling and pressed them together in front of her. The naked emotion radiating from Cassidy's eyes was almost too much to bear.

"You...you sound as though you actually hate her."

"Hell, yes, I hate her!"

"But why? What did she do to deserve that?"

His mouth twisted. "I was nine. My brother was four. It was summer, and I had baseball practice. The sitter was sick, and my mother couldn't be bothered to find another one. I got the job of taking care of my brother. No big deal."

Karen had never seen him so cold, so controlled. It was only with difficulty that she staved off a shudder. "What happened?" she managed to say, even though she was almost certain he was talking about his brother's death.

"I made a mistake."

"A mistake?"

"I was in Little League. We had a good team, a chance at the series. The coach was pushing us pretty hard, calling practices every afternoon." His skin had paled, a sign of severe emotional stress that not even he, with his fierce will, could control. "My mother promised to be home early so I could make it to the field on time.'' His lashes flickered. "She was late, or maybe she just couldn't be bothered, so I took Johnny with me. The police said he must have been chasing a ball when he ran into the street. The woman who hit him wasn't even going the speed limit.''

"Oh, my God,'' she whispered, staring at him in an agony of shock and compassion. "I'm so sorry.''

He acknowledged that with the slight movement of one shoulder. "Johnny lived for a few minutes, five, I think, though I could be wrong.'' He took a breath, one that was ragged and harsh. "In spite of her neglect, my baby brother died crying for his mommy.''

Karen pressed shaking fingers to her mouth while tears ran down her face. "Oh, Cass,'' she whispered when she could force aside the lump in her throat. "No wonder you were so upset when we didn't know if Vicki was alive or dead.''

His face hardened. "Dammit, this isn't about me. It's about—''

He broke off, and for a moment the only sound in the room was the rasp of his ragged breathing. Somehow she managed to keep her knees from buckling.

"It's about me, you mean,'' she murmured, striving for those same flat, measured tones that had served him so well. "You think that I'm like your mother, don't you? That my career means more to me than my child or my husband? That...that I'm a cold-hearted, selfish bitch?''

When he didn't answer, she had her answer. "Of course, that would explain the things you said to me last June.'' She nodded her head slowly, feeling oddly disconnected from everything but the pain building inside her. "And if Vicki had died in that cave, you would never have forgiven me, just as you've never forgiven your mother.''

He flinched, and she wondered why he should react so strongly to the truth. When he would have said something, however, she cut him off with a jerky movement of one hand. "No, don't say anything more. You'd made your point very well.''

She smiled, a tribute to a physician's ability to become

detached from her emotions, she suspected. "Our marriage had been over for months. If it's all the same to you, I'd just as soon skip the funeral speeches."

His shoulders jerked, but his jaw seemed harder than ever. "You're telling me you want a divorce?"

Karen tried to take a deep steadying breath, but no matter how much oxygen she took in, it wasn't enough to stop the shudder that ran through her. "If I stay with you now, knowing what you really think of me, I would eventually end up hating myself—and you."

For a foolish instant, she thought he appeared shattered. But the curt nod he gave her proved her wrong. Before she managed another breath, he walked out.

Eight

As the sound of Cassidy's steps faded, Karen felt the anger stream out of her in a rush. Hugging herself, she took a shaky breath, then another. Her legs felt weak, and her skin was clammy. It was a textbook case of shock. She'd seen it often enough in others to recognize the signs in herself. If she moved very slowly, everything would be all right.

Rubbing her cold arms with her sweating palms, she stared stupidly at the cluttered surface of Cassidy's desk. She took a step forward, then another, moving like a woman twice her age, until her hip bumped the arm of Cassidy's big chair. Slowly, stiffly, she lowered herself into the still warm seat. Okay, now that she knew his true feelings, she would find a way to move forward. But first, she needed to get control of her emotions.

Hysterical laughter rose in her throat. No problem, she told herself, taking great gulps of air to steady herself. Dr. Karen Moore Sloane was one strong lady. A survivor.

During her internship, the chief of medicine had rated her as capable, clearheaded and unflappable. *It's called professional detachment*, a curmudgeonly professor had boomed on her first day of medical school. *Find it or get out now. Otherwise you'll end up burned-out or locked up in a padded room.*

Detachment. Yes, that was the key, she decided, nodding her head in short little jerks. "Physician, heal thyself," she muttered, staring straight ahead. Okay, this was a serious wound but far from mortal.

Her mouth trembled, forcing her to clamp her lower lip

between her teeth. Crying would not help. She wouldn't give Cassidy the satisfaction.

A plan. That's what she needed now. As thorough as a treatment regimen. Simple, but effective. Well considered and comprehensive.

Of course, she and Vicki would move in with her mother temporarily. Vicki already had a room there, kept ready for her frequent overnight visits. It was the same sunny yellow-and-cream dormer room Karen had used as a child, with the same bed where she'd dreamed of her Prince Charming.

Slowly, she reached for the phone, then remembered that it was much too early to call her mother. She would call later, before Mom left for church. First, she needed to get dressed. Then she would have to wake Vicki and...

"Oh, God," she whispered, her voice breaking as a wave of pain washed over her. It was so unfair. First Goldie and now this.

Vicki's happy world, the only one she'd ever known, was about to be ripped apart—not only once, but twice—and Karen had absolutely no idea how to cushion her daughter from the agony.

Should she stay a few days? Or leave today?

A change of scenery might be the best thing to help Vicki cope, since all of her memories of Goldie were centered around the ranch. And...and everything else, too. Her toys, her room, her books. Her father.

Karen swallowed something that felt suspiciously like a sob and reminded herself of her vow. Detachment. A reasoned step-by-step plan of action.

Yes, it made sense to tell Vicki as soon as possible. One deluge of pain, hitting all at once, like lancing a boil, for instance, might be better than letting the child start to recover from Goldie's death, only to whammy her again with her parents' plans to divorce.

"Oh, baby, I don't have enough words to make you understand," she whispered, her eyes filling with tears. She closed them for a long moment, then gave herself a mental shake and sat up. Her gaze fell on the desktop and she frowned, remembering the photo Cassidy had been staring at when she'd found him here.

With tentative fingers she reached out to lift the blotter. The photo was facedown on the desk's scarred surface. The pasteboard back showed signs of wear—smudges of dirty fingers, a ragged corner, a tear at the bottom edge.

What if it's another woman? a voice prodded. His mistress? A lost love?

The possibility shuddered through her like a violent fever.

At least she would know more about Cassidy than she knew now, she decided as she turned the photo to the light—and stopped breathing. It was their wedding picture, a duplicate of the one on her mother's mantel.

The woman he married, that young, starry-eyed girl desperately in love and eager to please, was gone forever, she thought sadly as she replaced the photo. On unsteady legs she rose, then walked with deliberate steps toward the door. When she gained the hall, she reached back and quietly closed the door behind her.

As Karen walked through the silent house, the sun filtered through the drapes of the living room that separated the hacienda's two wings. Dust motes danced with wicked glee as she pulled the lapels of her robe tighter around her. After she was gone, Cassidy would have to get someone to clean for him. And cook, too, although he knew his way around the kitchen better than she did.

Perhaps he could arrange to take his meals with the men in the bunkhouse where Billy's wife, Dora, was in charge of the kitchen. Or perhaps, if they divorced, he would marry again. Statistics said that most men did. And Cassidy had wanted more children. Three or four.

A silent sob shuddered through her, nearly bending her double. Stop it, Karen, she told herself firmly as she straightened. They weren't even officially separated, let alone divorced, she reminded herself as she headed down the hall toward the master bedroom.

Did they have a twelve-step program to help a person fall out of love? she wondered. A one-day-at-a-time sort of thing for a woman too besotted to realize that her husband held her in contempt?

The sound of heartbroken weeping coming from Vicki's room interrupted her thoughts, and she sighed. Cassidy must have told her about Goldie, she thought. Feet silent on the carpeting, she walked past the master bedroom toward Vicki's.

The door was open, and the light on the dresser had been switched on again. Cassidy was sitting on Vicki's bed, holding her against his big chest, his cheek resting on her head. Her small hands were clutching his shirt, and her shoulders were shaking as she sobbed. Cassidy's big hand made slow circles on her back even as his body radiated tension.

"I know it hurts, baby," he said in a low rough voice that seemed torn by force from his throat. "I know."

"I l-loved her s-so much," Vicki sobbed. "It's not f-fair."

"No, it's not fair."

Karen folded her arms and hovered by the door, wanting to help, but knowing that Vicki needed her father's comfort more than hers right now.

"C-can we bury her here, up by the big oak tree where we buried Tabbythecat's kitten when it died?" Vicki asked, glancing up at her father's strong face.

Karen saw his jaw firm and knew what he was thinking. A thousand-pound horse needed a big grave and a crane to lift the body into it.

"I'm not sure that's such a good idea, baby," he hedged, gazing down into Vicki's tear-filled eyes. His expression was wary, the planes of his tanned face taut.

Karen closed her eyes for a long moment. Victoria was a rancher's child, exposed to the basic side of nature in many ways. But since Cassidy hadn't lost a horse in years, Vicki didn't realize that on other ranches horses were considered livestock to be bred and sold instead of pampered pets like Goldie. Nor did she realize that dead farm animals were either burned or sold off for tallow or pet food.

"Please, Daddy" came Vicki's plaintive cry. "Goldie will be lonely if she's buried anywhere else."

Karen watched Cassidy take a deep breath. This was difficult for him, she realized. In spite of her bruised heart, she couldn't help feeling a certain sympathy for him. Cassidy was a good man, if not a flexible one. Maybe, if he'd had half the love and tenderness he lavished on Vicki when he'd been growing up, he might not have grown so hard inside.

"Honey, I'm not even sure it's legal. A horse is a big animal, and there are sani—"

"But, Daddy!" Vicki's tear-filled eyes sparked with determination. "This is *our* ranch, and you're the boss. Everyone does what you say."

"I suppose I could use the 'dozer to scrape a big enough hole," he said, flipping one of her braids over her back.

"I saw some of those pretty blue wildflowers growing by the pump house," Vicki said with a trembling smile. "As soon as I get dressed, I'll go pick a big bouquet, as big as the one Mr. Bidwell gave Grandma for her birthday."

"That's a good idea," Karen said softly, drawing the attention of both father and daughter. "Goldie loved to eat my nasturtiums, remember?"

Vicki's grin was wobbly, all but breaking Karen's heart. "And the apples from the tree by Billy's trailer! 'Member how she used to drag me over there?"

"Darn animal made herself sick gorging on apples," Cassidy muttered, his gaze holding Karen's for a moment before he looked away. He lifted a hand to smooth Vicki's hair. Karen noticed that it trembled. "She had a good life. Plenty of company, a nice dry stall, fresh hay. And you. Not many horses are so well loved."

Vicki stared at her father's face, looking for reassurance. For the security that a child needed. Deserved. Finally she offered a soft smile.

"Maybe an angel will ride her like I used to."

Karen saw Cassidy swallow hard. "I can just about guarantee it," he murmured, his voice thick.

Alone by the doorway Karen swallowed the lump in her throat. "I'll make breakfast while you dress, sweetie. Then you can go pick your flowers."

* * *

"Can you do it?" Karen asked as she absently twirled a bite of blueberry pancake around in the puddle of congealed syrup in the middle of her plate.

Cassidy washed down his last bite of scrambled egg with a sip of his third cup of coffee. Or was it his fourth? Karen had lost track. Cassidy drank coffee the way others drank water, the only excess he allowed himself.

"I can do it," he said, his tone grim. "I just wish she hadn't thought of it."

Karen glanced out the window toward the hill overlooking the ranch house where the old oak stood in solitary dignity, sunshine gilding its huge branches. Partially hidden by the dense shade, Billy was seated atop the yellow bulldozer, methodically moving earth and rock.

After bolting her breakfast, Vicki had taken off in search of a funeral bouquet, leaving her parents alone in a kitchen that was suddenly too small and too silent. Karen wished now that she had switched on the radio. A little soft music would be a nice distraction. Even a news broadcast would help take the edge off the tension that crackled between them.

"Perhaps the ritual of a funeral will provide the closure she needs in order to begin the healing process," she said quietly, thinking about the days ahead.

"You think so?" He sounded only mildly interested.

Very carefully she put down her fork and picked up her napkin to blot her lips. She'd eaten only a few bites, and the churning in her stomach suggested that even those might have been too many. As she carefully refolded her napkin, she realized her hands were shaking, and she lowered them to her lap where they would be out of sight.

"Vicki's needs are the most important, of course," she said with the same care she exercised when discussing a procedure with a patient. "I assume you agree?"

Cassidy regarded her with inscrutable eyes the color of weathered oak. A gray tinge underlay his tan, and the character lines bracketing his mouth appeared to have deepened since their conversation in his office. Karen felt the first tickle

of tears behind her eyes and reminded herself that professional detachment didn't include a disregard for suffering.

"I agree," he said after a long moment's deliberation.

"I realize that the timing is atrocious, but perhaps there is
really no good time to tell a child her parents are splitting
up."

He said nothing, simply watched her.

"Vicki and I can move in with Mother until I find an apartment," she went on. "Mother always keeps Vicki's room
ready, and there's plenty of space in the backyard for Rags."

"I want unlimited access to my daughter, and I intend to
pay for her keep."

"Of course you can see Vicki as often as you like. We'll
have to work out a schedule."

As Cassidy listened to the calm cadence of her soft voice,
he felt panic claw its way from the steel cage where he kept
feelings he couldn't control. Once loosed, it ripped into him
so hard and fast it took several long moments to shove it back
in the dark box where it belonged.

"When will you leave?" he asked, careful to keep his
voice level.

"It would probably be easiest if I just packed and left some
time today, but we have to consider what's best for Vicki.
Two major upheavals in her life at the same time would be
terribly traumatic."

"She's a tough kid. She'll manage."

As he had? she wondered. She tilted her head and narrowed
her gaze. Sunlight shafted across his face, deepening the harsh
lines bracketing his grim mouth. Beneath the lethal power
contained in that hard scowl, she sensed a deeply buried pain.
It had been one of the first things she'd noticed about him
when they'd met. At the time, she'd been so sure she would
be able to heal him. Now she knew better. The gentleness
she'd been so sure existed beneath his solid shell had merely
been a romantic fantasy. A virginal longing of a lonely, overworked young woman who had sacrificed her teenaged years
to her dream of becoming a doctor. She knew now that the
longing she thought she had sensed in Cassidy to love and

be loved had been merely a reflection of her own deepest desires.

The man she married—no, trapped into marriage—was first and foremost a hard, bitter man. A loner at heart. Whatever softness he had was offered only to Vicki, and almost always when he thought no one was around to notice.

"Funny, all these years, I thought we had something rare, something special." She sighed, then shook her head. "'The human psyche has a great capacity for self-deception.' I read that somewhere."

Instead of answering, he consulted his watch and frowned. "What time did you say your mom was coming?"

"Noon. She couldn't manage sooner because she'd already committed to teaching Sunday School."

He nodded. Telling Sylvia wasn't high on his list of pleasant experiences. In fact, he figured it would be pure hell—especially considering the things she'd said to him at the party.

"Are you going to tell her or shall I?" he found himself asking.

"I'll tell her. She'll be upset, of course. She thinks of you as a son, you know."

He didn't answer. How could he tell her how much that had meant to him? Or that he would miss Sylvia's easy affection?

"God, this is hard," she whispered, dropping her gaze to her plate.

Her hair tumbled past her cheeks, a short dark halo that teased a man's senses. When they'd made love the first time, he'd been enthralled by the warmth of its caress against his cheek.

His gut twisted painfully. Was this how his old man had felt when Myra walked out? Like he'd been gut-shot and left for the buzzards? Abruptly, he got to his feet.

"Anything else before I head out?"

She looked up. "I'll need a car."

"Keep the Blazer. I bought it for you." He pushed the

chair under the table, then gripped the high back with both hands.

"We'll each need an attorney. To...handle the details."

"Whatever."

"I was thinking I'd call Amos Bynner. He handled Lucy Martin's divorce last year."

"Guess one lawyer's good as the next."

She cleared her throat, looked down at her plate. "Let's not tell Vicki today, Cassidy. Tomorrow will be soon enough. Let her have this one last night thinking we're still a family."

He nearly shattered then, but only inside, where no one could see. "Fine."

He carried his plate to the sink and rinsed it before putting it into the dishwasher. Turning, he saw that she had left her chair and come up behind him. In her robe and slippers, with her hair more curly than styled and her mouth pale, she looked as though she'd just gotten out of a warm bed after a long, hot night of loving. He shoved his fingertips into the back pockets of his jeans. If he touched her, he would crack.

"Tell me the truth, Cassidy," she said in a strained little voice utterly unlike her normally calm tones. "Did you ever love me, or was I just fooling myself all these years?"

It was the first time she'd ever asked. Perhaps because it no longer mattered. "I care about you, Kari, more than I ever thought I could, but it's just not in me to give you the kind of love you want."

She nodded, then wet her lips in that quick nervous gesture that had always charmed him. "Thank you for not lying to me."

"I've never lied to you, Kari. At least give me credit for that."

"You're wrong," she said distinctly, her voice without emotion or depth. "You lied when you promised to love me. On our wedding day. And you've been compounding that lie every day since by letting me believe you meant it."

Cassidy felt his mind ice over. Soon he would turn cold inside and out, a trick he'd perfected years ago, a way of protecting himself from the pain he knew was coming. When the chill was on him, he could feel almost nothing.

It was better that way. Lonelier perhaps, but safer.

"I'll let you know when it's time for Goldie's funeral."

For the second time that morning, he walked out, leaving her staring after him with tears in her eyes.

Nine

In spite of all Cassidy's efforts, the smell of blood still lingered in the foaling barn, mingled now with the stinging scent of disinfectant. Goldie and her foal were lying side by side in the stall where they'd died, covered by a tarp.

It had taken every ounce of guts he possessed to stitch up the wound left by the vet's emergency C-section and wash away the clotted blood still clinging to their coats. It had taken almost as much courage to watch Vicki say goodbye to her friend earlier this morning.

Damn, but he'd been proud of her, he thought as he ran his hand over the distended belly of a mare in the last stall on the left. Beneath his palm, he felt the sharp outline of a tiny hoof and hoped to hell this little one made it okay.

"Soon, pretty lady," he crooned, patting the nervous mare's withers. "Tonight, I think."

Salome blew air, then snorted and swished her tail. A full ration of grain remained in her feeding trough, a pretty good sign that she was in the first stages of labor.

"Yeah, I know. Life's a bitch," he muttered as he stepped out of the stall and latched the slotted gate.

"I thought Karen looked lousy, but you look like death."

Cassidy stiffened at the sound of the familiar voice.

"Thanks," he said, walking toward the door where Sylvia stood, looking composed and stylish in a navy suit and pearls.

A woman of means and strength. Like his mother.

Suddenly he was ten years old and terrified. This time he refused to cower. "Go ahead and get it all said, and be done with it."

Her lips curved but her smile lacked its usual sparkle. "Don't I at least get a kiss first?" she asked softly.

"What?" He figured fatigue had made him stupid—or else the woman was out of her mind.

She took a step forward, adding a hint of perfume to the mix. "In my family, we greet each other with a kiss. I thought you understood that."

Though her words were clear, he couldn't seem to get them sorted out. "You don't hate me?" he asked, eyeing her warily. If she raised her hand to him, he would take the blow, because he had it coming, but he would never forgive her.

"Why should I? It's clear you're already sick with hating yourself."

He scowled. For a woman who looked about as tough as a cream puff, Sylvia delivered a hell of a wallop. "Guess you're disappointed I didn't take your advice."

"I know you well enough to know you have your reasons."

The lack of censure in her voice threatened a lot of inner walls, walls he couldn't risk anyone breaching. He didn't move, but he put distance between them.

"I ran out of fight," he said flatly.

Her expression was gently chiding. "Now, that does disappoint me. I never figured you for a quitter."

He let that pass. "I'm a realist, Sylvia. Nothing I can offer her has a chance in hell against the exalted—and lucrative—practice of medicine."

"That's unfair," she retorted, her voice taking on an edge for the first time.

He shrugged. "Life is unfair."

Her eyes flashed then, and he braced himself. "You've lived with Karen for ten years and you can still stand there and say that my daughter sacrificed her youth and nearly worked herself into a nervous breakdown simply in order to make money?"

"It wouldn't be the first time a woman walked down that road."

The back door slammed, and Sylvia cast a startled glance

over her shoulder. Vicki and her mother had just emerged and were walking toward the grave site.

"If you truly believe that, there's no hope for you," Sylvia said, meeting his gaze squarely.

"None whatsoever," he drawled, sickened by his own cruelty, but unable to prevent it.

"In that case, I feel sorry for you," Sylvia said with a deep sadness in her voice. "You've just thrown away the most precious commodity there is—unconditional love."

To his surprise, she reached out to touch his arm before turning on her heel to follow her daughter and grandchild toward the spot on the hill. He watched for a moment, then headed out to get the 'dozer, hating himself and the situation with an intensity that bordered on violent.

The old casement clock in the living room was just chiming two as Karen opened the oven door to check on the biscuits she'd put in to bake after returning to the house from the funeral. For a moment, she stood staring at the golden circles on the sheet, wondering where she would be the next time she made another batch.

In an apartment? Her childhood home?

"Are you all right, darling?" her mom asked, pausing in the act of shredding lettuce into a salad bowl.

Karen set her chin as she reached for the pot holder Vicki had made her for Mother's Day. "As all right as any woman whose marriage has just imploded," she said as she slid the baking tin from the rack. Always tactful, Sylvia returned to her task, but Karen was all too aware of the sad droop to her mother's shoulders. Her own were pridefully straight as she switched off the oven.

She glanced through the window where Cassidy and Vicki were sitting together under the oak tree. As she watched, he reached out a long, rough forefinger to swipe away a tear from their daughter's cheek, then pressed her face against his chest.

The mare and her foal had been laid to rest at noon, with

a southerly breeze wafting the scent of the reawakening land over the mourners. Looking a little lost, her hand clinging tightly to her father's, Vicki had given a eulogy of sorts, then sat on Cassidy's lap while he used the 'dozer to smooth the earth again.

"It was really a very lovely ceremony," Sylvia said, her gaze, too, focused on the tranquil scene. "Although when you first told me what you had planned, I must admit I was a bit worried about how Vicki would handle it."

Karen dropped her gaze and turned on the cold water tap. "Vicki is really very resilient," she said over the sound of the running water. "She'll be fine."

"Eventually. The question is, will you?"

Karen jerked open a drawer and rummaged the jumble of contents for a potato peeler. The two extra-strength aspirins she'd gulped down right before her mother had arrived had only served to upset her stomach while leaving her headache untouched.

"It'll be rough for a while—change always is—but I'll be fine," she declared firmly, already practicing her positive self-talk. Of all people, physicians knew the value of an optimistic attitude, which was why, when counseling patients with life-threatening disease, she always urged them to look on the bright side.

"I, um, think I'll look for an apartment on the east side," she said brightly. "One of the obstetrical nurses just had a housewarming for the condo she bought on East Garden Green. Three bedrooms and a private yard with a small patio. Of course, there won't be room for a horse, or even much room for Rags, but we'll manage."

"I'm sure Vicki and Rags will appreciate that," Sylvia commented dryly.

Karen gave her mother a swift look. "Thanks for the support, Mother."

Even her mother's heartfelt sigh carried a touch of elegance. "Believe me, I know how badly you're hurting. Never think I don't." She hesitated, then added in a softer voice, "I was lost for months after your father was taken from us.

Sometimes I think that if it hadn't been for you, I would have sunk into a black pit somewhere and just shriveled up to nothing."

Karen blinked. "I never knew. You were always so upbeat."

Her mother's smile was bittersweet. "That was a front I put on for your sake, my darling. But at night, when I closed the door to my bedroom, I simply dissolved." Her smile faded. "In today's parlance, I was a basket case."

"What helped you get through the pain?" she asked, the potato in her hand forgotten for the moment.

"Coming to terms with loss, I think." Sylvia put down the salad tongs and shifted her attention to the picture of father and daughter framed by the window. "In a way, it was easier for me because your father was gone forever. I didn't have to walk down the street and wonder if I was going to run into him." She returned her gaze to Karen's face, and her eyes were dark with compassion and understanding. "And I didn't have to face the fact that he might find another woman to take my place."

Though well intentioned, her mother's words cut to the bone. For an instant, Karen couldn't catch her breath. "That would be difficult, yes, but I'll manage."

Her mother abandoned the salad and came to stand next to her. "Go ahead and cry, sweetheart."

"I wouldn't give him the satisfaction."

"When are you going to tell Vicki?" her mother asked when Karen began attacking a potato with the peeler.

"Tomorrow evening. I work six-to-two tomorrow, so I'll be home in time to make a start on packing. Just the basics. Enough for a week or so, until I can sort things out."

"Can I help?"

Karen tried to summon a grateful smile. "Yes, please. I…I admit I'm having trouble concentrating. Before you got here, I'd gone into the bedroom for something and couldn't remember what. Then I realized I was standing there with one of Cassidy's old shirts in my hand, shaking so violently my teeth were chattering."

She stopped, realized she'd been babbling and took a deep breath. "Helping Vicki deal with all the changes in her life is what matters now." She frowned, sniffed, then whirled around. "That and dealing with burning chicken," she added as she made a grab for the skillet. In her haste, she forgot the hot pad. Pain shot through her fingers and she jerked back her hand. Unfortunately it was still attached to the skillet, which crashed to the floor.

"Don't move. I'll get an ice cube for the burn," Sylvia ordered, rushing into motion.

"No, I can manage," Karen said, already moving. With twin gasps of surprise, they collided in front of the refrigerator. Karen's elbow jabbed her mother's side, while Sylvia trod on her foot with a spiked heel.

It was at precisely that moment when Vicki and her dad walked through the back door, followed by the ubiquitous Rags, who gave one joyous "woof" before attacking the nearest chicken breast with doggy glee.

"Anyone for takeout?" Karen said brightly, then promptly burst into tears.

Karen closed the tattered copy of *Little Women* and smiled. Vicki's face was shiny from her bath, and she smelled of bubble bath and clean little girl.

"Can't we read just one more chapter, Mommy?" Vicki wheedled with a look designed to melt any and all obstacles.

Karen was tempted—not by her daughter's obvious attempt at staving off bedtime, but because Vicki hadn't requested a bedtime story in years. Of course, she knew why—Vicki was feeling very much alone and lost without her equine best friend, and talking her mother into reading to her helped assuage that empty feeling.

"Honey, it's already past ten, and tomorrow's a school day." Karen herself had to be up at four in order to make it to the hospital in time for the 6:00 a.m. staff meeting.

Vicki's mouth drooped. "School's boring."

"Really? In what way?"

"It just is, is all. I'd rather stay home and help Daddy fix

the gate on the corral he built for the new bull.'' Vicki set
her jaw, which was a softer, more delicate version of Cassidy's. Two peas in a pod, she thought—one sweet and
tender, the other as tough as baked leather.

Karen placed her old and much-beloved book on the night
stand before reaching for one of her daughter's hands. ''I
know exactly what you mean. Sometimes I feel the same way
about going to the hospital and working when I'd rather be
puttering around the house or digging in my garden.'' She
thought wistfully of the neat rows of vegetables she'd planned
to put in when the ground warmed. ''I intended to try a new
variety of tomatoes this year.''

Vicki looked confused. ''You mean you're not now?''

Karen realized her error and covered it over with a grin.
''Let's make sure winter is really gone before we move on
to spring, okay?''

''Kay.''

Karen dropped her gaze to the small, tanned hand curled
in hers. In spite of the bath Vicki had taken earlier, there was
still grit under a couple of the fingernails, no doubt acquired
when she'd smoothed the crumbling red dirt over Goldie's
resting place.

''Sweetie, about going to school—''

''I can stay home tomorrow, right, Mom?'' Vicki's face lit
up. Clearly, she thought she'd won. Karen hated to dash her
hopes, but pampering Vicki now would only lead to trouble
later.

''Vicki, I didn't—''

''If you say it's okay, Daddy will, too,'' her daughter broke
in with the skill of a born negotiator. '''Cause you know more
about raising little girls than he does. Daddy said.''

She actually smiled then, and Karen's heart did a little jig.
In spite of the sorrow gripping her now, Vicki had a natural
joy in living that would carry her through a lot of tough times.
Karen's satisfaction faded, however, when she contemplated
the fresh hurt awaiting her innocent little girl.

''Honey, if I really thought staying home tomorrow would

be the best thing for you right now, I'd say yes without thinking twice, but you need to be with your friends right now.''

Vicki's eyes clouded, and her chin added a few more degrees to an already defiant angle. ''But, Mom, I'm all caught up on my work and—''

''Mom's right, peanut.''

Karen's breath hitched at the sound of Cassidy's voice. She'd always loved the husky overtones to the rich baritone drawl. At night, in their private world, his gruffly whispered words of lovemaking had taken on a sweet tenderness that was otherwise absent, as though he felt safe saying things in the dark he didn't dare risk in the daylight.

She knew better now.

''You always take her side,'' Vicki complained to her father, her mouth drooping at the corners again.

''Not always, but when she's right, I'd be a pretty sorry dad if I didn't.''

Karen didn't turn toward the door, but she sensed him coming closer. The energy in a room always seemed to change when Cassidy walked in, as though the molecules were realigning in response to some unspoken command.

After stopping on the other side of the bed, toward the head, he flicked Karen a shuttered glance before bending to kiss Vicki on the forehead. ''How's it goin', peanut?'' he asked as he straightened.

His face was drawn with weariness, and he had fresh contusions on the backs of both hands, the result of his assisting in the delivery earlier this evening of another foal, this time successfully.

He'd been in the shower when she'd begun reading the story and was now dressed only in clean Wranglers, zipped but left unbuttoned at the waist, and a crisp white T-shirt. He'd shaved and shampooed his hair, which was tousled by the towel he'd used to swipe away most of the water. Cassidy and hair dryers were still perfect strangers and always would be, she suspected.

''I don't see why I have to go to school,'' Vicki groused

up at him, her mouth forming a downward curve. "Elizabeth was out for three days when her grandpa died."

"Since you don't have a grandpa, that's not relevant, is it?"

Vicki frowned, but she didn't protest. Karen wished she possessed even a small measure of Cassidy's influence over their daughter.

"Besides, you have a report to give tomorrow, remember?"

"I forgot," she muttered, averting her gaze.

"On the history of this ranch," he continued, folding his arms and looking down at his daughter with that steady affection he reserved for Vicki alone. "With pictures from the museum, remember? You liked the one of Josiah Barlow and the bull he'd brought up from Mexico."

"Oh, those." Vicki sounded utterly dispirited. Karen watched Cassidy's jaw tighten.

"Yes, those. Last I heard you were fixin' to pass them around and talk about the bullfight that Josiah held out in the corral to celebrate Josiah Jr.'s birthday."

Interest flickered across Vicki's face, but she kept her gaze turned down. "Guess so."

He unfolded his arms and used the callused tips of one large hand to tip Vicki's face up toward his. "Trust me, peanut. It won't hurt forever."

Won't it? Karen wondered, watching Vicki respond to her daddy like a fragile blossom touched suddenly by a warm shower. For all his rough edges and laconic approach to life, Cassidy had turned himself into a marvelous dad.

"How's Salome?" she asked as Vicki sat up straighter and tugged her hand free from her mother's grasp.

Cassidy directed her a wary glance. "Good. Delivered a pretty little black-and-white filly."

"I'm glad," she said quietly.

Salome was the newest of Cassidy's mares, bought from the same stock breeder in California where he'd contracted to buy the bull. Karen had ridden the pretty horse a time or two last fall. Smaller than the other mares, yet with more stamina,

Sally had gone into labor shortly after Karen's mother had driven away around five-thirty.

"What are you gonna name her?" Vicki piped up, her brown eyes sparkling with renewed interest.

"That's up to you."

"Me? But you always name the horses."

"I name *my* horses. This new baby is yours."

An awed look appeared in Vicki's eyes, followed closely by the sheen of welling tears. Conflicting emotions waged a struggle in eyes as dark as her father's before her face crumbled.

"I don't want another horse. Goldie'd be upset."

Tears began rolling down her too-pale cheeks again, and Karen saw a quick look of panic race over Cassidy's rugged features.

Glancing her way, he shifted, then shoved his hands into the back pockets of his jeans, palms out, the only way they'd fit. Though he'd been in this cheerfully cluttered room countless times before, he suddenly looked acutely uncomfortable, as though he didn't belong.

"Guess that was a dumb idea," he muttered, his voice rough.

"No, just a little premature." Last night Karen would have stood up and walked into his arms. Tonight she remained rooted to the mattress edge, the arms she would have slipped around his waist stiffly at her side.

Looking unconvinced, he drew a breath, then withdrew his hands and walked to the dresser for a handful of tissues from the box by the night-light before returning to the side of the bed. Karen could tell by the sway to his walk that he was close to exhaustion. And why not? She, herself, was feeling wrung out, and she'd managed four or five hours of sleep last night while he'd had less than that.

"Here, sweetheart. Use these," he said gruffly when Vicki started to wipe her tear-drenched face with the edge of the sheet. Looking mutinous and miserable at the same time, she snatched the tissues from his hand and swiped her wet cheeks.

"I'll never love that new filly. Never, never, *never!*"

Looking grim but determined, Cassidy leaned forward to knuckle away a few stray tears. "Just be glad you have the choice," he said in a clipped tone before he straightened quickly and left the room.

Vicki glared after him, then burst into tears as soon as his tall form was out of sight. With a sigh, Karen scooted forward to take her daughter's small shaking body into her arms.

"That's it, honey. Cry it out. You'll feel better afterward."

She wasn't sure Vicki heard her. It didn't really matter, anyway, she thought as she smoothed a hand over Vicki's flyaway bangs. What mattered was assuring a scared and hurting little girl that her parents would always be there for her—even though their own lives were about to go in separate directions.

"M-mommy?" Vicki's voice was muffled and drenched with tears.

"What, dear?" Karen asked quietly, her heart aching.

"Will you stay here till I fall asleep, just like last night?"

"Of course."

Silently, Vicki drew back, her dear, sad face ravaged by an inner pain that wouldn't be wiped away so easily as her tears.

"O-only for a little while," she amended quickly, as though afraid her mother would think she was a scaredy cat. Or worse, a baby.

Karen kissed the top of her head, then stood up and drew back the covers. "Snuggle down and I'll just slip in here next to you for a few minutes."

"Just until I go to sleep, okay?"

"Okay."

Apparently satisfied, Vicki scooted sideways on her bottom, then turned on her side, facing the window.

Karen bent to remove her slippers. "Do you want the light on or off?"

"On, please. Just for tonight."

Karen removed her slippers and edged in beside Vicki's small body. Looping one arm over Vicki's sturdy little waist, she let out a long sigh. "Sweet dreams, sweetheart."

Vicki sniffled. "I hope I dream about Goldie."

"I hope so, too."

Silence settled around them for a few moments before Vicki asked quietly, "Did you dream about horses when you were my age?"

"Only the one ridden by Prince Charming when he came charging up to sweep Cinderella into his arms."

"Except Cinderella was really you, right?"

Karen smiled at the back of her daughter's sleek, dark head. "Yes, I was Cinderella."

"I don't believe in stuff like that anymore."

"I'm sorry to hear that, sweetie."

Karen felt Vicki stir a moment before she twisted to look at her mother. "You sound like you do."

"When I was just a few years older than you are now, I used to gather up the little bits of cotton fluff that fell from the trees outside Grandma's house and put them under my pillow."

Vicki's forehead pleated into a frown. "Why'd you do a silly thing like that?"

"Because I thought it was magic fairy dust and it would make me dream about my own special Prince."

"Did it work?"

Karen hesitated. "In a way, yes."

"You mean you dreamed about Daddy, right?"

"Well, I didn't know it was Daddy at the time, but, yes, I dreamed about a tall, handsome cowboy with black hair and a wonderfully shy smile who would carry me off on his big white horse and love me forever."

"Only Daddy's favorite horse is buckskin."

"That's true, but not everything in dreams comes true exactly the way you think it will."

Vicki eased to her back and regarded her mother with a thoughtful expression. "Is Daddy your really-and-truly Prince Charming?"

Karen fashioned the smile her daughter clearly expected. "Really and truly."

"Forever and ever?"

It was difficult to speak past the lump in her throat. "Close your eyes now, sweetheart. No more talking."

Vicki yawned, then drew a tired-little-girl breath. "I still think I'd rather dream about Goldie. Besides, Daddy says there's no such thing as real magic—just pretend, like in books and on TV. He said I should never forget that, especially when I was all grown up and meeting boys."

"Meeting boys?"

"Uh-huh. He said boys say stuff just to get a girl to kiss 'em, and that I should be real, real sure I loved a boy before I kissed him back. He said a lot of people end up awful miserable if they're not careful about stuff like that." She gave a drowsy little blink. "But you let Daddy kiss you, right? And you're not miserable."

"I said 'no more talk,' remember?"

Vicki yawned again, her questions already forgotten. While the empty feeling inside her spread, Karen watched her daughter's eyes close and her face relax. She didn't realize she, herself, was crying until a tear slid down her cheek and onto the cheerfully striped sheets.

Ten

Karen gave the already spotless bathroom sink another swipe with the pale blue towel before returning it to the old porcelain rod she'd found buried under a pile of castoffs in the barn loft. Then, for the next few minutes, she made sure all the other towels were lined up perfectly.

After leaving Vicki's bedroom twenty minutes ago, she'd made one last tour of the house to make sure the doors were bolted, though she knew full well they were—Cassidy was meticulous about security for his family—and then she'd brushed her teeth until her gums were stinging painfully. She was stalling and knew it.

Walking carefully, as though the colorful cotton hall runner was strewn with ground glass, she made her way down the short passage to the master bedroom. After switching off the hall light, she opened the door and slipped inside. Illuminated by only the small reading lamp on her side of the large Victorian bed, the room was shrouded in shadows.

Cassidy was sitting up in bed with the sheet pulled to his waist, his reading glasses sliding down his nose, the way they always did when he was absorbed in something. He glanced up as she entered, watching her over the rims. It never failed to intrigue her at the difference those glasses made. He still looked ruggedly appealing, but his harsh features seemed gentler somehow when he was peering through horn-rimmed lenses—especially when he was reading to Vicki.

"Is she asleep?" Though his gaze was direct, his expression was remote.

"Yes, poor darling. She's had a pretty rotten day, all in all."

One side of his mouth edged upward. ''All in all, she's not the only one.''

''No, she's not the only one.''

He hesitated, then closed the magazine he'd been reading and set it on the night table. His glasses followed. Though he always slept nude, even on the coldest of winter nights, she saw that he was still wearing the white T-shirt, and she suspected, his briefs.

''Thanks for backing me up about school tomorrow,'' she said as she went to the closet and slid it open.

''I didn't do it for you,'' he said to her back.

''I realize that.'' She went to her tiptoes and reached to the second shelf for the spare blanket she kept there in anticipation of Colorado's frequent sub-zero nights.

''She's my daughter, too, Karen,'' he said as she slid the door closed again. ''Don't ever forget that.''

''I don't intend to. And if you're suggesting I'd use her as a weapon against you, forget it. I wouldn't do that.'' Bristling at his arrogance, she turned to glare at him. ''Like it or not, we have a responsibility to Vicki to be civilized about this separation.''

''Separation?'' One black eyebrow rose in a lazy arch. ''Thought you intended to divorce me.''

She told herself it couldn't be pain in his voice. Not when his eyes were clearly rejecting her. ''I don't have much choice, do I?''

''You had a choice and you made it.''

Now live with it, she heard in the silence that followed. Her already raw emotions seemed to bleed a little.

''Get this straight, Cassidy. I do not intend to listen to one more snotty word about the choices I've made. Or my right to make them. Just as you've had the right to make yours.''

''What choices, Kari?'' His voice was silvered with sarcasm. ''What kind of choice does a man have when a woman comes to him with his child in her belly and all but begs him to marry her?''

Karen heard a gasp and realized it had come from her

throat. At the same time she saw shame race over Cassidy's hard features.

"I think it would be best if I slept on the couch." She didn't care that her words were brittle or that her legs were shaking. No matter what happened later, she intended to get through this with her dignity intact. "I'll set the alarm on my watch to wake me up before Vicki's up. So you see, wearing armor to bed was totally unnecessary."

"What the hell are you talking about?"

She meant to shoot a pointed glance at his chest, but somehow her gaze ended up lower, at the distinctive mound made by the sheet. Even unaroused, Cassidy was impressive.

"Is that an invitation?" The angry red flush that appeared on his cheeks like the burn left by a vicious blow took her by surprise.

"No. An observation."

Cassidy tossed off the covers and stood up. "Sure you're not interested in one last time for the road?" he drawled, moving around the end of the bed toward her, his eyes glittering now with a barely controlled emotion she couldn't have named if her life depended on it.

"For Vicki's sake I'm going to pretend you didn't say that," she said, dying inside.

"Come on, sweetheart. Give the poor suffering sucker a break." He reached out to take a lock of her hair between his callused fingertips. "I'll make it good for you."

"Stop it." She tried to pull away, but he simply moved his hand to the back of her neck. Though his grip wasn't rough, she knew all too well the strength in those long, sinewy fingers. With one twist of that powerful wrist, he could snap her neck. No fuss, no muss.

She refused to let fear take hold. Cassidy was responding to some inner need to hurt her. She could understand that. What she couldn't do—wouldn't do—was forgive him.

"Let me go, Cassidy," she said firmly, putting as much steel in her tone as she could summon.

"I know what you like, Kari. All the places where you like to be petted, the spots where you want my mouth." He brought his other hand up and used the pad of his thumb to trace her lower lip. His eyes glittered, and his breathing was ragged. "Lie down for me, Kari, and spread your legs."

She felt a killing rage and hoped it showed in her eyes. "I hate you for this."

"Go ahead and hate me. It makes it easier that way." He bent his head, his intention to kiss her burning in his black eyes. She reacted instinctively, jerking backward and lifting her hand at the same time. Driven by fury, her palm hit his cheek with a loud crack, snapping his head back.

He reacted like a wild man, his hand snaking out to grab her around the waist. "You...bitch," he growled. "I won't let you destroy me the way she destroyed my father, saying she loved him, saying she loved me...and all the while she was cutting my old man off at the knees. Emasculating him inch by inch—but *I'm not my father!*"

Karen knew fear then, the icy, uncontrolled kind that took the strength from her bones and set her heart racing. She'd seen Cassidy angry before, but never like this. Never vicious. He was a man driven by something beyond his control.

Tormented.

"Let me go," she ordered, trying to blank out her fear. "Or I'll have you arrested."

He flinched, but his gaze bored into hers. "Go ahead, Kari. But I promise you'll live to regret it."

"Nothing you could do to me would be worse than you've already done."

"No? How about suing you for custody of our daughter?"

The room filled with a gray mist and began to revolve.

She hauled in air and tried to force herself to concentrate. Dimly she was aware of Cassidy's face twisting. Of his eyes changing, growing alarmed.

"Oh, God, Kari, I didn't mean—"

"M-mommy?"

With a low cry, Karen jerked an anguished gaze toward the sound and saw her daughter standing barefoot and trembling by the door Karen had neglected to close. Ignoring Cassidy, Karen jerked away and went to her daughter, who was now as rigid as a statue, her skin parchment pale and her eyes dull with shock. Karen was afraid to touch her. Instead, she knelt in front of her, bringing them eye to eye.

"Vicki. Baby, it's…it's all right," she managed to say with soothing calm despite the wad of remorse lodged in her windpipe.

"I…I don't like it when D-Daddy shouts at you."

"Daddy wasn't really shouting, sweetie. We were just having a heated discussion." She shot Cassidy a look. "Weren't we, Daddy?"

It seemed to take him a moment to find his voice. When he did, it came out ravaged and abrupt. "Yeah, a discussion. Nothing for you to worry about, peanut."

Vicki darted a stricken gaze back and forth between them several times, while her small white teeth worried her bottom lip. Karen had never seen her looking so desolate, not even in those sad hours after Goldie's death.

"T-Tommy Secord said that when mommies and daddies fight, it means they're going to get a divorce," Vicki eventually said in a tiny voice.

"Sometimes, yes, but not always." Karen felt her stomach begin to quiver, and she felt a vicious jolt of self-contempt. Thanks to her own selfish need to lash out and Cassidy's outburst of rage, time had just run out.

"Are…are you guys gonna get a divorce?" Vicki persisted in the way of unusually perceptive children.

In the periphery of her vision, Karen saw Cassidy stiffen and swallow hard. "Yes, we are," he said before Karen could force the words past her constricted throat. "But that doesn't mean either of us will ever divorce you, sweetheart." He moved then, going to kneel next to Karen. His body radiated tension, every muscle taut, every sinew lashed with restraint.

"Daddy's right, darling," Karen added, desperate to make Vicki understand. "We both love you very, very much."

Vicki's gaze mirrored a grief-stricken confusion that broke her mother's heart. She looked so vulnerable in the fuzzy pink pj's with her one rosy cheek still bearing the imprint of her pillow. "That's what the daddies and mommies on TV say, and then they end up doing awful things to each other."

Like now, Karen thought as a tearing guilt settled over her like a thorny shirt. "Vicki, sweetie, listen—"

"Tommy said his daddy went away because he didn't love his mommy anymore. He said his daddy has a girlfriend who's nicer than his mommy." Her eyes pleaded with Cassidy an instant before she asked plaintively, "Is that why you were yelling at Mommy? 'Cause you don't love her anymore?"

Cassidy dropped his head for a moment before returning his gaze to his daughter's pleading gaze. "That's between your mom and me, Vick," he said softly but firmly. "What's important for you to know is that we intend to do all we can to help you get through this."

"But I don't *want* you to get a d-divorce," she cried, her voice soaked with the tears that were now streaming down her cheeks. "Please, Daddy, tell Mommy you're sorry and you won't ever yell again."

"Oh, baby, don't." Cassidy took in air, then reached out to draw Vicki into his arms. "We can't always have what we want." For the first time since she'd been old enough to control her own actions, their daughter resisted her father's embrace.

"Vicki, I know it hurts now, but it won't always," Karen ventured as she gently took one of her daughter's hands in hers. The small fingers curled trustingly around hers, then gripped hard.

"Wh-what will happen to me'n Rags?" she asked in a small voice. The tears were running down her cheeks now, but, when Karen tried to wipe at them, Vicki flinched away.

"You'll live part of the time with me at Grandma's until we find our own new house," Karen told her gently, lowering her hand. "And part of the time you'll live with Daddy here at the ranch."

"It'll be okay, peanut," Cassidy added, his voice thick. "Mom and I won't ever walk away and leave you alone, no matter what."

Karen heard the rough emotion in his tone and realized that his need to reassure her had come directly from his own experience as an abandoned child. For a moment she couldn't speak. When she finally found her voice, she had to pull the words from deep inside, one by one.

"Vicki, listen to me. Daddy is telling you the absolute truth. We will never, *ever* abandon you."

Vicki glared at her father, her eyes blazing, and yet so filled with hurt Karen had to bite her lip to keep from crying out.

"I don't care what you do!" she cried before wrenching her hand free and bolting back down the hall to her room.

The silence that settled into the dimly lit room was painfully tense. Neither moved for a beat, then Cassidy slowly got to his feet. The athletic grace that had always characterized his movements was absent, and he looked older somehow, as he ran an impatient hand through his tumbled hair.

"Kari, I know there's nothing I can say—"

"No, there's nothing more either of us can say to erase the hurt we just caused an innocent child."

With the economy of movement so characteristic of a man who rationed out his life in patterns of his own, he turned his back on her and strode to his side of the closet, his bare feet making no sound against the carpet.

"Why are you getting dressed now?" she asked as she watched him grab a pair of jeans at random.

"I'm going to sleep in the barn," he said, jerking on the old Wranglers one long leg at a time. "First thing in the morning I'll make arrangements to fly to Stockton to pick up the bull."

Karen moved with stiff strides to the bed and sank down on the mattress. "I thought you were going to wait until the end of the month." Not that she cared. It was just something to say. Anything to keep her mind from replaying the last few minutes.

"Vicki needs time to heal. She'll do better without me around." He zipped his fly, then grabbed a shirt, shrugging into it with savage movements. "I'll be gone four or five days, depending on how fast I can make arrangements to ship him back.''

Karen managed a shaky breath. ''I have a staff meeting at six tomorrow morning. It...it's too late tonight to call the chief resident, but—''

''Keep your schedule. I'll make sure Vick gets off to school all right.'' He walked to the bureau and jerked open his sock drawer.

''No, I'll do it,'' she said, numbly watching him take out a pair of thick boot socks.

He closed the drawer and turned. She waited for him to make a scathing remark about her career. Instead he nodded wearily before sitting down in the old cane chair under the window to pull on his socks.

When he was finished, he simply sat, his elbows resting on his thighs as though he was suddenly too weary to move. ''I behaved like an ass,'' he said, lifting his head to look her way. ''Nothing I can say or do will change that.'' He swallowed, glanced down at the floor, then straightened his shoulders and stood up. ''Set up the divorce any way you want. I won't fight you.''

Cassidy saw the surprise on Karen's face and wanted to fall to the floor at her feet and beg her to forgive him. But the memory of another time when he'd done that and more rose like bile in his throat, choking off the pleading words.

''All I ask is that you let her spend as much time as possible with me, and that you let me support her—and you— until you're established in a practice.''

''I don't want your money. I never did. All I wanted was your love.'' She smiled then, a sad, beautiful, cold smile that ripped into him like sizzling shrapnel. ''Thank you for showing me what a fool I was.''

''Don't say that.'' His voice was that of a man stretched on a rack of his own making. It shamed him, as did the look of numb disinterest she gave him.

Somehow he managed to hold it together long enough to leave the bedroom, to jam his feet into his boots in the utility room and slam out of the house.

Alone in the bedroom, Karen heard the violent sound and wondered idly if the door had splintered. Not that it mattered, she thought with a dazed detachment that seemed to be growing stronger with each breath she took. If the door was broken, that was Cassidy's problem. At least that could be fixed, she thought as she got to her feet and forced herself to move toward the bathroom.

Behind the closed door, she reached inside the shower stall and turned on the water, adjusting the taps to a temperature that was just short of scalding. Then, standing frozen on the other side of the curtain, she waited while steam filled the tub and rolled over the curtain rod to cloud the mirror and clog her lungs.

Only then did she slip out of her robe and strip off her nightgown. Staring straight ahead, she stepped into the tub, gasping only when the hot water hit her bare skin. She stood it as long as she could, long enough to wash away the last of her childish dreams. Long enough to let the determination to drive Cassidy out of her heart take root. Long enough to sob until there were no more tears left to fall. Only then, when her skin was red and stinging painfully, did she shut off the water and step from the tub.

As she dried herself she marveled that so much heat could leave her so cold inside. Detachment. That was the key. Blessed healing detachment.

The sooner she left the ranch—and her place as Cassidy's wife—the sooner she could start to get on with the rest of her life.

"Sweetie, you have to eat," Karen chided gently when Vicki sat with her hands in her lap and stared down at the strawberry waffle on her plate.

"Not hungry," the little girl muttered. Her lower lip was stuck out in a rare pout and anger radiated from her small body. Karen stifled a sigh. Explaining to the chief of residents why she wouldn't be in today had been a piece of cake compared to dealing with a little girl who had inherited her father's temper and her mother's determination.

It was just past seven-fifteen. The school bus was due in three-quarters of an hour and Vicki wasn't yet dressed.

"Sweetheart, I thought we'd talked all this out last night."

"I'm not going to school," Vicki declared mutinously. "You can't make me."

"Oh, but I can, Victoria," Karen reminded her softly but firmly. "I can carry you out to the Blazer in your robe and jammies if I have to. And I can sit in the classroom and make sure you stay there."

"I'll scream. Ms. Grant will report you to the principal and he'll throw you out."

"Don't count on it. Ms. Grant is not only a good teacher; she's also a mother."

"I *hate* Ms. Grant," Vicki cried, slipping from her chair. Before Karen could react, she'd turned and was racing through the mudroom to the back door.

Karen heard it creak open at almost the same time as Cassidy's deep voice. "Whoa, there, peanut. It's awful cold out there for just a robe and pj's."

"Let me go" came Vicki's strangled cry.

"In a minute. First tell me where you're tearing off to in such a rush."

Karen closed her eyes, willing herself to ignore the rush of emotion evoked by the sound of her soon-to-be-ex-husband's voice.

"Make Mommy let me stay home. She'll listen to you."

There was a moment of silence, then Cassidy spoke again. "Vick—"

"Tell her you're sorry for what you said. Then she won't be mad at you anymore and we can stay a family."

Karen froze, her hand creeping to her throat. She thought she heard Cassidy sigh before he spoke again. "C'mon, peanut, let's go get you dressed while I try to explain why that's not going to happen."

"But, Daddy—"

"Do what I say, sweetheart." Cassidy's voice was firm, and yet, Karen heard a note of terrible weariness, as well.

"Oh, okay, but you can't make me go to school."

Karen closed her eyes. Stubborn, stubborn, stubborn.

"Good morning."

She opened her eyes to find Cassidy watching her from the open doorway to the mudroom. Shadows rimmed his eyes, and his shirt was wrinkled and flecked with bits of straw, as though he'd tossed and turned his way through the night. Vicki was standing next to him, her hand in his, and her chin angled defiantly in her mother's direction.

"Good morning," Karen returned quietly, folding her arms over her wildly beating heart.

His gaze skimmed her robed figure, then returned to her face. "You're really taking the day off?"

"Yes. Tomorrow, too, if I need it."

He nodded, one side of his mouth moving. His tan seemed to have faded overnight, and she couldn't recall ever seeing him look so tired, so utterly spent.

"Vicki seems to think she deserves a day off, too," she said, smiling at her sulking daughter. Vicki responded with a disgruntled look that had Cassidy's mouth twitching.

"We're just on our way to her room to have a talk about that."

Karen glanced at the clock. "You have exactly thirty-six minutes before she has to be at the bottom of the lane. Otherwise, she'll miss the bus."

Cassidy glanced down at Vicki's glossy head. "Hear that, peanut? Time's wasting."

"Don't care."

Cassidy's expression smoothed, a sure sign he was up to something. "If you hurry, you'll have time to visit with the new foal before you leave."

"Don't want to," she declared fiercely, but Karen noticed that her eyes were alive with curiosity, and her posture wasn't quite as rigid.

"Prettiest little filly you ever saw," Cassidy went on as though Vicki hadn't responded. "Has a white blaze and three white feet. And the brightest green eyes."

Vicki glanced up at her father with a look of outrageous disbelief. "Horses don't have green eyes!"

Cassidy crooked one black brow and gave every appearance of looking surprised. "Is that a fact?"

"Oh, Daddy, you're just teasing me, right?"

He tilted his head, his eyes crinkling, giving him an oddly boyish look. Karen felt something tear inside. "Am I?"

"I'd check it out if I were you," Karen said, drawing the attention of both father and daughter. "Stranger things have happened."

"No way," Vicki declared, drawing her brows together.

Karen made a stab at looking guileless. "Guess you'll have to prove us wrong, then."

"Oh, pooh," Vicki muttered, but she tugged on her father's hand as though to drag him from the room. "Come *on*, Daddy," she ordered when he just stood there, his gaze locked on Karen's. His attempt at a smile failed miserably, as did her stab at hardening her heart.

"I called the breeder from the barn phone. He can have the bull ready to travel by midweek."

She realized she was twisting her napkin and relaxed her fingers. "When will you leave?"

"As soon as I throw a few things in a bag. Billy'll drive me to the airport." He glanced past her at the window, as though making sure his ramrod's old blue truck was still parked outside the shed. "The guy in California's going to make arrangements for me to ride the same train that brings the bull back to Grand Springs," he added as he looked her way again.

"When..." She stopped to clear an annoying thickness from her throat. "When will you be back?"

"Probably not before Friday."

"Dad-dy. Hurry up!"

He glanced down at the scowling little girl trying to jerk his arm from his socket. "I'll leave the breeder's number on my desk. He'll know where I can be reached in case you need me."

Karen had to force herself to breathe. "I won't," she said, her voice mild but her meaning clear.

A shadow crossed his face before those privacy shutters

slid silently, implacably in place again. "I understand." His mouth slanted, and he nodded slowly, before letting Vicki drag him from the room.

After they were gone, Karen sat quietly, knowing that she was in no fit state to move just yet. Slowly, feeling as limp as the first batch of spaghetti she'd cooked in this same kitchen as a bride, she turned her head toward the window where another glorious spring day was busy being born.

Blue skies and sunshine and the end of a marriage, not necessarily in that order. The thought gave rise to a ridiculous urge to laugh, which she suspected would quickly turn to a sob. She took one breath after another until the urge passed.

She was still looking out the window when she heard the pounding of boot heels on the hall carpet. Seconds later, Vicki came barreling through the kitchen with her windbreaker in one hand and her Ninja Turtles backpack slung over one shoulder. The now neat braids showed a few irregular patches where the silken strands had snagged on Cassidy's rough fingers, and the tips of her bangs were wet where she'd most likely swiped a washcloth over her face.

"I've got twenty minutes left," she shouted as she disappeared into the mudroom.

The door slammed, and the sharp crack of wood hitting wood made Karen wince. Like father, like daughter, she thought, and had to fight to keep from breaking into a thousand pieces. Later, she told herself as she rose slowly to gather up the remains of the special breakfast she'd fixed for Vicki and herself.

She had just scraped the waffles into Rags's dish and was opening the dishwasher door when she heard Cassidy walking down the hall. It occurred to her then that most likely she'd spent her last night under this roof, and she closed her eyes on a wave of pain before making herself turn to face him.

He was dressed for traveling in a tan Western-cut corduroy blazer over a blue plaid shirt and reasonably new jeans. To her shock, he was wearing the rawhide belt with the turquoise-and-silver buckle she'd bought him for their first Christmas together. Though he'd professed to love it, she soon noticed that he rarely wore it. Too ornate, she'd figured out after a time. Cassidy had simple tastes and an aversion to pretense.

In one big hand he carried his best fawn-colored Stetson, an old army satchel in the other. He'd shaved, she noticed, then sucked in her breath at the sight of the handprint now purpling on his cheek, hidden earlier, she realized now, by his morning beard.

An image of his expression as his head had snapped back rose to taunt her. For an instant he'd looked shattered. Utterly bereft.

He deserved it, she told herself before an irrational guilt could take hold.

As though sensing the turn of her thoughts, he scowled. "Vicki's still pretty raw," he said, his voice strained. "Maybe you should call that shrink you took her to last time."

"I already have—right after I called the hospital. Vicki has an appointment for tomorrow after school." She reached for a towel to dry her hands, but in reality to keep him from noticing how badly they were shaking.

"Sounds like you have everything under control."

"Not everything, but I've made a start, anyway." She gestured to the pad covered with scribbles only she could read.

"Another of your lists?" he teased, only to have his words come out harsh and accusing.

"Yes, another of my lists," she said coldly. "But after today, you won't be bothered with my little quirks any longer."

Cassidy shifted his booted feet and wondered if a man could choke to death on his own pride. He should be so lucky, he thought grimly as he glanced at the clock. It was time to leave, but he couldn't make himself walk away.

"Kari, can't we get past this? I'm...I'm willing to try again if you are."

The gaze she turned on him was only mildly interested. "Why?"

Because I don't want to be empty again, the way I was before I met you. "For our daughter's sake."

"Vicki would only suffer more if we tried and failed."

He gritted his teeth. An urge to haul her into his arms nearly overpowered him before he mastered it. He could almost see her shedding her feelings for him. The way everyone else had. Everyone but Vicki. And maybe, after today, she, too, would start to despise him.

"You'll miss your flight," she said very calmly, as though it didn't matter one way or another.

He wouldn't beg. Not even for her. "Take...care of yourself," he said, his voice suddenly raw.

"Goodbye, Cassidy," she said before she turned away.

He left her then, carrying the image of that stiff, brave back with him as he slowly, painfully started to bleed inside.

Eleven

Cassidy propped one foot against the carved wooden railing, looking past the beer bottle in his hand at the bright lights spelling out the name of the motel near the entrance. On the small, mission-style patio table at his elbow was the bucket of chicken he'd bought earlier—along with the six-pack he was steadily pouring down his throat.

It was almost dark, he realized without really caring. Scowling, he tipped the bottle to his lips and drank. His stomach recoiled, and a shudder of revulsion ran through him.

God, he'd hurt her.

After all those years of telling himself he'd shucked off his past like dead skin, he'd let old memories and buried resentments twist him into a sadistic bastard. A sorry, selfish shell of a man who'd been too busy making sure he never let anyone close enough to hurt him the way his mother had hurt him to realize what he was throwing away with both hands.

His chest hurt at the memory of the bruised disbelief in Karen's beautiful gray eyes. Day and night, awake or tossing through the occasional hours of sleep he managed when exhaustion finally claimed him—he couldn't stop remembering.

He was sick with it. Almost as sick as when he'd seen his father slumped over in a pool of sticky blood. That afternoon, while he'd waited for the cops to arrive, he'd made some hard and painful decisions. No woman was worth that kind of pain, no matter how pretty or seductive or kind. No matter how much he needed to feel her arms around him at night.

He knew now he'd been the worst kind of coward—afraid to love the one woman who could have healed him. He'd sell his soul to make it right. The thought had him spitting out a vicious curse. Even that was denied him, he realized, because his soul was already destined to burn in the fires of hell.

The hell he was already living.

The Bank of Grand Springs was nearly as old as the town itself. Like most of the early structures, the first building had been little more than rough-planed planks covered with tar paper, necessitating an around-the-clock guard in order to preserve the fledgling bank's assets while a larger, sturdier building of brick and stone was being erected two lots down.

That structure was still in use, though with extensive renovations and security measures added along the way.

This was where Sylvia had found work after she'd been widowed, and where she was now an executive. Over the years, Karen had spent a lot of after-school hours in the employees' lunchroom, doing her homework until her mother was ready to leave. Even as an adult, she'd headed for the bank whenever she had news that couldn't wait.

Just walking through the heavy double doors evoked a myriad of memories, almost all of them worth cherishing, too, like the first time she'd brought Vicki in, wrapped like a plump, cooing mummy, to be admired and praised by her mother's friends.

Thursday was usually a quiet day, and this Thursday was no exception. Seated in front of the new accounts desk, Karen let her gaze trail over the gleaming brass fixtures that had once held gas jets while the clerk processed her application for a new checking account.

The bank was supposed to be haunted by the ghost of a crusty old sourdough, shot down by the bank robber who'd left his mark on the wall. Her mother swore she'd seen him once, standing in front of one of the windows with a poke of nuggets clutched in one grimy hand. Cassidy had simply laughed. He didn't believe in anything he couldn't test with his senses.

"That should just about do it, Karen," the clerk said as she added the signature card Karen had just completed to the account folder and closed it with a soft pat.

Cassidy had been gone four days, during which she'd moved Vicki and herself into the house on Gold Rush Street, cleaned out her closet and decided which of Vicki's possessions should stay and which should go. Frank Bidwell had insisted on sending a couple of men to help her with the boxes, while Billy had taken Vicki on a long ride in order to spare her the sight of her things being carted away. Today, after she picked up Vicki from school, she planned to return to the ranch in order to give the house a thorough cleaning while Vicki spent time with the pretty little filly she'd named Domino. Domi, for short.

Although Karen, like her mother, was a woman who prided herself on taking care of herself, she was beginning to feel overwhelmed by all the threads that needed to be unraveled when a marriage broke up—things like changing the title on the Blazer and putting the insurance in her name, like removing her name from the checking and savings accounts she shared with Cassidy and opening one of her own where she would deposit her checks from the hospital. And of course, deleting her name from the title to the ranch.

"You should have your imprinted checks in a week or so," the clerk went on, her gaze going automatically to the small calendar on her desk. "In the meantime, these should do fine."

"Thanks, Glenda. And thanks for not asking any questions."

Glenda Newman was a large, sturdy woman a few years older than Karen, with an air of quiet competence and a careworn face that still retained hints of a once spectacular beauty. It was common knowledge inside the bank that she'd been both an abused daughter and wife for far too many years before she'd found the courage to fight back. Karen admired her strength and grit, and had told her so more than once.

"If you ever need a friendly ear, mine's available," Glenda said as Karen rose from her chair.

"Thanks. I just might."

After tucking the new checks into her purse, she skirted Glenda's desk and headed for the area at the rear of the lobby where her mother had her desk. On the way, she spotted Peggy Stockwell just turning away from a teller's window. A smile spread over her pretty face as she caught sight of Karen and changed direction.

"Hello, Dr. Sloane," she said with a shy smile. Her glossy red curls were piled atop her head, and her green eyes sparkled with a vibrancy Karen envied. Her own eyes were shadowed from too little sleep and too much stress.

"Hi yourself, and it's Karen, please."

"Takin' the day off from the hospital?"

Karen smiled. "Actually, I traded shifts with one of the other residents so I could help carpool Vicki's class on a field trip to the *Herald* this afternoon."

"How was it—besides chaotic?"

Karen laughed. "We didn't go because the *Herald*'s mainframe crashed just before we were getting ready to leave the school. No computer, no presses running, and most important, nothing to show twenty-seven inquisitive third-graders besides blank monitors. No fool she, their teacher decided to reschedule."

"Aha, so you're playing hooky."

"I guess I am at that—although it feels more like I'm running all over town taking care of errands."

"Join the club," Peggy said with a rueful downward glance at the shopping bag gripped in one hand. "I've been to five different places so far, with two more to go before I can head on home."

"Is Travis watching the twins?"

Peggy nodded. "I figure that's a surefire way to make a man appreciate his wife."

Karen hoped her answering grin revealed nothing of the leaden unhappiness that was her constant companion these days. "What are they now? Ten months?"

"Almost—and getting bigger every day." Karen saw the blaze of happiness in the younger woman's eyes and wanted to warn her to cherish every moment of that joy. "Which is one reason why Travis and I have decided to rent a house for the time we'll be in town," Peggy continued brightly. "That trailer is getting a bit small for all four of us."

"Have you found a place yet?"

Peggy nodded. "It's nothing special, just a tract home on the edge of town, but it has a small shed where the landlord says Travis can stable his horses and a fenced yard for the twins when they're old enough to toddle around."

She paused, a smile blossoming as though she were picturing the scene in her mind. "Right now we're sitting on lawn chairs and eating off of an old card table. Like Travis keeps saying, we have to wait for him to win more prize money before we can afford real furniture."

Karen nodded. "I remember those days all too well. When we were first married, Cassidy and I had to choose between a new roof for the barn or living room furniture."

"Let me guess. You got the roof."

"Yes. We got the roof." The furniture had come later, after Cassidy had shipped a hundred head to market. They'd celebrated with pizza and soda, then made love on their brand new sofa.

Over the years, they'd made love on those same cushions more times than she could count. And planned for the future between kisses. Vicki had napped on it and thrown up on it and smeared Easter candy into the nubby fabric. As a piece of furniture, it was probably worth a dollar and a half at a swap meet, if that.

"Sorry," Karen told Peggy, realizing her mind had been wandering. "You were telling me about your new house?"

"Actually, I was trying to work up the nerve to ask you and Cassidy to the housewarming we have planned for three weeks from Saturday."

There it was, that first sharp reminder, Karen thought with sad resignation. Sooner or later everyone had to know about the failure of the Sloanes' marriage. She knew enough divorced couples to know that the invitations invariably stopped for one or the other. It would be the same for them.

If not right away, soon enough. She could spread the word slowly or quickly—either way it was going to hurt.

"Sounds lovely," she said with what she hoped was a warm smile. "But Cassidy and I are getting a divorce."

Peggy's shocked expression said volumes. "I'm so sorry. If there's anything I can do—"

"No, but thank you."

"Travis had a feeling…I mean, well, a couple of times he mentioned that Cassidy didn't seem like himself—" she broke off, her face turning a fiery red. "Shut up, Peggy," she muttered.

Karen laid a hand on Peggy's arm. "It's okay. I'm getting used to the idea." It wasn't really a lie, she told herself. After all, she'd managed four hours of sleep last night, hadn't she?

"Please think about coming to the party, anyway. I'll tell Travis not to say anything to Cassidy, just in case."

"I appreciate the thought, but I'm spending as much of my free time with Vicki as I can right now."

"Of course, I understand."

"Please don't look so stricken, Peggy. It's okay, really. And tell Travis not to feel the least bit hesitant about inviting Cassidy to your party."

Peggy nodded. "I feel so terrible for you, Karen. I know what you're going through. After…after Clyde abandoned me, I felt like so much used Kleenex until I met Travis and realized I had a beautiful new life just waiting for me."

"I'm happy for you, Peggy. You deserve all the happiness I know Travis and those babies will give you."

Peggy's smile came easier now, Karen noted with satisfaction. "I hope so. But sometimes I have to pinch myself to make sure I'm not dreaming, you know?"

"Yes, I know," Karen said softly.

"Well, I should be going." Peggy hesitated, then reached out to give Karen a fierce hug. Shopping bags crinkled between them, and something hard clanked against Karen's shin, but she didn't care. It felt good to know that someone understood.

As though embarrassed, Peggy drew back, muttered a hurried goodbye and headed for the door. Karen glanced toward the far end of the lobby and saw that her mother was still with a customer. Just as well, she thought, turning on her heel and heading for the rest room in the back.

Two minutes later she was safely locked in a stall, tears running down her face, mourning the loss of a stupid, ugly sofa.

Cassidy was tired and hungry and smelled like cow dung and sweat. Forty-seven hours bedded down next to a mean son-of-a-bitch bull in a crowded cattle car had honed his already foul mood to a dangerous edge. The fact that he was still suffering the lingering aftereffects of a head-shattering, gut-busting hangover didn't help.

Grand Springs's best cattle hauler, Mac McWhorter, had wrinkled that big eagle's beak of his when he'd caught a whiff of his human passenger, but wisely kept his own counsel, for which Cassidy was grateful.

"Guess you put down a bundle on that ugly critter back yonder."

Cassidy roused himself long enough to grunt. Mac was a hell of a teamster, but he had a tendency to gossip about his customers more than was wise.

Undaunted, McWhorter leaned forward to spit tobacco juice into the coffee can he kept wedged between two coils of rope on the floor. "How many head you runnin' these days, anyway?"

"Enough." Cassidy closed his eyes and tried not to speculate about the next few minutes. Either she'd be there or she wouldn't.

"Place looks damn good, Cass. Better'n it ever looked under the JB brand."

Cassidy felt a rush of pride. Bathed in the glow of sunset, the land had a serenity about it that never failed to soothe him. "Got a long way to go, though." He slitted his eyes and watched the familiar contours of his land drift past. The aspens had budded during his absence, and the snow level on the distant peaks had climbed a good thousand feet by his reckoning. Wouldn't be long before spring hit full force. Before then, he had a lot to do.

Before he'd left, he'd issued orders to have the fences re-
paired and the tack mended by his return. Spring was always
hectic on a ranch, especially this year. And the trip to Stockton had put him behind. Still, a man would be a fool to pay
big bucks for breeding stock he hadn't seen with his own
eyes.

"Don't mind tellin' you, Cass. I ain't never seen an animal
as mean as that there Brahma back there. Woulda kicked that
dumb railroad greenhorn clear into the promised land if you
hadn't manhandled the kid out of the way." McWhorter
rubbed a rough hand against his stubbled jaw before leaning
forward to spit again. "If it was me, I'd have that bastard
dehorned first thing I did."

Cassidy let that pass. He was too busy wondering if the
house would be as cold and empty as his gut.

"I gotta figure that you have yourself a plan, seein' as
though most of the other ranchers have gone to artificial in-
semination."

His reasons for buying the hide-and-guts bastard with an
attitude were entirely practical. Once word got around about
the primo quality of beef he was raising on the Lazy S, he
was bound to make a fortune in stud fees.

"Mind the ruts, Mac. I haven't had time to grade the lane
yet this year."

It was McWhorter's turn to grunt. "Where do you want
me to unload?"

"The corral behind the equipment shed."

"Gotcha."

As the buildings came into sight, Cassidy felt his gut
tighten. Work would help. Work always helped.

The lights were on in the house, and Karen's Blazer was
parked in its usual spot. He told himself not to hope, but he
did, anyway, hoped desperately, with all the force of a man
seeing a glimmer of light in a dark, cold prison.

"Daddy's home!" Vicki had passed through the kitchen
and was running pell-mell toward Mac McWhorter's huge
cattle transport truck before the sound of her voice faded.

Karen gripped the edge of the sink and waited for her suddenly galloping heart to slow the frantic pace. Cassidy wasn't
due home until tomorrow at the earliest. But there he was,
climbing down from the truck's tall cab, his jacket rumpled
and his hat pulled low. He moved warily, as though the sinewy muscles of those long legs had gotten stiff from inactiv-
ity, and he carried his shoulders differently, like a man struggling under a weight that was almost more than he could bear.

He turned at the sound of his daughter's voice and held
out his arms. She flung herself against him with a trust Karen
hoped never faded.

Telling herself she had to get this first awkward meeting
behind her, she threw down the rag she'd been using to clean
the counters, wiped her hands on her jeans and walked outside.

Though he had Vicki a good two feet off the ground,
wrapped in a bear hug while she chattered away, his gaze
locked with Karen's the moment she stepped from the back
door. It was a good fifteen yards to the truck, yet she felt
herself react to the sheer power of his presence.

In spite of that—or maybe as a result of it—she dug deep
for a friendly smile. He didn't return her smile, nor, she realized sadly, had she expected him to. Instead, he gave Vicki
a quick kiss on her nose, then set her on booted feet that were
already pointed toward the back of the trailer where Mc-
Whorter was standing, fishing in his pocket for the key to the
padlocked door.

"I see you were successful," she called when they were
only a few yards apart.

"Enough so's I'll have to eat beans and rice for the next
year."

Already he'd made the transition from married man to
bachelor. Karen felt a chill and resisted the urge to hug herself
warm again. "Good thing Dora has been busy filling the
freezer with casseroles."

"Sounds good, but it'll be a while before I can eat it. Gotta
get this valuable capital asset settled in his new home first."

"What's his name, Daddy?" Vicki asked, literally hopping

up and down with impatience as McWhorter took his own sweet time removing the padlock.

"Man who bred him called him 'that mean son of a...gun.'"

Vicki's bangs moved as she wrinkled her forehead. "That's not very nice."

"But accurate, little lady," McWhorter contributed with a grin that showed off tobacco-stained teeth. "That old boy darn near kicked in the side of my truck afore me and your daddy got him chained down real tight."

"Daddy! That's awful."

Karen saw Cassidy flinch under his daughter's rebuke and stepped forward, between the two. "Honey, Daddy and Mr. McWhorter weren't trying to hurt him. They were just trying to keep him from hurting himself."

Cassidy strode to McWhorter's side. "Wait until I get the gate open, then back up to the opening."

McWhorter nodded. "You best get the twelve-gauge out from behind the seat and have it ready." He pocketed the padlock but left the door closed while he returned to the cab and climbed in.

Karen felt a shiver of fear tap-dance down her spine. Though she loved animals, she wasn't crazy about meeting one the size of a freight train head-on. Nor was she about to let Vicki anywhere near that bull once he was unchained.

As though reading her thoughts, Cassidy pinned her with a look. "Go inside, both of you."

"Works for me," she muttered, reaching for Vicki's hand.

"I wanna watch," Vicki declared, pulling away.

"Now, Vicki—" The reasoned argument Karen was about to offer was cut short when Cassidy hefted Vicki against his side like a sack of wheat and strode off toward the porch, with Karen hurrying along behind.

"Inside," he ordered again as he set the sputtering little girl down next to the door.

"I can watch from here," Vicki countered, setting her jaw in a perfect imitation of her father.

Cassidy cast an impatient glance toward the truck, now

idling noisily and spewing out blue smoke in a noxious cloud. Two of the hands were already mounted and hovering next to the gate. They were also armed, Karen noted with alarm.

"Vick, pay attention, because this is important," Cassidy ordered, his voice only marginally softer. "That's more than a half ton of mad bull in that truck, not some cuddly little calf bawling for his mama."

"But—"

"An animal like that is just purely cantankerous."

Like most males, Karen longed to interject, but didn't, because she didn't want Vicki to think she wasn't taking Cassidy's warning seriously.

"You won't let him hurt me," Vicki declared firmly, her trust in her father shining from the eyes nearly identical in color and shape to his.

"Accidents happen on a ranch, Vick."

Karen bent down to bring herself eye to eye with her daughter. As she did, her thigh brushed Cassidy's arm, and he shifted away, as though burned. She noted the subtle rebuff with regret.

"Remember I told you how Daddy and I met," she said quietly.

Vicki nodded. "Daddy got his ribs busted by a horse."

"And Daddy's always very careful, right?"

"Yeah, but—"

"No buts, Victoria. Daddy and I don't like to forbid you to explore new things, but neither can we allow you to get hurt."

Resignation drifted across Vicki's freckled face, but her jaw remained stubborn, giving her mother a glimpse of the strong, self-assured woman she would become. It would take an equally strong man to win her heart.

"Later, when he's not so mad, can I take a look at him?" Vicki's question was directed at her father, who scowled.

"Okay, but only when I'm right there with you." He reached out a hand to tug on the end of one pigtail. "And don't think you can make a pet of him, either, by sneaking sugar to him when nobody's looking."

"No, Daddy," Vicki promised solemnly.

He grunted something unintelligible as he got to his feet. Pulling his worn leather gloves from his back pocket with one hand, he opened the storm door with the other. "Inside, both of you."

"Remember those broken ribs," Karen couldn't help saying before she followed Vicki inside.

Something very like hunger flashed in his eyes for a split second, and then...a leashed anger. "I didn't expect to see you here."

"Vicki wanted to spend time with Domino, and I had a few loose ends to tie up."

As though pondering her words, he pulled on one glove, then the other. She'd worn those same gloves once, while helping him with an injured calf. They'd all but swallowed up her fingers, just as his personality had all but swallowed up hers.

"You get settled at your mom's okay?"

"Yes." She took a breath and caught the familiar scents of hard work and cigar smoke coming from his clothes. Cassidy rarely smoked, and only when he was under an unusual amount of stress. "I saw that attorney I told you about. He's drawing up the papers. All he needs is the name of the person you want to handle your side."

He glanced up, then away, toward the east. "I trust you, Kari. Whatever he sends me, I'll sign." He brought his gaze down slowly, then shifted it her way. "If that's what you really want."

"It's what has to be."

His mouth thinned. "I blew it big-time, didn't I."

She shoved her hands into the pocket of her apron and managed a sad smile. "We both did."

He nodded. "For what it's worth I'll always be here for you, Kari." With that, he took the porch steps at one powerful leap.

Twelve

The hospital cafeteria had closed at eight. The tables had been wiped, the stainless steel warming table and salad bar scoured and disinfected. Now, at a few minutes before nine, only the squat, gray-haired custodian industriously waxing the floor and a few sleepy-eyed visitors and staff members remained.

Slumped in her chair at one of the corner tables, Karen poked at the dried-out remnants of her tasteless ham-and-cheese sandwich and wondered if Cassidy had hired a cook yet. Vicki had come home on Sunday night after her first weekend with her father to say that her daddy's cooking was "rank."

From what Karen had been able to glean from the hyper confusion of her daughter's comments, they'd eaten mostly steak and eggs with an occasional feast of peanut butter and banana sandwiches—and "gross" store-bought cookies for dessert. Not exactly haute cuisine, but reasonably nourishing. For Vicki, anyway. Cassidy worked so murderously hard most days that he needed a tremendous number of calories to sustain him.

She pinched off a piece of stale crust, popped it into her mouth and reminded herself that his intake of power foods—or lack thereof—was no longer her concern.

It had been two endless weeks since she'd left the ranch, and life post-separation was not progressing at a tranquil pace. In fact, she could count the things that were going right on one hand and still have enough free fingers to make a fist. On the other hand, the list of things that were going wrong seemed to grow hourly.

Usually as reliable as the sunrise, the Blazer had developed an oil leak, she hadn't had time to get her tax records to Cassidy's accountant, who'd taken to calling twice a day with tactful reminders, and so far, Vicki had hated every rental they'd looked at.

"Mind if I join you, Dr. Sloane, or would you rather brood in peace?"

Karen glanced up and smiled at the pleasant—and she, ruefully admitted, welcome—surprise.

"Sit, please," she urged, sitting up straighter.

Lindy Chung had piercing black eyes, a figure that had strong men stepping on their tongues when she passed, and the softest heart of anyone Karen had ever known. Past forty now, she had been practicing psychiatry for fifteen of those years and had never shied away from tackling the hard-core cases her fellow shrinks generally—and some said wisely—avoided.

"Thanks." Lindy deposited a paper cup filled with rancid-smelling coffee onto the table before settling into the hard chair with a heartfelt sigh. "Would you believe this is the second night in a row I've had to get dinner from a machine?" she muttered, pulling a plastic container from her expensive leather tote bag.

"Another emergency?"

"Same one. Postpartum syndrome." Lindy broke the seal with one long red nail and flipped open the lid. She took a delicate sniff of the contents, then wrinkled her patrician nose. "Lord, what do those food service people put into these things, anyway?"

"Noah Howell swears he got boar meat in one of his sandwiches last week."

Lindy chuckled. "That man's so besotted with his new wife he couldn't tell boar meat from shoe leather."

It was an effort to smile, but Karen managed somehow. "If ever I saw two people who were meant to be together, it's Noah and Amanda."

"Me, I'll reserve my judgment until they make it past the

first seven years." Lindy bit down on one corner of her sandwich and grimaced. "Noah might be on to something here."

The muted chimes of the paging system sounded through the almost-empty room, and she paused to listen to the paging operator's calm voice.

"Dr. Petrocelli to Admitting, please. Dr. Tony Petrocelli."

"Poor Tony," she murmured, glancing at her watch. "Last I saw him, he was making rounds around seven-thirty."

"The rewards of being in demand," Lindy muttered, chewing.

Karen decided she didn't want anything more to eat and shoved aside her plate in order to rest her forearms in front of her. At least once per shift she made it a point to call Vicki and chat for a few minutes. Tonight, when she'd called, Vicki had refused to speak with her. Another snit, her mother had informed her with more than a little exasperation in her usually unruffled tones.

"Guess Cassidy and I beat the odds, then, because we almost made it to ten," she mused aloud.

Lindy put down her sandwich and reached for her coffee. "Are things smoothing out yet, or are you still in that shell-shocked state?"

"A little of both," she admitted. Telling her co-workers about her separation had been easier than she'd expected. It seemed that many of them had suspected problems in the Sloane marriage. "Most days I don't have much time to brood. Vicki, on the other hand, seems to be doing nothing but."

"Adjustment problems?"

"Big-time." She raked her hand through her hair, a gesture of agitation Lindy acknowledged with a measuring look. "Her teacher has called twice in the past two weeks to 'communicate her concern' about Vicki's behavior. She was very nice about it, but bottom line, my darling, headstrong, bull-headed daughter had better shape up—and fast—or she's about to become well acquainted with the principal's office."

"I take it you've had a talk with Vicki about this?"

"Several, in fact, and I've discovered that my sixty-pound

bundle of joy has inherited Cassidy's ability to stonewall along with his temper."

"Now, that is worrisome," Lindy muttered with a grin designed to soothe rather than mock.

"Phil Potter, Vicki's psychiatrist, assures me it's normal behavior in children with newly separated parents."

"Acting out."

"Yes." Karen drew a breath. More and more she was feeling disconnected from her body, as though trying to escape a reality she couldn't bear to face. "He told me to give her plenty of reassurance but not to give into her when she had one of those tantrums." Karen sighed. "Easy for him to say, since he's not the one battling wits with a determined eight-year-old."

"Phil's an excellent kiddie shrink. And for what it's worth, I agree."

"Yeah, well I know how you therapist types stick together."

Lindy pushed aside the half-eaten remains of her dinner and settled back in her chair. "Similar to the way you resident types stick up for one another, I expect."

"Touché," Karen allowed with a tired smile.

"Karen, Vicki's in good hands, yours included," Lindy declared before snatching a napkin from the dispenser on the table. "I'm more worried about you."

"I'm coping—just," Karen replied as the other woman blotted her lips. "Work helps. And Mother and Frank have been there for me from that first awful moment."

"And Cassidy?"

She shrugged. "According to our…his foreman, he's driving himself and everyone else into the ground. Billy claims the ranch has never looked better or been more productive, and yet Cassidy finds fault with everything and everyone. A couple of the hands have spoken privately to Billy about taking other jobs if Cassidy doesn't ease up."

Karen dropped her gaze to the table with its dull Formica top and collection of scratches. Slowly, she reached out to press her fingertip to an errant crumb, which she carefully deposited on her abandoned tray. Across the table, Lindy watched and waited.

"He swears he doesn't love me, and yet he's acting like he's the one with the broken heart," she declared indignantly. "I could strangle the man for making me waste precious time worrying about him."

Lindy grinned. "You could always stop."

"Ha. A lot you know!" She took a breath, and her indignation slipped away like so much hot air. "Damn him, why does he have to be so pigheaded? He works as many hours as I do—more, sometimes, especially in the spring when the babies are being born. I spent a lot of nights alone because he was busy, but I understood. And I never, ever tried to make him feel guilty for putting his work first." She took an angry breath, her stomach in turmoil and her energy coming back in jerky spurts. "Does that sound like the behavior of an emasculating bitch to you?"

Lindy's beautifully formed lips twitched. "I take it that's a direct quote."

"I'm paraphrasing, but in essence, yes."

"Sounds like the man has a great many unresolved issues from his childhood."

"What he has is a mean temper and a blind, self-centered, arrogant, chauvinistic attitude about a woman's so-called place, and I'm *sick* of it." She didn't exactly stamp her foot, but she thought about it.

Lindy blinked, her mouth twitching. "You've certainly got me convinced."

Karen glared at her, then burst out laughing. "Oh, Lord, Lindy, I think I'm losing it."

"Hmm, it occurs to me that father and daughter aren't the only Sloanes in Grand Springs with a hot temper."

Karen felt her anger slip away and the dull misery surge back. The two emotions were equally strong, but the one protected while the other clawed at her raw insides. It occurred to her that she would do just fine if only she could live the rest of her life in a constant state of simmering rage. On the heels of that bemused observation came another, far more disturbing suspicion.

Was that Cassidy's way of protecting himself from the pain of his past? By turning an angry face to the world whenever he felt threatened? And if he did, was that anger directly proportional to the depth of the pain he was fighting?

"What?" Lindy prodded in a quiet voice.

Karen turned her thoughts outward as a frown tugged at the network of tiny muscles surrounding her eyes. "Lindy, I think I've just had one of those epiphanies you shrinks talk about all the time."

"I'm listening, if you want to run it by me." The other woman shifted her tray to the side, then leaned forward and crossed her arms on the table. Something about the angle of her chin and the contours of her mouth had Karen suspecting that her friend had just slipped into her professional persona.

Karen took a breath, then as succinctly as she could, laid out her theory.

"Very possible," Lindy said after a moment's thought. "In my practice I've treated a great many men who grew up equating tenderness and sensitivity to weakness." She tapped one finger against the tabletop, clearly lost in thought. Then she nodded and said, "I know it sounds hackneyed, but it's been my experience that a man's ability to handle the softer side of his psyche is directly related to his relationship to his mother."

Isn't everything? Karen thought with a weary sigh. "I was afraid you were going to say that," she muttered before going on to tell Lindy everything she knew about Cassidy's early years. When she was finished, Lindy sat with her chin propped on one fist, her gaze focused somewhere to the right of Karen's left shoulder.

"Not the prettiest story I've heard, but far from the worst." With a small sigh, she lifted her head and sat back. "I assume he wouldn't agree to counseling?"

Karen made a show of shuddering. "Not in a million years. He's the most private man I know."

"Understandable. Issues of trust are quite common with

traumatized children, compounded in this case, I suspect, by his history of losing everyone who mattered to him.''

Karen took a moment to think about that. As she did, she idly watched a gray-haired couple walking toward the exit. The woman's step was faltering and she was leaning heavily on the man's arm. His concern was obvious as he matched his steps to hers, and his gaze was soft when he turned to look at her. Though both appeared well into the twilight of their lives, Karen sensed that the bond between them was as strong and as vibrant as a new day in spring.

The weight pressing her heart grew heavier. "And now he's lost his wife," she said softly, achingly.

"Did he? Or did he deliberately drive you away?"

"Is there a difference?"

Impatience crossed Lindy's lovely face. "Of *course* there's a difference. Think about it. If he makes it impossible for you to stay, he's still in control, still making the rules. In other words, he's safe."

Karen tested that in her mind and couldn't find a flaw in the logic of it. But her heart wasn't so sure. "In other words, he was willing to sacrifice our marriage in order to keep from feeling too much?"

"That's one possibility, yes."

Karen noted her friend's careful phrasing and smiled sadly. "On the other hand, we just might be making excuses for a man who's exactly as he seems—a decent, hardworking guy who got a virgin pregnant and did the honorable thing by marrying her, but when he finally got tired of putting up with a woman he didn't love, he took the easy way out and pushed her into doing exactly what he wanted all along."

"True, in which case it would be fairly easy to prove that hypothesis, wouldn't it?"

Karen rubbed her tired eyes. "It would?"

"Sure. If the guy is out dating night after night or whistling while he works, or celebrating the fact that he's free again, it's a good bet he was never emotionally attached. On the other hand, if he looks anything like you, I'd say he's pretty much dying inside and fighting it the only way he knows how—with anger.''

Karen inhaled slowly and exhaled the same way. ''Does driving himself and his men into the ground count as celebrating?''

The look Lindy sent her way was comprised of both humor and compassion. ''What do you think?''

''I think I'm going to have to take some time to mull this over.''

Lindy leaned forward, her expression earnest. ''Fight for him, Karen. Find a way to shock him into seeing what he's doing to himself and to you. Make him face whatever demons he's battling.'' Her voice softened. ''Help him see that for once in his life he's not alone.''

Karen drew a shaky breath. ''What if he won't let me?''

Lindy pushed back her chair and reached down for her belongings. ''Think of it this way,'' she said as she rose. ''Do you really want to hang on to a guy who's too emotionally crippled to appreciate what you're offering?''

Yes! Karen wanted to shout, but deep down she knew Lindy was right. Much as she hated to admit it, she wanted more for herself than a man who was too frozen inside to love.

A week later Karen was still mulling over Lindy's words while sitting alone in her mother's kitchen at midnight after a hectic Saturday night helping out in the ER.

She'd seen Cassidy only once since the conversation in the cafeteria—this morning when she dropped Vicki and Rags off for the weekend. His face had been impassive beneath the familiar Stetson as he'd nodded in her direction. As far as she could tell, he wasn't exactly pining for her. In fact, he looked magnificently confident as he stood in the small training corral adjacent to the big barn, working an unfamiliar black gelding on a lungeing line.

Though it had been early by her standards, only a few minutes past eight, his jeans and buckskin vest were streaked with grime and sweat.

Stifling a yawn now, she forced herself to take another bite of the quiche she'd heated in the microwave and thought about the meeting she'd had that afternoon with the divorce lawyer. Terse to the point of rudeness, the man had asked a series of questions, then asked her to compile a list of assets she considered exclusively her own, and those she shared with Cassidy.

Assets, she thought with a sad shake of her head. Property. Things.

But what about her dreams? What about the threads of her life that were so firmly braided into Cassidy's dreams?

And what about her daughter?

The attorney had sounded almost bored when he'd asked what kind of custody arrangement she wanted to set up. As though Vicki, too, was an asset to be divided.

She felt pressure in her sinuses, a sudden difficulty with her breathing. As she'd done too many times in the past few weeks, she banished the need to cry to the list of things she would do later, when she had some spare time.

Time? *To spare?* she thought glumly. What was that?

A nasty, sadistic gnome with a whip who hated her, she decided with a whimsy that was far from comforting.

"You look like a lady who could use a slug of my famous double strength cocoa," Frank said, flashing that rogue's smile of his as he came into her mother's spotless chrome-and-glass kitchen, bringing a rush of vitality and leashed power with him.

"The man is a saint," she said, fashioning a smile of her own as she straightened her slumped shoulders and made an effort to force down another bite.

"Not even close, darling Kari," he said as he rattled through the pans in the cupboard until he found one he liked.

"No doubt that's a big part of the reason Mom is so crazy about you."

A chuckle rumbled from his deep chest. "That and the fact that I've never tried to change a hair on that gorgeous head of hers. Not that I'd want to, you understand."

"A refreshing attitude in a male," she muttered.

Frank let that pass as he opened another cupboard and took down three mugs, then fetched the cocoa, sugar and the milk—all with the easy familiarity of a man very much at home in the kitchen in spite of the aura of lethal toughness surrounding him.

"Of course, your mom is wise enough to offer me the same courtesy," he said, prying open the lid on the cocoa tin.

"I assume you're talking about Mom and you exclusively," she said evenly, watching him.

"Who else would I be talking about?" he asked with a bland look that made her scowl.

"Haven't a clue," she said, struggling against a leaden need to throw her tired body into his arms and absorb some of his strength, the way Vicki ran to her father for comfort.

"Mother said you're trying to talk her into a June wedding," she said, deliberately changing the subject to one less troubling. "Again."

"Yeah, well, sooner or later she's going to get it into her head that I'm not giving up, no matter how many jumps she puts me over."

Karen felt the skin of her face pulling into a frown. "Are you saying that my mother is deliberately keeping you... uh—?"

"Dangling." His voice blended a wry humor into the firm declaration.

"Now, that's flattering," she grumbled.

His eyes crinkled as he dug into a drawer for a wooden spoon. "I'm in love with your mother, Karen. I've been in love with her for years, but I'm not blind to her faults."

"Faults? *My* mother?" She clucked her tongue. "Shame on you, sir."

His grin flashed. "A stubborn streak a mile wide," he said in his rough baritone as he pulled open the door to the fridge and took out a gallon of milk. "A tendency to fuss over the smallest things, a penchant for worrying about people she loves." The door closed with a quiet thump as he added softly, "And a deep-seated fear that if she lets herself love me, she'll lose me."

Karen rubbed at her suddenly cold cheek. "Because she loved my father and he died, you mean?"

"Smart girl. Excuse me, *woman*. I've spent five years proving to that woman she's stuck with me, no matter how hard she tries to drive me away."

"But Mother loves you."

"Sure she does, but that doesn't mean she can keep herself from testing me." He measured the cocoa by his own mental rule and added milk before turning on the burner. Only then did he turn to look at her. "She's a special lady, my Sylvie. And dammit, she's going to marry me if I have to toss her over my shoulder on June 1 and carry her to Judge Patrick's chambers kicking and screaming every step of the way."

Karen laughed at the image of her impeccably groomed mother dangling upside down over Frank's broad shoulder. "If you do, promise me you'll give me enough notice so that I can find a ringside seat."

"You got it," Frank said, grinning as he stirred the cocoa that was already beginning to smell sinful. He would make a wonderful husband for her mother and a great stepfather, she decided, watching him lift the wooden spoon to his well-shaped mouth for a taste.

At least, she was pretty sure of that—though she'd heard someone say once that he'd been a real hell-raiser as a young man. Abandoned at an early age by his teenage mother, he'd grown up in series of foster homes—until he'd slugged one of his foster "fathers" for taking a belt to one of the other kids. After that, he'd lived on his own, supporting himself by working in one of the silver mines that had been prevalent in the area thirty years ago.

Though he was nothing like the image she held of her own gentle, intellectual father, he'd knocked around enough in his early years to acquire a rough sort of charm that Karen found endearing. Add to that the fact that he was sensitive, funny and a whiz at making her mother blush, and you had one terrific man. Even dressed casually in jeans and a luscious burgundy-and-cream cable-knit sweater that probably cost more than she made in a month, he exuded a quiet air of authority that had nothing to do with his well-padded bank account. Immediately she thought of Cassidy and waited out the fast little flurry of pain that always accompanied thoughts of him.

"So how's it going?" he said, turning down the heat before leaning against the counter and crossing those huge miner's arms.

"Do you want the truth or a soothing evasion?"

He lifted one silvered brow. "Let's go for the truth first."

She dropped her fork onto her plate and pushed it away. "Vicki's miserable, I'm miserable, and Rags is driving everyone crazy with his own version of misery."

Raised from a tiny pup on the ranch, the sensitive shepherd had developed signs of severe homesickness almost immediately. Night after night he sat in the backyard and howled. When he wasn't howling, he was barking or trying to dig himself an escape route under the tall redwood fence. Sometimes he barked *and* dug simultaneously.

Sylvia had already received two complaints from neighbors and a not-so-veiled threat to call Animal Control from old Mr. Hornutt on the corner. They'd tried bringing Rags into the house, but the independent canine hated confined spaces and nearly wore himself out pacing from the front door to the back. It seemed he was only happy at the ranch.

"You neglected to mention Cassidy."

Karen swiveled to the side and hooked her sock-clad toes onto the rung of the chair. "Cassidy is…like those big old boulders on that ranch he loves so much. It would take an earthquake to move him so much as an inch."

"Obstinate, is he?"

"You have no idea," she assured him with a heavy sigh.

A twinkle appeared in his sky blue eyes. "Oh, I think I have a glimmer," he said before reaching into yet another cupboard for a bottle of very old, very expensive brandy that her mother kept just for him.

"You think I'm being too hard on him?"

He poured the now steaming chocolate into the cups. "What I *think* is, I'd be ten kinds of a fool to answer a question like that,'' he said as he rinsed out the pan and up-ended it in the drainer.

"Coward,'' she accused with a fond smile.

"Absolutely.'' He added a generous amount of citrus liqueur to two of the cups, then, bottle poised over the third, lifted a brow in question.

"Sure, why not?'' A nice little alcohol buzz might let her sleep through the night for once without dreaming of Cassidy.

"Not on duty tomorrow?'' He poured the same amount into hers before corking the bottle and returning it to the cupboard.

"I'm working swing this month,'' she said, thanking him with a smile as he set the steaming mug in front of her. The rich scents of chocolate and citrus curled upward, and she inhaled with pleasure.

"Lovely,'' she murmured after taking a sip.

"Thank you, ma'am,'' he said with a dip of his silvered head.

"Welcome,'' she managed to say before treating herself again. The taste was both tart and sweet—and just a little wicked. Exactly like Cassidy's kisses.

Seconds ticked by, unnoticed, until finally she realized Frank was watching her. No, *measuring her*. She lifted her brows and tilted her head.

Frank seemed oblivious to anything but her. Finally he sighed heavily and straightened those big shoulders. "Karen, did you know that my company had the listing on the Barlow ranch before Cassidy bought it?''

She shook her head, puzzled that he would bring that up now.

"He still had his army haircut when he showed up with everything he owned in the back of a third-hand pickup and a chip on his shoulder the size of Pikes Peak.'' Frank wrapped his big hand around the mug and brought it to his lips for a quick sip. "He had no credit, no friends to recommend him and, sadly, not nearly enough cash to cover the down payment Sue Ellen Barlow was demanding for her daddy's place.'' His mouth twitched. "I took one look and told myself I'd be crazy to waste my time trying to put together a deal that didn't have a chance in hell of getting past a reputable loans officer.''

She must have looked bewildered because he chuckled. "I quoted him a down payment that he could afford, made up the difference from my own pocket and swore Charlie Too Tall down at the bank to secrecy.''

"You did what?'' she blurted out, her mug frozen halfway to her mouth.

"I took a calculated risk, nothing more.''

She blinked, trying to understand. From the family room came the sound of music. Vivaldi, she registered absently. "Why?'' she asked finally.

"Now, that's a question I asked myself a lot during that first year when it came time for him to make his monthly mortgage payment.''

"He was late?''

Frank shook his head. "Not once, but I suspect there were a lot of months when he had to choose between eating and meeting his obligation.''

She stared at him, seeing the kind eyes and the strong features. "But the risk...you must have had a reason.''

"He had hungry eyes.'' Something flickered in his own eyes, and for an instant, his jaw tightened. "Nobody had to tell me he'd had a rough time as a kid. Or that he was desperate for a place of his own, a piece of earth and sky and security where he could put down roots, a place no one could take from him.'' His smile was sad. "It's hell growing up knowing no one wants you.''

"Oh, Frank,'' she whispered, deeply touched, for him, for Cassidy—and more than a little confused. "Does Mother know what you did?''

"No one knows, except Charlie and me—and Cassidy.''

That threw her. "When did you tell him?''

"I didn't. He found out a few weeks before you two were married, when he went to the bank for a second mortgage in order to finance some renovations on the house.''

"He was angry?''

"You might say that, yeah," Frank drawled before lifting the mug to his mouth again. "Had this notion I felt sorry for him, and his pride wouldn't let him accept charity."

Karen rubbed her toes along the chair rung. "Men and their pride."

Instead of grinning as she'd expected, Frank responded with a frown. "Sometimes, when a man's had a lot to overcome, pride's the only thing holding him together." Absently he rubbed at a thin white scar along his jaw.

"*Did* you feel sorry for him?"

"No." She heard the trace of annoyance in his deep voice and knew he'd put it there deliberately. "I told you I understood him, but what I told *him* was the truth, too. What he got from me was a loan, nothing more—with enough interest tacked on to have him sucking in hard."

I'll bet, she thought, seeing Frank in a new light. "And?"

"And he chewed on the furniture for a while, added a couple of points to that interest and told me to write it up as a separate note." He grinned. "Made me a tidy bit of change on that cowboy of yours."

She smiled, but it seemed he wasn't finished. "I've made a fortune on reading people—what they say they want and what they really want. Cassidy wants you. I'd stake every penny I made on that."

She held the mug to her cheek and wondered if she would ever be able to talk about her failed marriage without feeling sick inside. "Then why am I sitting here talking to you instead of out at the ranch where I belong?"

He arched a brow. "Good question. Got an answer you'd care to run by me?"

"A lot of them, some that even make sense." She took another sip and held her breath against the intoxicating heat sliding down her throat. "He just wore me out, I guess. I got tired of defending myself for wanting to do what I could to make the world a better place."

He nodded. As practically a member of the family, he knew all about the problems that had led up to their separation.

"I have pride, too, Frank. Maybe more than I should, but

I simply couldn't stay with a man who held me and my goals in contempt.''

''Are you so sure he did?''

''He...he told me I reminded him of his mother and that he hated her.'' She felt her stomach lurch as she revisited the scene in the den in her mind. ''He used our daughter as a weapon to blackmail me into doing what he wanted, and when that didn't work he threatened to take my daughter away from me.''

''And you can't forgive him for that?''

''No. Yes.'' She frowned. ''I don't know.''

''Poor kid, you're really hung up on the guy, aren't you?'' He slipped the words out so softly that it took her a moment to react.

When she did, it was with a bleak smile. ''Does it show?''

''In neon lights.''

She drew a shaky breath. ''All I was asking was that he bend just a little,'' she said in a small voice.

He regarded her in sympathetic silence for a long moment, then picked up both mugs. ''It's just an observation, Kari, but it seems to me Cassidy was doing nothing but bending from the moment you decided to go back to med school. And he's been bending ever since.'' He paused by her chair to drop a kiss on her hair. ''You might want to think on that some when you get to feeling lonely.''

Thirteen

Cassidy had just turned off his computer on Monday morning and was thinking about the week just starting out when the phone rang, demanding his attention. Since it wasn't yet 6:00 a.m., he figured the call was important. With a scowl, he snatched up the receiver before the second ring.

"Sloane here."

"Cass, it's Rio Redtree."

He'd met the Grand Springs native a few years back when Rio sat in for Bren Gallagher during one of their poker nights. Never one to warm to a stranger quickly, Cassidy had found himself liking the younger man immensely by the end of the evening. Since that time, they'd spent many a night glaring at each other across a steadily mounting pot. More often than not, to Cassidy's chagrin, Redtree had gone home with more money in his jeans than he'd brought while Cassidy's pockets tended to be all but empty.

Curiosity surfaced in his mind as he leaned back in his chair and made a stab at massaging away the hard ache at the base of his skull that was his constant companion.

"How's it going?" he asked, because it was expected.

"Can't complain. And you?"

"Overworked." And missing his wife so much he was sick with it.

Redtree chuckled. "There is that."

"You got a reason for calling a hardworking rancher in the middle of the night?"

"Like you were asleep." The other man cleared his throat. "Something's come up I think you ought to know about."

Instantly alert, Cassidy narrowed his gaze. "I'm listening."

There was a brief hesitation, as if Rio was searching for words. Cassidy felt the first prickling of concern and sat up straighter.

"It concerns Vicki, mostly," Rio confided finally.

Fear stabbed deep. He warned himself not to bolt before he knew where he was heading. "Concerns her how?"

"Easy, Cass, it's probably not serious, but—"

"Answer the question, Redtree." He heard the threat in his voice and made a conscious effort to control himself as he added, "What do you know that you're not telling me?"

Rio's sigh did little to stem Cassidy's growing alarm. "Vicki's class was here at the *Herald* last week on a field trip, and while the other kids were learning about computer pasteup and design, she slipped away to talk to me. Said she recognized me because I played poker with her daddy."

Cassidy heard the crunch of gravel outside and glanced at the clock. Billy was a few minutes early. The other hands wouldn't be arriving for another half hour or so.

"Go on."

There was the sound of rustling paper before the other man continued. "It seems she's decided I should do an article on the effect of divorce on little girls and dogs."

Cassidy indulged in a curt oath that had Rio chuckling. "Yeah, well, I told her that it might be a better idea if she wrote it, seeing as she's had experience."

Because he was alone, Cassidy let his head drop. "Why do I think I'm not going to enjoy this?" he muttered, digging harder into the knotted muscles of his neck.

"You have a fax machine, right?"

Cassidy already knew where this was going. "Yeah."

"Hold on a minute while I get a pencil."

Cassidy heard drawers opening and Rio muttering. "Okay, what's the number?" he asked when he came back on the line.

Cassidy recited the digits, waited until Rio repeated them, then asked a little too brusquely, "She didn't, uh, cry or anything, did she?"

"Like a bubbling little fountain," Rio said cheerfully, earning him another rude comment. ''But I had her laughing again before they left.''

''Hell, Redtree, I didn't think you had a sensitive bone in that pitiful wreck you call a body.''

Rio's chuckle would have been infectious—if Cassidy wasn't busy bracing himself to read his daughter's words as soon as they spilled out of the fax. ''Funny what living with a good woman can do for a man, ain't it, Sloane.''

Cassidy closed his eyes on a knife-thrust of pain. ''What is this, Redtree, a damned conspiracy to rub my nose in my own stupidity?''

''Something like that, yeah. Is it working?''

''It's working.''

''Going to try to get her back?''

Cassidy thought about lying. A man had his pride. ''I'm considering it.''

''Want some advice from a man who's been there?'' Redtree's voice was subtly altered, as though he was grinning.

''Might as well, since I figure you're gonna give it whether I want it or not.''

Rio laughed. ''Well, hell, you're smarter than I figured.''

''You gonna tell me or insult me?''

Cassidy heard a long-suffering sigh that had his teeth grating together.

''Get yourself all duded up, buy her a coupla dozen roses and maybe some candy—to get her in the mood, you know. And then, get down on your knees and grovel. Works every time.''

Karen woke a little before noon, still groggy from the aftereffects of a long and stressful weekend as a resident-on-duty. Exhaustion still buzzed in her head, and her arches ached.

Just over seven more months and her days as an ill-paid, overworked resident would be at an end. Then, after surviving the worst, she could look forward to private practice as a better-paid, but still overworked doctor.

With a heartfelt sigh, she sat up and threw off the covers.

Though her bedroom was the smallest of four on the second floor, she'd chosen it because its two dormer windows looked out on the snow-capped Rockies marking the western horizon. It was the same view she'd had from the master bedroom at the ranch, and it didn't take much thought to realize why she favored it.

Three weeks down and a lifetime to go, she thought as she glanced at the thick packet of legal papers on the small desk between the windows. She must have signed her name two dozen times in the past weeks, each signature taking her closer to a final act of separation from the man she loved. And couldn't have, she reminded herself as she climbed out of bed.

Without bothering with a robe, she padded across the chilly floor to the door. The second floor was wrapped in silence as she gained the hall and turned left, heading toward the bathroom at the end of the hall. Halfway to her destination, she was startled to hear a heavy footfall behind her. Turning quickly, her heart suddenly pounding, she was stunned to see Cassidy coming toward her from the direction of the stairs.

He was wearing a sky blue Western-cut shirt that she'd never seen before, and his jeans were clean, though far from new. His jaw was shiny from a recent shave, and he'd made an attempt to tame the unruly curl from his glossy black hair.

Her body responded before her mind, and desire was already racing through her as she stood frozen, unable to move. How long would it take before she stopped acting like a giddy schoolgirl with a crush every time they happened to meet unexpectedly? she wondered as she fought to regain her composure.

When the earth stops spinning or that untamed sex appeal that he exudes suddenly disappears, came the answer from the more primitive part of her woman's heart.

Cassidy, too, stopped dead when he caught sight of her, and for an instant, she was sure she saw a naked look of longing flash across his carved-granite features, but when he spoke, his voice was as controlled as ever.

"I rang the bell," he said, shifting his stance. "I figured you wouldn't mind if I let myself in."

Karen resisted the urge to huddle deeper into the oversize Broncos jersey that served as her nightshirt. She hadn't missed the hot lick of arousal that had appeared in his eyes when he first caught sight of her standing there with her legs bare and the neck of the big shirt hanging over one shoulder. That, at least, hadn't changed. Cassidy found her sexually appealing.

"Of course not. You're always welcome in my mother's house."

He narrowed his gaze, but not before she saw a slice of frustration in those dark depths. "But not in yours?"

"You're Vicki's father," she said evasively. "You'll always be welcome in her house."

His mouth slanted. "I came up to see if you were awake yet. I tried to be quiet, just in case."

She couldn't help smiling. Cassidy was too big and too impatient to be quiet—unless he was sleeping. And even then, he had a tendency to mutter disjointedly. Though she'd never managed to make out more than an odd word or two, the urgent tone of his rambling suggested that he was pleading with someone only he could see.

Early in their marriage, she'd tried to get him to talk about the problems that followed him so tenaciously into sleep. After a few abrupt but icy rebuffs, she'd let him fight his nocturnal battles alone. Now she wondered if the pleading words had been directed at the mother he claimed to hate.

"You didn't wake me," she assured him, endeavoring to make her voice as cool as his. "Or, if you did, it was time for me to get up, anyway."

He nodded, then glanced back toward the stairs. Probably planning his escape route, she thought. These days they rarely managed more than five minutes of conversation before one or the other walked away. This time she decided to make it easy for him.

"Was there anything particular you wanted?" she murmured politely. To her surprise, he scowled and turned red.

"I had a call from Redtree this morning. It seems that our daughter has taken up journalism." He reached behind him and pulled a folded piece of paper from the back pocket of his jeans. "She wrote this article after her class visited the *Herald*."

Cassidy saw the quick look of puzzlement come into Karen's still sleep-drowsy eyes as she took the fax. Though he kept his gaze resolutely fixed on hers, he was all too painfully aware of the familiar outline of her small, firm breasts beneath the thin covering of her orange-and-blue sleep shirt. One look and he wanted her with an intensity that could weaken him, if he gave into it.

"I was one of the chaperones for that trip," she said, unfolding the paper. "I do recall seeing her talking with Rio at one point, but she didn't say anything to me about an article."

"Yeah, well, she wrote one." Cassidy shifted, far too aware of the growing desire in his lower body. "Look, why don't I make some coffee while you read it? We'll talk when you're finished." And dressed, preferably in something that a nun might consider conservative, he added silently as he turned and beat a hasty retreat.

The coffee took four minutes to brew. She was back in six, dressed in old jeans and an outsize University of Colorado sweatshirt the color of a strawberry roan colt he'd once had.

The shirt he could handle. It was too baggy to do more than whet a man's imagination. But those damn jeans—now, they were giving him big trouble. Something about the way they cupped her backside and caressed her thighs, he suspected, wrenching his gaze to her face.

He'd accepted his sexual need, but his craving for her affection and warmth just seemed to grow stronger the longer they were apart. He thought he'd had this leftover ache tucked safely away, but he'd been wrong.

For a lot of years he'd fooled himself into thinking it was strictly sex he wanted, and sex he offered. But now, even as his body stirred and swelled behind the barbed constriction of his button fly, he knew that he would take a vow of celibacy for the rest of his life if she would look at him with love in those pretty gray eyes just one more time.

Before either of them had a chance to speak, he picked up the mug he'd just filled with coffee and silently held it out to her. He knew her fingers would brush his, told himself he was braced to feel her touch. Even so, when her fingertips whispered against his, heat raced through him like a fever, leaving him weak and wanting inside.

"Thanks," she said, drawing the mug to her so quickly a few drops slopped over the side and onto her shirt where the big C curved over her breast. His mouth went dry, and he focused his attention on tasting his own coffee. He waited until she took a greedy sip before suggesting that they sit.

"You look exactly the way I felt earlier," he drawled, watching her carefully, his gaze narrowed to hide the hunger that prowled inside him every minute of every day.

"Actually, I feel as though I just might shatter if I breathe too hard," she said, pulling out a chair. "And you?"

"Like I've been kicked so hard my belly button got shoved into my backbone." He took the chair opposite and dragged it back far enough to allow room for his long legs. Maybe, with the width of the table between them, the need to hold her would settle. Or maybe not, he realized as he tried to adjust his large frame to the medium-size chair.

Beyond the sunny bay window his mother-in-law's garden was bursting with color and life. There were flowers on the table, too, yellow trumpety things with long stiff stalks like the ones Kari had planted beneath the bedroom window. One of the frilly petals had a torn edge, as though it had been attacked by some garden pest.

Feeling raw, inside and out, he let his gaze find hers across the table. The spark of life and intelligence in her gray velvet eyes was a mere flicker, now obscured by a mother's anguish.

"Her penmanship is atrocious," she said finally, breaking the silence.

"Especially since she printed most of it," he drawled, his throat so tight it was a miracle he could draw breath, let alone speak.

Her smile was a ray of sunshine, but before he felt its warmth reach his cold face, it was gone, swallowed by the torment reflected on her face. "Imagine, promising to give up her allowance forever if we got back together."

"Take my advice, and take her up on it. It might be your only chance."

"You're probably right." Eyes downcast, Karen fiddled with the mug's thick handle, turning it one way, then another. Since reading Vicki's plaintive words, she'd been heartsick. A wry smile bloomed in her mind for a brief span at the layman's terminology.

Heartsick. Heartbroken. Heartsore.

Words coined by poets to describe the feeling that now filled her to bursting. And yet, she knew that the human heart was incredibly resilient. Even hers.

And Cassidy's? Had his past layered his heart with so much bitterness it was no longer capable of doing anything other than pump blood?

She hunched forward and pressed her hands around the mug. The daffodils were new, and she realized her mother must have picked them after Karen had seen Vicki off to school and gone back to bed.

"I'll talk to her." She lifted her gaze to his hard, unreadable, beloved face. "Unless you—"

"You read the article, Karen. I'm not exactly her favorite person at the moment." His words were raw, his expression savage. "'My daddy won't let my mommy be a doctor and that makes Mommy sad. And he says I can't be a rancher 'cause I'm a girl, which is the most special thing I can be.'" He shook his head. "Guess that pretty much sums it up."

"Children see things in simple terms, Cass. When she's older, she'll understand."

"Maybe. But she'll always carry scars." His mouth twisted. "How's that for irony? I was trying to protect her from hurt, when all along, I should have been protecting her from myself."

"Time will help her heal. That and knowing we love her."

Cassidy saw the faith shining in his wife's eyes and wished

he had the same trust. But life had taught him a long time ago that trust was a trap. "Yeah, well, she's not real sure about that right now, is she."

Her face twisted and tears welled in her eyes. "I hate to cry," she grumbled, wiping them away with hurt, stabbing gestures.

He slid his own rough, range-ruined hands from the table-top and fisted them on his thighs. "You're entitled."

She sniffed, then glared at him across the fussy tips of the ridiculous-looking flowers. "Men always say that when a woman breaks down in their presence, but they never do it themselves."

"Some do. Depends on the man."

The fire was back in her eyes. For now, anyway. Fury he could ride out. It was the hurt that tore him apart. "What about you, Cassidy? When was the last time you cried?"

Across the table Karen saw a trapped look come into his eyes and allowed herself a tired smile. What was the use? Cassidy was never going to trust her with anything more than his scorn—and, maybe once upon a time, his affection. "Never mind. Forget I asked."

An errant muscle jerked in his rugged jaw. "I cried. When my mother came into my room on my tenth birthday and said she was leaving."

"On...your birthday?"

His gaze bored into her, as fathomless and cold as that hidden pit at the bottom of Devil Butte. "Why not? That was as good a day as any to tell me she hated my guts for killing my baby brother and couldn't stand to be in the same house with me one more minute."

"Oh...my...God," she whispered. "That's a contemptible way to treat your own child. *Any* child."

He stirred, restless, as though desperate to escape, yet steeling himself to stay. He wasn't sure why he needed to tell her about those dark times. He only knew he did. "It was only a damn practice game. A warm-up for the play-offs. I could have missed it, but I wanted to be there, wanted to show off for the girls who always crowded around to watch."

He swallowed, and his eyes grew darker, bleaker, as if the memories were pressing closer. "Johnny wanted to stay home and watch cartoons. I threatened to beat him to a pulp if he didn't shut up and do what I said."

Karen saw the reflexive movement of one corner of his hard mouth and suspected he was reliving the scene in his mind. It staggered her to realize the enormity of the hurt he must have suffered, not to mention the terrible burden of carrying that alone and in silence for more than two-thirds of his life.

Fresh tears filled her eyes and she longed to go to him, to offer her comfort and her understanding, but she was afraid to move. Lindy was right. Cassidy needed to purge himself of this poison, and she would listen, no matter how his words sliced at her.

After a moment, his big chest heaved and he settled his shoulders straighter. "I must have warned him a dozen times to stay on the grass. He had those stupid little trucks he was always playing with and a couple of books. One of the girls shared her potato chips with him." One side of his mouth curled. His gaze was focused unerringly on hers, but she doubted he really saw her. "Johnny was crazy for potato chips."

"Was he?" she asked softly, encouragingly.

He didn't respond directly. The look in his eyes made her wonder if he'd even heard her speak. "I'd just hit a double to right and was doing a stupid victory dance on the bag when I heard brakes squealing. I knew then. I just...knew." There was raw pain in his eyes now, and a terrible yawning grief that she suspected was only a small part of the agony he'd carried for so long.

"Let it go, Cassidy," she urged, her voice thick with the tears she didn't dare shed. "You've been in purgatory long enough. You don't deserve to spend the rest of your life paying for a mistake you made when you were a child."

His eyes turned hot with a depth of savage emotion that stunned her. "You don't understand, Karen. My brother would be alive if I hadn't been such a show-off."

She schooled herself to be calm, the same calm she exhibited in the face of terrible suffering in the sickroom. "You were nine years old. Vicki's age. How could you be expected to take care of yourself and your brother?" She inhaled swiftly, feeling a surge of anger at a woman who would neglect her own children so shamefully. "You were right to hate your mother."

"I didn't have to take Johnny to that field with me, but I did. And then I just forgot about him." His chest heaved as he dragged in a great stream of air. "I loved my brother, Kari. I was supposed to take care of him, and I didn't. It…changed me. Twisted things up inside."

"Cassidy—"

"I tried to punish you for my sins, Kari. I know that now." He raked his hair back, resettling the raven thickness. "I had no right to do that, and I'm…sorry."

"The point is that you do know it. We can build on that."

The look he gave her was so full of longing, so deeply emotional that she wanted to shout with joy. It was going to be all right! The burst of happiness died when he spoke again.

"It's too late."

"You're wrong. It's never too late."

His smile was terribly sad. "That's my sweet optimist."

"But it's true," she exclaimed softly, desperately. "I know it won't be easy. Change never is. You won't be alone, darling. I'll be there."

His mouth twisted, and for an instant she thought that awesome control would crack. "I'll always be alone, Kari. That's my punishment."

He slid his chair backward and stood up. It took her a moment to realize he was leaving. "That's it? You won't even try?"

"I *have* tried. For nine years I've tried. But it's not in me to love you the way you deserve to be loved."

"There you go again," she said with plenty of impatient indignation in her tone. "Taking responsibility for someone else's well-being."

His eyebrows drew together in an ominous frown. God,

how she loved the power of this man, she thought as she, too, got to her feet. "I'm not going to argue with you," he declared in steely tones.

"Fine, then I'll argue with you." She settled her fists on her hips and glared at him. "I love you, Cassidy Sloane, and I'm not going to let you shut me out."

He went rigid, and she sensed a savage struggle going on behind those black, forbidding eyes. "You don't have a choice, Karen."

"Oh, but I do. I can call my attorney right now and tell him not to file the papers."

"Then I'll file them," he said, his face shutting up.

Shutting her out. "Like you said, our marriage is over."

He let his gaze roam her face for a moment before he settled his shoulders into a rigid line. And then he was gone.

Karen waited until bedtime to have a talk with her daughter. She began by showing Vicki the fax and complimenting her on her writing skills. Vicki beamed, but her glowing smile dimmed when Karen told her that Cassidy, too, had read the article.

"Is Daddy mad 'cause I put in that stuff about him not wanting you to be a doctor?"

Karen passed a gentle hand over her daughter's hair. She felt a fierce need to protect her child. But how? "No, sweetheart. Daddy understands why you wrote what you did, but I think it hurt him a little, too."

"Oh." Vicki's big brown eyes grew wary.

"Which brings up an important point. I know Mr. Redtree promised to print what you wrote in the paper, and if you still want him to, he said he would keep his promise, but here's something you might want to think about. Once it's printed, people will know that you're disappointed in your daddy, and your mommy, too. Your friends might even tease you."

Vicki drew her eyebrows together in a poignant imitation of her father's ominous scowl. "They'd better not. Specially that dorky Brooks Gallagher."

"It's something to think about, though." When Vicki remained silent, Karen plowed on. "Particularly since you might come to change your mind about some things in the future."

"You mean like what I said about Daddy saying bad things to you and all?"

"Yes, exactly."

Vicki seemed to be struggling with something before she admitted in a little voice, "Maybe I didn't really mean that." She thought a moment longer, then added, "Guess maybe I don't want Mr. Redtree to print it, either."

"I'm glad, Vicki. Very glad. And I think that's something you might want to tell your Daddy when you see him on Wednesday night."

Vicki looked a little scared. "Maybe—" she hedged, then asked plaintively "—are you still mad at Daddy?"

Karen shook her head. "No. I'm not mad."

The sudden blazing of hope in Vicki's soft brown eyes tore at the wounds in Karen that hadn't even begun to heal. "Then we can go back to being a family again, right? Me and you and Daddy and Rags?"

Trailing her fingertips over a stuffed bear that lay atop the coverlet beside her daughter, Karen took a moment to reply.

"Daddy and I can't live together anymore, sweetie," she said with a sad finality. "We disagree on too many important things."

"Like you being a doctor 'stead of just a mommy like he thinks you should?"

"No, Daddy admits that he was wrong about that." Once she might have felt a great satisfaction in that. Now the validation he'd offered paled in comparison to the other things he'd said. Or hadn't said.

"Then we can go home, right?"

"It's not that simple, sweetheart," she hedged, wishing her head wasn't buzzing with tiredness and her mind wasn't sluggish.

"Why not?"

Karen rubbed her aching temple and tried to focus her

thoughts. "Remember when you dropped Grandma's favorite piggy bank and broke it?"

"I was just a baby," Vicki said defensively.

"Yes, and Grandma wasn't angry with you because you didn't mean to drop it. But that didn't mean anyone could put it back together, either, because the pieces were too small."

She could see Vicki struggling to understand, and the little girl's efforts were painful to watch. "Well, Mommy and Daddy's marriage is like that piggy bank, sweetie. Somehow it got broken, and now it can't be fixed."

Vicki's chin trembled. "Are you sure?"

"Pretty sure."

"What about Daddy? He's real good at fixing the tractor when it breaks down."

Karen cleared her throat. "In this case, not even Daddy can fix what's broken." But he could, a little voice reminded her. If only he wanted to do the hard work it would take to repair the damage done to him when he was scarcely any bigger than Vicki. "Do you understand what I'm saying, sweetheart?"

Though she still looked sad, Vicki nodded. "I guess so. But I still wish we could be a family."

Karen smoothed a dark curl from her daughter's cheek. "Oh, honey, I know you do, and I wish with all my heart that I could make that happen. But I can't."

"Is that why I hear you crying sometimes in your room at night, and Daddy gets this awful sad look on his face whenever I talk about you?"

Karen nodded, her eyes burning with tears she refused to shed in front of her daughter. "Daddy and I tried hard to make our marriage work. And when we didn't succeed, it made us both sad." She reached out to straighten Vicki's thick bangs. "Most of all it makes us sad to know that you wish things could be the way they were. But they…can't."

Vicki looked crestfallen. "Not ever?" she asked plaintively.

Karen shifted her gaze to the night table and the framed photo of the three of them taken in happier times. A family on a picnic, snapped by her mother. Karen was wearing a halter top, shorts and a bemused smile. Cassidy had his shirt off and had just leaned down to give her a possessive kiss on her bare shoulder while Vicki looked on, radiant with good health and a child's innocent joy.

A shiver had run through her then. A shiver ran through her now. A man who truly loved her would have fought for her and the life they might had together.

"No, sweetie," she whispered sadly, "things will never be the same again."

Fourteen

The snow on the lower peaks was mostly gone by the end of April, and the sun was riding higher and higher in the sky with every day that passed. Like the land itself, the ranch was coming alive. The winter's ravages had to be evaluated and tended. Fences needed mending, and hay hauled to the high pasture.

Day after day, Cassidy worked himself into a state of blind, dumb exhaustion, coming home only when he finally figured he was numb enough to enter the empty house without wanting to put his fist through a wall. But even as he hung up his hat and shouldered out of his down vest in the mudroom, he was listening for the sound of Karen's voice calling his name.

When he showered, he let the hot water massage his tired muscles and longed to feel her small, capable hands running over his body just one more time. When he turned over in bed, he swore he could smell her scent on his pillow. But when he woke, he was alone, just as he'd always been.

Not even the satisfaction of delivering three healthy foals on three successive nights could lift the hard weight of depression that had settled over him since Karen had left.

He didn't want to miss her. He didn't want to desire her. To do both would weaken him. But in the quiet hours of the night when his resistance was low, he felt the old loneliness seeping into him, tearing at his willpower.

It was then that the weight of his past mistakes pressed hardest. It had been years since he'd had the old nightmare, the one that had come to him every night for years after Johnny's death, but suddenly it was on him again, wrenching him from sleep and sending him outside to pace for hours until the sick guilt eased its hold on his gut.

Like a man possessed he took on more and more of the workload. He was in the saddle so much he'd been forced to buy another horse to add to his personal string. Named Lucifer by a breeder who'd given up on him, the beast was a mean sucker, black as original sin except for a white lightning bolt blaze. The hands had a fine old time watching the boss pit two-hundred-and-five pounds of muscle and will against a thousand pounds of pure cussedness.

Cassidy had gone through two bottles of liniment, his entire lexicon of swear words and a year's supply of patience, but the horse refused to break. He would, though, or one of them would end up with a broken neck. Sometimes, when the loneliness settled in with a fierce vengeance, he didn't care which of them came out the winner.

The papers from Karen's attorney came to him on a gray Friday, served by a pasty-faced kid with a smirk. His first inclination had been to shove the papers down the little bastard's throat. Instead, he threw them on the dining room table, grabbed his hat and headed for the barn.

On the way, he stopped by the holding corral to check on the Brahma who pawed the ground at his approach, his straggly tail jerking back and forth in a purely mean challenge. One male to another.

Whitehorse was there, along with two of the other men Billy had set to shoring up the corral's north section where the bull had tried to kick his way to the larger pasture where his "ladies" were waiting.

Cassidy rested one booted foot on the corral's lower rail and stared back at his twelve-hundred-pound gamble. Whitehorse looked up and grinned around the nails clamped in his teeth. "Can't rightly blame the bastard for trying, considerin' all those pretty little heifers sashaying back and forth in front of him all hours of the day and night."

"Yeah, Toro's got all the equipment and the yen to use it, all right. All he needs now is the chance."

The third man, a recent hire that Cassidy had put on at the

request of his ramrod, stood up to stretch out his back. Pushing fifty, Rex Simon was a Vietnam vet who'd tried to medicate himself into oblivion for so many years he had trouble communicating with humans, though he had a real way with horses.

"Spanish, is he?" Simon asked, jerking off his hat to scratch his shaggy gray hair.

"Nah," Whitehorse said, pounding another nail in place.

"Boss's little girl named him that after a story she read about the feller who homesteaded this place back in the 1880s. Had him a Texas longhorn by the same name."

Cassidy frowned. "Wanda hasn't been letting Vick hang around here, has she?"

Whitehorse ducked his head, but not before Cassidy saw the dull blush on his high cheekbones. "Not much, and me and her made real sure Miss Vicki doesn't climb on the fence."

Cassidy narrowed his gaze. "Get this straight, Whitehorse. I don't want her within a dozen yards of this corral."

"Yes, sir." The young hand drew another nail from his mouth and drove it home with three hard blows. Simon shot Whitehorse a speculative glance before reaching for another length of board.

"Wanda June, either," Cassidy added when he figured he had Whitehorse's undivided attention.

"Yes, sir."

Cassidy felt his temper stir and kicked the fence post with the toe of his boot. "Guess you know Wanda's like another daughter to Karen…to me. I would take it real bad if she got hurt, physically or otherwise." He waited. When the kid didn't answer, he prodded, "Understood?"

"Understood" came the mumbled reply.

Cassidy didn't like the defensive edge on the young hand's voice and made a mental note to talk to Wanda when he had a spare minute or two.

"Stockwell's comin' out sometime this afternoon to check out the bull. Let me know when he gets here." With one final look at the bull, who had gone back to grazing, he turned and headed for the barn.

"You fixin' to go a few more rounds with that black devil?" Billy asked when he glanced up from the tack he was mending to see Cassidy bearing down on him.

Skirting the pile of leather lying at Billy's feet in the center aisle, Cassidy spit out, "Something like that."

Because of the dreary weather, most of the interior lights had been turned on, even though it was still daylight outside. A soft glow bathed the aged gray of the planks with amber and made the bits of hay strewn over the packed earth floor shimmer like gold.

The familiar and much-loved scents of horses, alfalfa and grain filled Cassidy's senses, but they no longer soothed him as they once had. Just as seeing all the horses, every last one of which he owned free and clear, no longer filled him with a sense of accomplishment.

Irritated at the direction of his thoughts, he ran his gaze over the stalls, then headed for the one on the end where Lucifer stood watching him with the equine equivalent of pure hatred.

"Spoiling for a fight, aren't you, you stubborn son of a bitch?"

The horse bared his teeth and whuffed out air. Hell, why not? Cassidy thought as he reached for his favorite bridle. Wrestling with Lucifer for a few hours might be a darn sight more satisfying than fighting with his conscience.

"You gonna give Vicki her new mare when she comes this afternoon or wait till tomorrow?" Billy asked, his head bent over his task once more.

Cassidy spared his ramrod a sour look before throwing the blanket and saddle onto Lucifer's muscular back. Every extra hour with his daughter was precious to him, and he had rented a couple of her favorite videos for the occasion.

"I figure she'll head for the barn first thing tomorrow morning. I'll show her the mare then." Cassidy brought up a knee to nudge the horse over. "Easy boy," he said, gentling his tone and shifting the saddle. Then, to Billy, he remarked, "It's too wet to let her ride tonight."

"Hell, boss, she ain't no sissy." Billy scoffed. "I seen her comin' home lots of times looking like a drowned puppy. Her 'n' Miss Karen both. Right feisty ladies, if you ask me."

"I didn't."

Cassidy took another jerk on the cinch, then waited. As soon as Lucifer was forced to let out the air he'd trapped in his belly, Cassidy gave the cinch another hard jerk. Lucifer tossed his head, jostling Cassidy until he regained his balance. Automatically, he reached back to stroke the animal's velvety muzzle, the only soft part on the ornery animal.

"Too bad you 'n' Miss Karen broke up the way you done. Woulda been comforting to know she was close by when that sorry excuse for horseflesh tosses you on your keister again. Lord, but she's a cool hand in a crisis." Billy chuckled. "Remember the time you sliced your leg open muscling a steer into that old chute we shoulda torn down before then? Lordy, but that little woman did order us around."

She'd also sutured the gash with a rock-steady hand and gleam in her eyes as she offered to trade him the prettiest scar in two counties in exchange for a kiss. She'd gotten her kiss, all right. And more. He'd ended up with a neat row of tiny stitches bisecting his hamstring—and a satisfied smile on his face.

Bracing himself for the inevitable nudge of Lucifer's nose against his shoulder, Cassidy stopped in front of his ramrod and narrowed his gaze. "Is there a point to this walk down memory lane, Russell? Or are you angling for unemployment?"

Billy's mouth twitched. "Just recollectin' some, that's all."

Pulling a bandanna from his back pocket, Cassidy met the younger man's gaze, his gut constricting as the pain of loss and bitterness seared through him.

"Take my advice, Billy. Don't push your luck."

"Guess this is the wrong time to ask you to put on a new hand for a few months?"

Cassidy paused to direct a narrowed gaze at his ramrod. "What, another one of your reclamation projects?"

Russell shook his head. In his spare time he volunteered at the Rescue Mission in town. As a sort of a payback, he'd told Cassidy once. "Not this time. It's Dora's nephew. He got into some trouble in Denver and her brother figures a couple of months on a ranch might just open his eyes some."

Cassidy tested the square knot he'd tied in the blindfold, then slipped it over the horse's eyes. Lucifer jerked his head back, then shook it, trying to dislodge the bandanna. Cassidy tightened the grip on the reins and murmured to the animal until he calmed. Only then did he return his attention to his ramrod. "What kind of trouble?"

"Same as me. Drugs."

Cassidy frowned. "How old is this kid?"

"Twelve."

Cassidy offered his opinion in one crude, explosive word that had Russell nodding. "Hell of a note, Cass. According to Dora's brother, Ryan—that's the kid's name—has been using since he was Vicki's age."

"You know my policy on drugs and alcohol," Cassidy said, rubbing the gelding's taut neck. "I give one chance, that's all. But with a kid—" He shook his head. "Maybe Vick's not here every day, but—"

"You have my word, Cass," Russell hastened to reassure him. "He won't be using. As for working, I know you can't really hire him. I was thinkin' more of odd jobs for an hour or so after school."

Cassidy took a moment to think it through. He knew he should refuse, but he kept remembering himself at twelve. "Anyone ever tell you what a soft touch you are, Russell?" he said with a scowl.

"'Bout as many as say the same about you, Cass."

Cassidy used another word—equally foul and succinct— before leading Lucifer toward the door.

Russell just laughed and stood up. "Guess if you're contemplatin' another suicide attempt at tamin' that so-and-so, the least I can do is stand by to pick up the pieces.

* * *

Karen downshifted for the last hill before the top, grateful that Cassidy had graded the access road since last Friday. The worst of the winter ruts had been smoothed to more manageable grooves that were easier on the Blazer's shocks.

Behind her, Rags had suddenly come to life, standing in the back well with his nose pressed to the window and his plume of a tail beating the air eagerly.

"Mommy, do we really have to leave Rags?"

Karen heard the plaintive note in her daughter's voice and reached over to smooth Vicki's perpetually tumbled bangs. "You know we do," she said quietly. "Otherwise, Grandma will have to pay a lot of money in fines to the noise abatement people."

"Maybe we could try keeping him inside again," Vicki proposed with a hopeful glance at her mother. "I could keep him in my room at night, so he wouldn't hurt Grandma's things."

Karen thought about her mother's prized china collection which had been smashed beyond repair when the exuberant shepherd had skidded across the priceless Oriental rug to smash into the cabinet at full speed.

"We tried that, Vicki. Rags hates being shut in."

She sensed rather than saw her daughter slide her a look. "But he could get used to it."

"Honey, be fair. Rags isn't happy in town." Karen tightened her grip on the wheel and braced for the rush of sadness that always greeted her when the old white house came into view.

After an initial confusion with scheduling, the weeks had fallen into a routine of sorts. Vicki spent alternate Wednesday nights with her father and three out of four weekends. Though she could take the bus to the ranch on Wednesdays, Karen drove her on Fridays so that Rags could go, too.

Now that Rags was to be in permanent residence at the ranch again, she supposed that her own trips to the ranch would be far less frequent. For Vicki's birthday, of course, which was coming up in just two weeks, and other special occasions, though what those would be, she didn't have a clue.

The ranch seemed busier than usual, she noted as she drove between the 'dozer and Billy's truck. Instead of pulling into her old spot in the shed, she had taken to parking in the visitor's spot under the massive oak tree where Vicki's rope swing still hung, looking oddly forlorn as it swayed in the sporadic wind gusts. After all, that's what she was now, wasn't she? A visitor?

"Hurry and park, Mommy," Vicki exclaimed, straining to see over the dashboard. "Daddy's trying to break Lucifer again."

"Lucifer?"

"His new mount. Billy says Daddy's already been bucked off twice."

Karen frowned as she caught sight of the group of cowboys gathered in front of the main corral. Beyond the wall of denim shirts and worn jeans, she spotted Cassidy leading a huge black gelding around the perimeter of the corral.

Dressed in chaps and a buckskin vest over his usual working clothes and his battered workaday Stetson, he seemed to be talking quietly to the nervous horse, as though reassuring him. Presently blindfolded with a bright red bandanna, the animal was at least sixteen hands high, with only a lightning bolt blaze to soften the inky coat.

"Are you sure he's not just training the animal, sweetie? Daddy doesn't usually have to break the horses he raises."

"This is a new one he bought from Wanda's daddy. A real son-of-a-bitch hellion."

"Vicki," she chided softly, sparing her daughter a look.

Vicki immediately stuck out her lower lip and frowned. "Well, that's what Billy calls him."

"When you're Billy's age you use words like that. Until then, watch your language, young lady." Karen braked and shifted into neutral. "Don't forget your things. I'll see you when Daddy brings you home on Sunday."

"Don't leave yet, Mommy," Vicki said quickly, her gaze darting back toward the barn where several of the men had climbed onto the railing for a ringside seat. "Come watch, okay?"

"Now, Vicki—"

"Remember when Daddy got his ribs busted and you helped the doctor patch him up?" Vicki's attempt at looking innocent was so pathetic Karen had to laugh.

"I guess I can stay for a few minutes," she conceded, shoving the floor shift into reverse before switching off the engine.

"You could stay for dinner, too," Vicki bargained as she reached for the door handle. "Daddy wouldn't mind."

"I'm sure he would," Karen said as she, too, opened the door.

"Uh-uh. I asked. He said you were always welcome here." Vicki reached behind the seat for her backpack and schoolbooks before slamming the passenger door. As she turned, Karen noticed a rip in the sleeve of her new sweatshirt, and the seat of her jeans were dirty, as though she'd sat down hard in the midst of mud puddle.

"Victoria Sylvia, have you been fighting again?" she asked over the sound of Rags's impatient yapping.

Vicki shrugged thin shoulders that seemed far too vulnerable.

Give me patience, Karen prayed to whatever deity looked after exasperated moms and troubled little girls.

Though it was a mild day under the lowering clouds, the wind still carried a bite, causing Karen to huddle into her bulky wool sweater as she went around to release a now-frantic Rags, who all but exploded past her in his eagerness to be home again. With an exuberant yelp, the sturdy Aussie streaked at full speed toward the corral.

"I know how you feel," she muttered under her breath as she joined Vicki, who was waiting impatiently a few feet away, her gaze darting back and forth between her slowpoke mom and the nearly irresistible sight of her father handing the still skittish gelding's reins to Billy before vaulting himself to the top rail.

Still laughing at something Cassidy had said, Billy turned

his head their way. Seeing them approaching, he grinned and lifted a hand in greeting while at the same time saying something that had Cassidy twisting toward them. Even with a good thirty feet between them, she felt the impact of his gaze before he turned away.

Seconds later, she saw him tug his hat lower, watched Billy hand him the reins and saw him slip from the fence to the saddle in one fluid, controlled movement of muscle and sinew and bone.

Her heart gave a traitorous leap before resettling into the erratic rhythm of arousal. How long would it be, she wondered, until she no longer reacted to the sight of that magnificent body with a dizzying hunger? Or longed to pull that proud head to her breast and stroke away the hard lines of bitterness and self-hatred his past had seared into that rugged face?

"Uh-oh, there he goes!" Vicki shouted, breaking into a run. At the same time, Cassidy gave a curt nod, and Billy leaned forward to strip the bandanna free.

With a shrill scream that seemed to tear at Karen's eardrums, the horse went straight up in the air, only to crash down on stiffened legs. Karen saw Cassidy's head snap back, saw his back muscles ripple under the buckskin as he controlled the horse's head with the reins. She was running before she realized it, her heart racing and her breath coming in harsh gasps.

"Just in time for the show, Miss Karen," Billy said as she squeezed into a spot between him and Vicki, who was screaming like a banshee while Rags barked steadily at her side.

In the corral, the frenzied horse was spinning wildly, side-stepping, plunging, going high in the air again, determined to dislodge the equally determined two-hundred-pound man clinging to the saddle with powerful legs and sheer cussedness.

"He's crazy," she muttered, her fingers trying to dig handholds into the rough wood rail.

"The boss or the horse?" Billy drawled, his gaze still welded to the action in the arena.

"Both," she muttered, then gasped as the horse reared, pawing air with those lethal steel-shod hooves. Still Cassidy hung on and even managed to keep the horse moving forward between bouts of bucking, drawing a ragged cheer from the men gathered to watch.

"Hot dang, I do love a good tussle," Karen heard someone say over her right shoulder. Twisting to look, she saw Travis Stockwell, his grin a white slash in his bronzed, weather-beaten face, his chocolate brown eyes glittering with excitement and—if she wasn't mistaken—envy.

"You're all nuts, every one of you," she told him scathingly, only to have his grin widen.

"Yeah, ain't it great?" he said as he brought his hands down on Vicki's shoulders in a surprisingly gentle gesture that had the little girl grinning up at him.

"Hi, Travis," she said before returning her excited gaze to the center of the corral. At that moment, the enraged animal bucked, not once but a half dozen times. More.

It seemed to Karen that man and animal were perfectly matched, each throwing his all into a battle that only one would win. The maddened gelding's eyes showed white, then flashed with black fury. Cassidy's determination was more controlled, and all the more lethal, Karen decided. He seemed driven, she realized as the horse and rider spun crazily, sending Cassidy leaning far out over the saddle until he seemed airborne. Yet his boots remained hooked in the stirrups and his thighs seemed made of steel.

"Why is he doing this?" she blurted out, her voice shaking.

"Three parts 'can't quit' and a stiff measure of black temper," Billy said, turning to look directly at her. In his world-weary gray eyes she saw a gentle reproach mingled with the humor and understanding.

"You're saying he's doing this because I left him."

"More like he's mad 'cause he couldn't ask you to stay."

Karen scowled. "Damn him, doesn't he know the kind of damage he could do to his spinal column?"

"Reckon he's more concerned with his tailbone at the moment," Billy replied with a chuckle. But Karen noticed that the tough little man's knuckles were white where they curved over the railing.

Karen's jaw ached as she watched Cassidy gently tap his spurs into the black horse's side, urging him into a ragged trot, punctuated now and then by the animal's renewed attempts at escape. The cheering grew louder, and in the periphery of her vision, she saw Randall Whitehorse consult a stopwatch, then scowl as he dug into his jeans for a wad of folded bills, which he handed over to a gray-haired cowboy she didn't know.

"All right! He's got 'im now," Travis shouted, looking almost as excited as Vicki, who was now jumping up and down.

It did look that way, Karen decided as the intervals between bucking and rearing grew longer. Cassidy was no longer leaning forward, but the rigid line of his shoulders and the angle of his head signaled a focused caution as he urged the exhausted mount into another circuit around the octagonal enclosure.

As he passed in front of her, his head down, his expression fierce and his brows drawn, she had the oddest feeling that he was watching her, and had been watching her the entire time.

She drew in air and forced her fingers to relax. As soon as Cassidy safely dismounted to accept the congratulations of the now laughing, cheering hands, she would slip away and—

"No, Rags," Vicki screamed suddenly, but the excited dog suddenly bolted under the bottom rail and headed straight for the gelding's flashing legs, apparently taken with a notion to play tag with the intriguing creature.

Then everything happened at once. Travis grabbed Vicki by the scruff of her sweatshirt an instant before she, too, would have slipped between the rails. Billy vaulted to the top of the fence, poised to leap to the sodden corral floor. The gelding stopped dead, then with another scream of pure animal fury, leapt into the air, and at the same time twisted in response to the iron control Cassidy exerted.

Rags dodged the flailing hooves, barking ecstatically. The horse came down hard at the exact moment Cassidy tugged on one rein, intending to bring the animal's head around. The result was an inevitable tumble.

"Kick free, boss!" Billy shouted. Other excited voices called similar warnings. But it was too late. The gelding was already going down, carrying Cassidy with him. Just before the horse hit, Cassidy managed to pull his feet from the stirrups, but the collision with the ground sent him flying over the horse's head. A collective gasp rose from the spectators as he hit with a sickeningly loud thud—and lay still.

Billy was off the rail and running while the others were still frozen in shock. The gray-haired man was also moving, splashing mud in his wake as he pounded earth. He and Billy reached Cassidy at the same time. The new hand grabbed the trailing reins just as the struggling horse gained his feet. Rid of the man on his back, he was surprisingly docile, allowing the man to lead him toward the barn.

"Daddy!" Vicki screamed, struggling against Travis's iron grip.

All this Karen saw in the blink of an eye while her heart lodged in her throat. And then training kicked in and a welcome calm came over her.

"Keep her here," she called to Travis as she climbed through the fence. "Get the first aid kit," she shouted to Whitehorse, who spun around and headed for the barn and the well-stocked medicine cabinet.

"Help me," she shouted to the nearest man who reached up to catch her as she surged through the rail. On her feet again, she ran, oblivious to the soupy mud beneath her sneakers.

"Out of my way," she shouted to the wall of big male bodies between her and her husband's inert form. Like magic, they jumped sideways, knocking into one another, slipping in the mud, muttering curses.

"Give him room," someone ordered, and the anxious, hovering men drew back en masse, as though pulled by an invisible magnet. Already bending over his boss, Billy made room for her at his side.

"He's breathing regular, and his pulse is strong."

Karen sank to her knees, already running an assessing gaze over Cassidy's sprawled body. To her great relief, he was already moving, lifting one gloved hand, flexing a knee, scowling, and though his eyes were closed, his color was good. Red clay and bits of brown mud were smeared across his wide forehead and along one side of his face.

Beneath her probing fingers, she felt the edema pushing up under skin that was already darkening to an angry purple-tinged redness. There was blood, too, she noted as she saw the crimson smear on her fingers. Possible concussion, she thought as she withdrew her hand. Worse case, a hematoma.

"Here's the kit, ma'am," Randall said, squatting beside her and setting the large white box within easy reach. She nodded her thanks as she laid two fingers to the pulse tripping like crazy at the side of Cassidy's strong neck.

"Strong like I said, right?" Billy asked, his expression anxious.

"Very."

"Don't look like anything's broken, either."

Karen grunted. She was too busy shoving aside the buckskin vest in order to run her hands over his ribs. "Careful, honey," Cassidy grated between clenched teeth. "I'm ticklish, remember?"

Billy snorted, and Karen froze as Cassidy's thick black lashes fluttered, then lifted. As the light seared his retinas, he groaned and quickly slitted his eyes while a frown gouged lines into the bronzed skin above drawn ebony brows.

"Don't move," she ordered, embarrassed to her doctor's soul by the tears of relief gathering in her eyes.

"Lucifer?" he asked, shifting his gaze toward Billy.

"Intact, and damn proud of himself."

Cassidy snorted. "Too bad...Mick Peavy already...took a

gelding knife to the…black bastard," he muttered between testing breaths.

"I hear ya, boss," Billy said, chuckling.

Next to her, she saw Whitehorse break into a grin. "Cowboys," she said in shaky disgust.

"Lousy…husband material," Cassidy said, trying to sit up. Agony splintered the surface of his onyx eyes and leeched the weathered tan from his skin.

"Watch your language," Karen warned, seeing her daughter approaching, her hand clutching Travis's like a lifeline. "Vicki's here."

"Help me sit up," Cassidy ordered, his mouth barely moving, as if even that small movement was more than he could bear.

"Better not," she countered, only to have him shift his attention to Billy, who shrugged, then bent down to loop an arm under Cassidy's shoulders.

Cassidy's skin went from gray to white as his wiry ramrod eased him into a sitting position. As soon as Vicki reached him, however, his face changed, and the suffering that had been in his eyes and in his voice was muted, as though he'd suddenly dug deep for some inner strength.

"How'd you like the show, peanut?" he asked, his hard cheeks folding into a decent enough grin—if a person wasn't close enough to sense the toll it was taking on his control.

"Are you hurt, Daddy?" she asked, her voice trembling.

Though Cassidy was well within arm's length, Karen noticed that Vicki seemed reluctant to touch her dad.

"Nope. Just a few bruises and a bi—a whopper of a headache."

Vicki giggled, but quickly sobered. "Please don't be mad at Rags, okay? He just wanted to play."

Cassidy's mouth quirked. "Remind me to have a talk with him soon," he said before turning to Billy to snarl coldly, "Last I heard, Friday was still a workday around here."

"You heard the boss," Billy called over the murmur of male voices. "Y'all get on back to what you were doin'."

After good-natured grumbling and a few parting words of encouragement for the boss, the hands did as they were told.

"You sure you don't want to try the circuit with me this summer?" Travis asked, his grin firmly in place again. "Way you stuck to that bronc, you'd be a cinch for major prize money."

"Or a split skull," Karen said with acid in her tone.

"C'mon, honey, weren't you just a little bit impressed with this poor beat-up cowboy?" Cassidy asked, watching her with still-narrowed eyes.

"Not a bit. Macho stupidity has never been high on my list of desirable character traits."

"And here I nearly killed myself showing off for you," Cassidy said mournfully. His tone said that he was joking. Something in the shifting currents in his eyes planted a doubt. Had he changed his mind and decided to fight for them, after all? Realizing she was scowling, she rearranged her features into the stern look she reserved for particularly difficult patients.

"Vicki was impressed, weren't you, darlin'?" Travis interjected, surprising Karen with his perceptiveness.

Vicki nodded vigorously. "Can I try that when I'm older?" she asked eagerly, her earlier reticence apparently forgotten.

"Nope," Cassidy said, reaching out to tug on one of her braids. "But you can give your old man a hello kiss."

Vicki complied with gusto, before asking permission to go find Rags, who had wisely made himself scarce. "Take your things into the house first," Karen said, casting a nervous glance at the clouds gathering above. "It looks like rain."

Already running, she tossed a cheery "Okay" over her shoulder that had Travis and Billy exchanging grins.

"Don't stand there looking like identical idiots," Cassidy grunted. "Help me up."

Before they could comply, Karen laid a hand on Cassidy's thigh. "I want you to let Billy take you into the hospital for a thorough work-up," she said quietly.

His face closed up. "No."

"You could have a concussion. Or a hematoma. A blood clot."

His jaw turned to granite. "I know what a hematoma is, Karen."

She bit off a sigh. "Fine. I'll just leave you to your headache, then." She started to rise, only to have his hand shoot out to grip her forearm.

"I'm sorry, Kari. I didn't mean to sound...ungrateful."

"Be careful not to jar his head," she said, slipping free of Cassidy's grasp. Or rather, he allowed her to go free, she thought as she stood. Anything Cassidy really valued, he held on to with an unbreakable grip.

Fifteen

Forty minutes later, Karen was alone with Cassidy in the bathroom, where he'd insisted on going in order to shower off the muck and mud. Now he was sitting on the closed lid of the toilet with only a towel around his waist while Karen busied herself disinfecting the small wound on his temple.

The two extra-strength aspirins she'd forced down his throat had done little to take the edge off the pain that had him grunting with every movement of his head.

Outside, the rain was coming down in windy gusts, which had sent most of the hands inside the various buildings to mend tack or clean stalls. Travis had jawed with Billy about the new bull for a few minutes before driving off, taking with him one of the hands who needed to leave early. Vicki and Rags were watching a video and eating cookies in the living room. Now and then, peals of delighted little-girl laughter drifted through the house like a soothing breeze.

"Hold still," Karen ordered, fixing Cassidy with a glare designed to quell even the most difficult patient.

He returned her glare with a cold, angry look that would melt a mountain. "Stop trying to drive a spike in my skull and I will."

"Some spike." Still glaring, Karen wafted the cotton ball she'd been using in front of his Roman nose. To her surprise, he took one look at the blood-soaked piece of fluff and flinched.

"Well, get to it, then," he said, his voice suddenly strained.

"Don't give me orders, Sloane. I'm not one of your hands."

He closed his eyes. "I know who you are, Kari. And who

you're not." His tone was suddenly laced with a weariness that hurt her more than his coldness.

Resisting an urge to smooth back the shock of thick, wavy hair tumbling over his forehead took almost as much concentration as staunching the still oozing gash. "This needs a couple of sutures."

"You're the doctor," he said, without opening his eyes.

She bristled, then realized that the sarcasm that usually accompanied a mention of her career was absent. In its place was a grim acceptance that she found oddly disturbing.

"Well, 'the doctor' still thinks you should spend at least one night under observation."

"Just what I need," he grumbled. "People running in and out of my room all night long, asking me stupid questions."

"I told you why that's necessary, Cassidy. Even a slight pressure on the brain from swelling or seepage can cause serious problems." Even death, she added silently with a slight shiver.

He slitted one eye open. "I've been through all that before. I don't intend to go through it again."

"At least let me make an appointment with a neurologist for tomorrow."

"No."

"Are you seeing double?"

"No, and I'm not queasy," he said before she could launch into the series of questions she'd already asked a half dozen times since Billy helped him into the house.

"Cassidy, this isn't a game."

His sigh was ragged. "Let it go, Kari. Rassling with you wears me out worse than any knock on the head."

"Since when?" she retorted, tossing the soiled cotton into the trash basket before reaching into the well-equipped kit for a packet of sterile gloves.

He didn't answer. Instead, he opened his eyes and stared straight ahead. Concentration tightened his facial muscles and added new lines to his forehead. "This will sting," she warned as she broke open the packet of suture materials.

He grunted and let his thick lashes drift closed. She busied herself preparing the needle and sutures, then drew a breath.

"Cassidy, are you okay?"

"Hell no, I'm not okay," he grated. "I just fell off a horse in front of half the county, my head aches like a son of a bitch, and I'm sitting here damn near naked, trying not to think about making love to my…doctor."

Karen blinked. "You can't be—" She broke off when she realized the direction of her thoughts—and her gaze. Below the low-riding knot of the towel, his body was surging to an impressive hardness.

"Aroused?" he supplied in a taut voice. "Sitting here wanting you so much I'm half out of my mind?"

Realizing she had no answer to that, she busied herself cleansing the suture area with antiseptic. "Ready?" she asked, poised to begin.

"Guess so," he said, setting his jaw.

"Try not to move," she warned, but she knew her words were unnecessary. Cassidy was the most controlled man she knew. She was the one who had to take several deep breaths to settle the sudden jitters in her stomach.

Five minutes later she was finished. Cassidy hadn't moved, though his face had turned ashen and sweat beaded his skin.

"All done," she said, dropping the used needle into its packet. When she left, she would throw it into the trash bin outside.

"What, no neon Band-Aid?" he said, his voice only a little hollow.

"Nope. Fresh air helps it heal."

His chest rose as he inhaled slowly, drawing her attention to the wedge of black hair covering his pecs. Now that her work was done and there was no need to center her attention on the practice of medicine, she was intensely aware of his potent masculinity—and powerless to withstand the sensual cascade of memories.

A terrible longing ran through her like the first slow heat of fever, and she felt herself flush. "If you think you can stand, I'll help you to bed."

He seemed half-asleep as he opened his eyes and looked at her. Between the midnight lashes, his eyes were disturbingly lifeless. "Thank you," he said in a voice that was scratchy and slightly slurred.

Alarm ran through her, crowding out the more personal thoughts. Even as she helped him to stand, she was searching for a way to convince him to let her drive him into the hospital.

"Okay?" she asked as he swayed, then leaned heavily on the shoulder she'd slipped under his arm.

"Let's get it done," he rasped, his expression fierce as he fought to regain his balance. Together they made it to the bedroom, but when Karen started toward the far side of the bed where he'd always slept, he stopped her.

"This side." Her side.

Without comment, she used one hand to pull back the covers, then eased him onto the mattress. The towel slipped open, giving her a glimpse of a hard muscled thigh—and more. This time, when the wild need ran through her, she simply accepted it.

With a sigh, he lay back against the pillow and closed his eyes. He frowned, then gradually relaxed, and his breathing evened into a quiet rhythm. It was as if he'd reached the end of his endurance and was instantly asleep.

Karen frowned. In and of itself, that wasn't a reason for alarm. Coupled with the blow to his head and the hard jolt his body had suffered, however, it could be significant.

You heard him, she lectured herself. He's fine. As tough as that thousand-pound specimen of fighting horse he'd battled to a draw.

Biting her lip, she reached for the knot cinching the towel and worked it free. He muttered something as she gently rolled him onto his side in order to pull the bunched towel from under his buttocks, then rolled him to his back again.

"Kari?" The sound of his voice startled her into dropping the towel.

"Yes, Cassidy?"

"When I said I was sorry, I wasn't...I meant for... accusing you of being like my mother. I was dead wrong."

"Thank you for that," she said softly.

For an instant he looked as though he intended to say more, then his expression hardened. "Just so you know," he grunted before closing his eyes again.

Cassidy woke to the sound of a groan in the dark, and for a moment, while his heart rate made a stab at a world's record for speed, fought to orient himself. It took him a few bad moments to realize that he was the one making enough noise to wake a dying man.

Damn that black bastard to hell, he cursed, then winced as a mountainside of viciously sharp boulders tumbled over and over inside his skull. He tried to concentrate on the wedge of silvery light formed on the coverlet by the moonlight streaming through the window. Bad mistake, he realized almost instantly, and then he slowly, carefully shut his eyes.

There were a few holes in his memory, but he remembered enough to know he'd hit the ground going the speed limit at least. Damn near dug to China with his head, he reckoned, lifting a hand to the lump on his temple.

Even thinking hurt. Breathing didn't help much, either, and as for moving—forget it. Maybe, in a week or two, he might try blinking his eyes. At the moment, however, even that seemed beyond him.

He touched rough skin and the sharp little edges of the sutures Karen had knotted into his scalp while he sat there trying not to wrap his arms around her and press his aching head against her soft breasts.

The thought gave rise to another kind of pain, and he groaned again.

"Cassidy?" Karen's hauntingly soft voice came through the gray cobwebs clinging to his brain. It took some doing, but he managed to pry open his eyes. He saw darkness, the patch of moonlight, a hazy outline of a woman's enticing body.

"Leave me alone," he ordered the shimmering image that

always seemed to float just out of his reach whenever she showed up to tear a few more chunks out of him.

"Do you know where you are?" the voice persisted, and he closed his eyes against the taunting sound.

"In hell," he muttered, turning his head away. Where there was no way out and no relief from the remorse that tormented him night and day, he thought as a cacophony of pain and self-loathing took up a familiar chorus.

He knew why he was dreaming of her again. She'd been in the house, in this room, leaving behind a hint of her perfume and a man who hadn't had a peaceful moment since the last night they'd spent together in this bed.

"Exactly where *is* hell?"

Now she was making him mad, and she wasn't even real. "Wherever you are," he grated through a clenched jaw.

"I'm serious, Cassidy. If you don't give me a straight answer I'm going to turn on the light and drag it out of you."

The soft voice suddenly had an all-too-human edge. Suspicious and more than a little wary, he forced open his eyes one more time, afraid she'd be there, even more afraid she wouldn't. The first thing he saw was a deliciously curved female hip, much too close to the side of his bed, and sheathed in jeans that seemed much too big. Inching his gaze upward, he found the alluring swell of womanly breasts covered in an old sweatshirt he belatedly recognized as his own.

Above the stretched-out ribbing of the neck, he saw the familiar tilt of a small chin with a cute little indentation and the stern line of lips that could also be soft and yielding. Only force of will and a lot of years keeping his emotions under tight rein kept him from groaning again, this time for reasons other than sheer exhaustion.

"Karen?" His voice came out as rusty as the hinges on an old corral gate, and he cleared his throat. "What are you doing here?"

That won him a frown. Scant comfort to a man starved for a smile. He'd stopped hoping for more somewhere high above the Rockies on his way west to pick up the Brahma. It was then that he'd realized just how out of control he'd been that last night. How ugly his words had been. How they must have ripped into her gentle soul.

"How do you feel?" The edge still rode her voice, but it was tempered by the instinctive concern of doctor for patient.

"Lousy, but it'll pass."

"Headache?"

"Some," he hedged. He shifted his gaze to the window, hiding a wince at the cost of even that small movement. "Looks like the rain let up."

"Around nine, and don't change the subject." She sounded exasperated and moderately testy. He felt one side of his mouth curve. Kari was cute as a spitting kitten when she was "managing" him.

"What time is it now?"

"Eleven. What's your name?"

He sighed. "Cassidy Rogers Sloane, but you can call me a gold-plated fool, since that's what everyone else has been saying I am this past month."

Her mouth turned down at the edges. He didn't blame her. As humor, it was damned pathetic. As truth, it was dead-on.

"Where are you?"

"Some godforsaken place in Colorado." He lifted a hand to tug at the edge of the sweatshirt. He took it as a good sign she didn't jerk away. "You should have left some of your clothes here."

"Can I get you anything? A glass of water, or maybe some tea?"

He let his hand fall away. "No, nothing."

"Go back to sleep, then. I'll be in to check on you at midnight."

Too wiped out to argue, he let his eyes close. Locked in his own private misery, he heard her feet brush against the rug as she walked to the door, heard the faint click of metal on metal as she touched the knob.

"Karen?" he asked softly.

"Yes, Cassidy?"

"Why did you stay?"

A sigh whispered between them. "Someone had to. I'm trained for it."

He heard the rustle of clothing, the quiet click of the latch, and she was gone.

Shortly after Karen had checked on him at twelve and found him in a surly but lucid frame of mind, she tried to catch some sleep on the couch—and failed. She tried reading but couldn't concentrate.

After that, she checked on Vicki and Rags, who'd been allowed to sleep at the foot of Vicki's bed in order to ease Vicki's mind about the poor, penitent creature's welfare, then headed toward the back door and a breath of rain-freshened air.

On the way through the kitchen, she stopped to refill her mug with coffee and managed a few sips before carrying it with her to the porch. The ranch looked deceptively peaceful, like a small village slumbering in the moonlight. Only the glare from the security lights and the ugly outline of the bull-dozer marred the pastoral scene.

Taking a breath, she willed her tired mind to numbness. Her body, she discovered, was already there. It took her a moment to notice Billy heading across the moon-washed yard toward her. It was then that she saw his truck parked under the light pole by the equipment shed.

"How is he?" the ramrod asked without preamble as he gained the steps.

"Okay so far," she said in a quiet voice. "He's sleeping."

Karen saw the flash of relief in his steel-colored eyes. "Best thing for him, other than you being here."

Though she shrugged, she felt a betraying tension in her stomach muscles. "He might give you an argument about that."

Instead of answering, Billy leaned his back against one of the posts holding up the roof and crossed both his arms and one booted foot over the other. It was a stance she knew well. Cassidy sometimes stood that way when he was untangling a particularly knotted problem. "He's started drinking. Heavily."

Karen blinked. "Drinking what?"

Billy moved a shoulder. "The empties I've seen have all been Scotch."

She frowned, sure she had misunderstood. "Cassidy hates hard liquor."

"Could be, but he's still pouring it down his throat like water every night—unless Vicki's sleeping over. Then he works all night, instead. Either way, I figure tonight's the first solid sleep he's had since you left."

Very carefully she wet her lips. "Have you...voiced your concern?"

Billy snorted. "I tried. It's an experience I don't care to repeat."

"He was angry?"

"Naw, just stripped a few layers of skin off my hide with a few well-chosen words."

Karen realized she was holding her breath and let it out slowly. "Thank you for telling me," she said carefully.

Silence settled between them, and beneath the wide brim of his hat, he seemed to be watching her intently. Something about the set of his chin told he was working up to something. Finally, he let out a sigh and pushed back his shoulders.

"I'm not much for asking favors, Karen, but I'm asking now. Give Cass another chance." He waited, braced.

"I offered to withdraw the divorce petition. He's the one who insisted I go ahead."

He compressed his mouth and nodded, his disappointment almost tangible. "Man's stubborn, no way around it."

"No, no way around it," she repeated, the tears she fought off all day welling again as she hugged him. "You're a very special man, Billy."

"Well, hell, Karen, any more of this and you'll have me bawling, too," he said with a self-conscious grin that faded almost as quickly as it had come. "If you ever need a friend, you know where to find me."

Sixteen

When she went to check on him at one, Cassidy was still lying on his back with one hand buried under the pillow, the other outstretched toward the empty half of the big bed. The sheet was bunched across his navel, revealing the impressive expanse of bare chest and shoulders that never failed to thrill her.

In the hour since her last visit to the bedroom, the moonlight had shifted, angling now across his face, which was turned toward the door. He was asleep, his stark black brows drawn, his too-gaunt features a mask of harsh bronze scored with bitter lines. He looked ten years older, ten years harder. And yet, there was a vulnerability around his mouth that she'd never seen before.

"Back so soon, Doctor?" His voice was heavy with defiance under the taut words, and he didn't open his eyes.

"Back again," she told him in a decent imitation of Nurse Tutt's military bearing. "And not in the mood to humor an ill-tempered grouch, so let's have it, buster. Name, address, the whole drill."

His mouth relaxed enough to erase some of the harshness from his expression. "Cassidy Sloane, I live in Colorado, and I'm not seeing double."

"How do you know if you don't open your eyes?"

"Give me a minute, and I'll see what I can do." His lashes lifted then, thick black crescents that cast shadows on the silvered bronze cheekbones. She felt the impact the moment he shifted his gaze to look directly at her. The pain was there, but muted, paled to insignificance by the hot lick of hunger in those dark, beautiful eyes.

"What do you see?" To her chagrin, her voice caught.

"A beautiful woman in my bedroom." He withdrew the hand hidden under the pillow and reached for hers. She wanted to resist. Would have moved. But his fingers were already tightening, drawing her closer. Shivers ran along the network of nerves under her skin. Though she knew the tiny tremors were fueled by chemical changes in the brain, she didn't want them to end. Not yet.

The air changed. Suddenly she was twenty-four and sure she'd just met the man whom she wanted to be the first to fill her body with pleasure.

"No," she whispered. Meaning it. Not meaning it.

"Yes, Kari."

"You need rest."

His hard, callused fingers tightened but gently, carefully, as if he were afraid of bruising her, while his thumb rubbed the spot on her wrist where her pulse pounded.

"I need you, Kari. So much I'm sick with it." His voice was rough, controlled.

She saw them then, the faded, worn rosebud pattern on the pillow beneath his black, tumbled hair, and her heart opened on a choked sob. "Oh, Cassidy."

"Kiss me, Kari. Please kiss me." His voice was so taut with suppressed emotion it seemed to vibrate.

Karen eased lower, careful to keep from jostling him as she fitted herself alongside his big body. Warmth from the fire inside him enveloped her instantly, and she sighed with the sheer pleasure of being with him again.

"Promise me you'll tell me if there's pain," she whispered, furrowing her fingers into the curly black hair on his chest. Beneath her eager fingers, she felt him suck in.

She froze. "Cassidy? Should we stop?"

A sound—half chuckle, half groan—rumbled in his throat before he urged her mouth closer with the gentlest of pressure on the back of her neck. "Don't stop," he begged an instant before their lips met.

She expected a sensory explosion, but the feeling that spread through her was achingly sweet, like the first taste of a sun-kissed peach. She felt herself melting, giving herself up to that sweetness.

Her hand trembled as she traced the line of sinew and swell of muscle along the slope of his shoulder, down to the massive biceps that rippled under her questing fingers. Drunk on her own pleasure, she raked her short nails along the upper curve and felt those ripples deepen to a sudden shudder.

"Easy, honey," he muttered against her mouth. "I'm a sick man, remember?"

"Mmm."

His lips curved, then parted, and she felt the slow sweep of his tongue between her lips. Tasting. Tempting. She moaned and sucked his tongue into her mouth. This time he was the one to moan before breaking off the sensual duel.

"Don't you dare stop now," she demanded in a husky tone that seemed to shiver like the most sensual caress in the silvery air.

"Not a chance." His mouth brushed her cheek with moist, testing kisses, then slid with a gentle pressure to the hypersensitive spot behind her ear. At the same time his hand stroked down the curve of her hip, the restraint in him almost palpable.

"Good, so good," he whispered hoarsely, even as she rubbed against him, annoyed at the layers of cloth between them. Need was like a hot, slick fist inside her, slowly relaxing fingers that stretched relentlessly deeper.

She struggled to get closer and felt him groan. A shudder ran through him, and she dug her fingers deeper into the resilient flesh cushioning the hard chest. His mouth found hers again, his tongue demanding access. Eagerly she met his demand with her own, her nails now raking where they'd only tested before.

Awash in his own raging need, Cassidy heard the soft sound of pleasure escaping from her elegant throat and wanted to shout. Instead, he reminded himself that he was on shaky ground, only one stupid mistake away from that black pit where he spent most of his nights lately.

With a strength he hadn't known he possessed, he ignored

the pain in his head and the even greater pain throbbing in the hard ridge of flesh wedged against her belly, and made himself concentrate on the small signals she was giving him, once as familiar to him as the sound of his breathing in the hell of night.

"Touch me, please, Cass," she pleaded, squirming against him. He gritted his teeth and eased backward, knowing he was close to exploding.

"Where?" he demanded, waiting.

"Everywhere," she panted. "Anywhere. I need to feel those rough cowboy hands on my skin."

The emotion that shot through him felt perilously close to hope. Wild, irrational, mind-numbing hope that he might be able to break free of the prison of his past, after all. Before it could take hold and weaken him, he fought it off and focused his attention on pleasing her.

"Seems like I recognize that shirt," he teased gruffly, sliding his hand beneath the soft material to caress the smooth skin above the curve of her bottom. Just the feeling of her warm flesh against his callused palm was almost enough to override his determination to go slow.

"My blouse was, ah, muddy," she whispered between soft little moans.

"Jeans, too?" He forced his mind away from the small forays her quick hands were making over his body.

"What?"

The bemused sound of her voice had him smiling, even as his body began sending urgent signals. "You're wearing my best Wranglers, honey."

"Your...oooh...your what?"

She was rubbing her pelvis against his thigh, and even through the sheet, the friction was an exquisite torture. He forced himself to block out everything but the need to please her. "Jeans," he said, kissing her forehead, her cheeks. "My jeans."

He drew up one leg in a desperate need to ease the pressure in his groin. At the same time he found the hook of her bra and prayed he remembered how to slip the hooks free.

"Help me, honey," he demanded when his rough fingers fumbled and failed.

She uttered a small sound of protest, and he felt the moist warmth of her breath on his chest a split second before her teeth scraped over one tiny nipple. He felt a hot pleasure shudder like fever through him, and his control frayed. Teeth gritted, he resisted the violent urge to flip her onto her back, rip open the fly on those damn jeans and surge into her with all the pent-up need of a man at the ragged end of a short rope.

Not yet, he panted silently, drawing her on top of him. Though the sheet, a layer of denim and—if fortune was generous—silk lay between his throbbing flesh and the hot, moist entrance to her womb, he felt an almost unbearable rush of pleasure before he tamped it down.

"Tell me what you want, honey." He damn near cried in relief when the bra gave way.

"Everything," she gasped out, between nibbling bites of his chest.

"This?" he demanded, cupping her breast with his palm.

"Yes, oh yes." He tested the hard nipple with his thumb and forefinger.

"And this?" He shifted his attention to the other soft breast and heard her breath hiss through her teeth. He allowed himself a fierce moment of satisfaction, only to gasp as her hand began a slow, deliberate exploration of his belly, apparently following the line of dark hair toward his navel.

Muscles jerking, he arched, then fisted his free hand in her hair. He couldn't seem to get enough air in his lungs, no matter how hard he tried, and his concentration was graying dangerously at the edges.

"Kari, wait…oh, baby, don't."

"You're so strong, so beautiful," she whispered, her breath hot against his chest. At the same time she insinuated her thigh between his, and he nearly came apart.

Forgetting his pain, he did flip her then, and at the same time jerked down the zipper that was keeping him from the warm, sweet treasure he needed so desperately. Using his hands and his mouth, he pushed the bunched denim over satiny thighs, past cute little knees, over world-class calves.

Between frenzied kisses, he rid her of the shirt. Panting, she tugged and twisted until her bra joined the rest of her clothes.

"The sheet," she demanded, tearing at it with both hands until it slipped free, leaving him naked and exposed. Vulnerable, as he'd never been vulnerable before.

Freed from restraint, his body sprang free, a throbbing shaft of hot blood and nearly unbearable need. He almost came off the bed when her hand closed over the rigid flesh. Release beckoned, tearing at his resolve. One quick, hard thrust against those small fingers and he would find relief from the agony that rode him unceasingly. It took every last scrap of control left to him to cover that hand with his, staying the maddening friction.

"You're not ready," he muttered through a clenched jaw as she lifted her head and looked at him with glazed, reproachful eyes. In spite of her protesting moans, he slid down her body, his tongue hot as he tasted satin skin, until the craving for more sent him lower.

Karen tossed her head on the pillow, her chest heaving, her mind fragmenting by the buffeting of sublime pleasure so intense she forgot where reason stopped and sensation began.

She heard herself pleading, felt the silken thickness of his hair against her clutching fingers, and still he licked and suckled, the suction of his mouth hot against her belly.

A gasp tore from her as he swirled that clever tongue into the tightly curled hair below her navel. She felt the exquisite rasp of whiskers as he sensitized every inch, leaving her quivering, her body soft and aching inside.

She heard a sharp intake of breath, felt his big hands nudging her thighs wider. And then his tongue was burrowing between the damp curls. Belatedly aware of the door that stood ajar, she buried her face in the pillow that smelled like him and bit her lip to keep from screaming.

When his mouth closed over the hot little nub, she splintered. Wave after wave crashed and swirled, and she sobbed in release and exhilaration. Then, only then, did he lift his head and move to cover her. She felt the hot lash of his need, the desperate hunger, the fierce drive as he slowly pushed into her, his hardness forcing her body to accommodate him. Through dazed eyes, she saw the flash of triumph in his eyes, a rare moment of yearning, a wild joy before his lashes swept down.

Cassidy felt the little tremors begin again, deep inside her body where he'd always felt safe and whole and wanted. Where the accusing voices stopped and his soul quieted.

He moved slowly, filling her, withdrawing to the limit of her moist heat, filling her again. And then she was convulsing, choking out his name, clutching at his shoulders.

He shuddered her name as the world gave way and he, too, convulsed, spilling deep. And for one precious shattering moment, hell went away.

Cassidy hated mornings. The loneliness was worse then, clawing at him. Taunting him with his own inadequacies. Aching and sore, every muscle reminding him of Lucifer's revenge, he lay very still, his eyes half-closed and staring at the ceiling, waiting for the pounding in his head to ease, for his mind to clear. For the energy to start another day.

It was then that he sensed a difference in the cloying thickness of dawn seeping into the bedroom. A presence. He turned his head so fast a wave of dizziness swamped the pain, and for an instant he froze. It hadn't been a dream, he realized, afraid to breathe, afraid to believe as he stared at the small, cuddly body, curled in tumbled bedclothes only inches from his outstretched fingers.

He felt his chest swell with an emotion he refused to name. It wasn't love. Even he, in his wildest dreams, knew that was beyond him. He simply didn't have the courage to take that risk.

Slowly, he lifted a hand to the raw wound on his temple and ran his fingertips over the prickly stitches that were already beginning to pull and itch. It didn't surprise him that she'd taken care of him. Or that she'd stayed. Kari had a way of taking care of hopeless cases.

She did not, however, sleep with them. That she'd slept with him gave him the first sliver of hope he'd had in weeks. The why didn't matter. Not anymore. She was here, that's all he cared about. In the bed they'd shared, with the scent of her on his hands and the taste of her on his lips.

Inch by inch he made himself relax. Between bouts of sodden oblivion and brutally hard work, he'd come face-to-face with a lot of hard truths. Some he could handle. Some he couldn't. Not yet. Maybe not ever.

One thing he knew now, absolutely. He would slice open his own belly and bleed out his life before he'd let himself hurt her again. God help him, he would work day and night to give her the moon and the stars and some of that fairy dust she'd told him about once, when she'd been tipsy on a few sips of honeymoon champagne.

With a slowness that cost him, he inched closer until he felt the warmth of her against his skin. He let the smile in his mind curve his lips as he bent his head to gently brush a kiss over her pale lips. Still asleep, she smiled, then snuggled closer, her hair tickling his chin and her small hands folding over his arm.

"Hey, wife," he whispered, watching her curly lashes flutter.

As though annoyed, she drew her golden brown brows together and murmured something unintelligible.

"C'mon, honey, open those gorgeous eyes for me."

Her frown deepened, and her tongue made a fast little trip along her lower lip, sending fire straight to his belly. His body stirred, and he bit off a groan as he folded his body over hers and pulled her closer.

"You'd tempt a dying man," he murmured against the sweet-smelling warmth of her neck.

Karen woke to find herself lying on her side, entangled in the prison of her husband's strong body. He was nuzzling her neck, and she was already half aroused. When she stirred, his arms tightened and he murmured something against her skin.

It took her a moment to realize he'd just made an extremely suggestive comment.

"Oh, no, you don't," she whispered, even as a smile broke inside her.

Somehow she managed to twist around until they were nearly nose to nose. The bruise on his temple had spread to include his eye socket. That and the dark blush of black whiskers on his jaw gave him an extremely roguish look that she found utterly enchanting.

"What?" he demanded, lifting one arrogant eyebrow.

"You look like a pirate," she murmured, lifting a hand to gently touch the edge of the truly magnificent shiner.

His eyes crinkled. "Never been on anything bigger than a rowboat in my life."

"I know. You'd rather risk your life on an insane horse."

His mouth quirked as he ran a slow hand through her hair, then fisted his fingers in the thick mass. "If it means I get to wake up with you in my bed, yeah."

Karen heard the possessive note in his graveled voice and felt the first pang of uneasiness. Making love had solved nothing. In fact, she had a terrible feeling it was only going to make things worse.

"How do you feel?" she asked, letting her gaze assess and gauge.

"Ready to take on that demon son of a bitch again—and before you start, I know exactly who I am and where we are." Though his voice had a teasing quality and his mouth had soft corners, he looked tired and just a little tense. His eyes were clear, but the lines framing them were disturbingly deep, and his skin was still too sallow.

The result of injury, trauma and pain? Or of something more dangerous? Like the first stages of alcoholism?

"What time is it?" she asked, stalling.

But his eyes narrowed, and she realized her voice had come out a little too sharp. "Dawn, or near to. Why? You got something you got to do?"

She hesitated, then hedged. "I'm off today."

"All day?" Buried deep in the gruff tones was an echo of

a little boy eager for a treat. Her heart turned over. How could he be hostile one minute and adorable the next?

"All day," she confirmed warily. "And lose that devil's gleam in your eyes, Sloane. Your day is already planned."

He lifted one eyebrow, his eyes suddenly wary.

"It is?"

It was silly, really, but she was almost positive that if she just kept talking, she could keep Billy's words at bay.

"First breakfast, and then you're going to take another antibiotic."

"I was thinking more in terms of a picnic. Out by the old line shack. Just the three of us. Vicki is always bugging me to take her out there to look for arrowheads."

She sat up, realized she was naked and blushed. "Cassidy, you're in no condition to get out of bed, let alone sit a horse." She made her tone brisk, but the impact was sadly diminished when she leaned down to scramble for the sweatshirt lying in a heap by the bed and nearly toppled over before he caught her.

He watched her with eyes that were suddenly hooded. "Karen, if you don't want to spend the day with me, say so."

She fought a sudden impulse to wrap herself around him and hold on tight. "It's not that," she denied, before wrestling her arms into the shirt. When her head popped free, she saw that he was now sitting up, his back propped against a pillow he'd mashed against the headboard.

The sight of those faded rosebuds had another spate of tears pressing against the backs of her eyes. Detachment, she intoned silently. It was becoming a classic stimulus-response cliché, she realized, and didn't care.

"I didn't force you to make love to me last night," he said very quietly. Suddenly the room seemed darker somehow, in spite of the rapidly brightening daylight streaming through the window.

"I know that, Cassidy. And I'm not sorry."

Cassidy allowed himself a moment to think about that. Whenever something didn't feel right to him, he tended to slow down. "You're afraid I'll hurt you again."

She bit her lip and looked down at her hands. "I...saw the bottles. In the trash bin outside the back door."

He'd kept himself from being snake-bitten once by freezing until the danger slithered past. He had the same urge now. "Counted 'em, too, I reckon."

She lifted her gaze. Her eyes were liquid with misery and something else that ripped him open all the way to the bone. Pity. He nearly gagged on it before he made himself go cold.

"Cassidy, listen to me. I'm no expert, but I understand—"

"Do you? I doubt it." He took comfort in the brittle sound of his anger.

"Your father was an alcoholic. It's an inherited trait. You're susceptible."

"Probably." He saw the beautiful gray eyes that had glazed with passion when he'd thrust into her now fill with frustration, and allowed himself a moment to mourn the loss before shuttering that away, too.

She tried again. He gave her credit for that. "There are programs—"

"No." Not even the pride that had protected him for so long could deflect the shame that was pouring into him with each word she uttered.

"I can talk to Lindy Chung. She could recommend a therapist."

"No programs. No therapists." He'd thought he'd reached the limit of the torment a man could take and remain sane when she'd walked out. Now he knew better. This was worse. Much worse. He wasn't sure he had the strength to push it away this time. To survive.

"I won't give up, Cassidy. No matter how many insults you hurl my way or how much you glower or threaten, I'm not going to let you drink yourself to death like your father did."

"My father shot himself."

She glared at him. "Is that the next step, then?"

He nearly reached for her then. Nearly crushed his arms around her and buried his face in the curve of her neck where he wouldn't have to face her. "What about Vicki, Cassidy?

Are you going to arrange it so that she walks in after you've done it?''

"Shut up!" he shouted, lashing out, knowing even as he did that she had every right to be concerned. A man who drank himself into oblivion every night was lousy father material.

"Not this time, Cassidy. This time you're going to listen to me."

The shame was like a cancer, eating at his insides, and the pain was unbearable. Worse than the anguish of watching his brother die. Worse than the whiplash agony of his mother's loathing. Far beyond anything he could ever have envisioned.

She thought he was a drunk.

His beautiful, brave wife looked at him and saw a sodden, slobbering weakling. A miserable whiner with a death wish. And she was right. He just happened to be sober at the moment.

But he would soon take care of that.

He was already pulling back the sheet, already steeling himself against the agony in his head that the movement stirred to life. "Get out of my way, Karen," he growled with a leashed fury when she moved to block him.

"Or what? You'll knock me over?"

"If I have to."

Karen saw the icy glint in his eyes and knew he would do just that if she didn't get out of his way. The woman in her was ready for a fight, but the healer knew he was in no fit shape to be out of bed.

"You win," she said softly as she rose. "This time."

His scowl was a masterpiece of lethal masculine beauty. And a facade. A carefully constructed, desperate barrier between hurt and the scared, guilt-ridden little boy who'd made a terrible mistake and didn't know how to make it better. The man that boy had become still bore the scars, still longed for the love that should had been his by right. And somehow, she would make him accept that love.

But all that would come later. After she figured out how to help him without driving him further into hiding. "I love you, Cassidy," she said, meeting those stony eyes calmly. "And it's because I love you that I won't give up."

"You're wasting your time," he whispered, his voice hoarse. "I'm a lost cause."

She smiled as she shook her head. "You're wrong. You're the most wonderful man I've ever known."

Before he could guess her intention, she framed his cold, wounded face between gentle hands and leaned down to kiss his hard, angry, vulnerable mouth. A shudder ran through him as their lips met, but he didn't move. He also didn't kiss her back.

"I'm leaving now, Cassidy," she said as she released him. She bent, picked up the jeans he'd torn off of her, then met his eyes with a quiet challenge. "I'm taking Vicki with me so you can get some rest. But hear me and hear me good. You might have given up on yourself, but I haven't."

"Then you're a fool."

"Stop it. You know better than that." She smiled. "I love you and I want to be your wife. To live here and fight with you and make love with you and have more babies. But I've gotten greedy since we've been apart. I want it all—your smile and your laughter and your love. It doesn't have to come all at once, but I have to know you're willing to try."

He ached to hold her, to smell the clean fragrance of her hair. To stroke the softness of her cheek. To experience the magic of her body fitting so perfectly to his. But he knew the futility of wanting something he couldn't have.

"Go home, Karen. Leave me alone." He knew she had to hear the defeat in his voice. The weariness he could no longer hide.

"I am home, Cassidy. But I will go back to Mother's. I'll lie in bed at night and wish you were there. And I'll wait for you to come for me."

"I won't."

Her smile was so sad he nearly reached for her. "Then we'll both lose."

Cassidy waited until she woke Vicki. Waited while Vicki got dressed and gathered her things. Waited until he heard the Blazer drive away. Only then did he leave his bed and stagger naked to the kitchen.

His hand shook and his head pounded as he reached into the uppermost shelf of one of the cupboards for the Scotch he kept there. With one violent wrench, he had the cap off and the bottle tipped to his lips. But he couldn't make himself tip it that extra fraction of an inch that would send the blessed relief pouring into him.

Something was wrong. Something that nagged at him through all the layers of blind rage and seething frustration and yearning hunger that were his constant companions these days.

She'd been shocked and upset and a bit of a bully. She'd chided him and lectured him and pushed him right to the edge of violence. But what she hadn't done was give up on him. And she'd kissed him, as though she really meant it, then left him to pull himself together in privacy.

God help him, she'd said she loved him, he thought in a blaze of disbelief and dawning hope. Even knowing the worst of it, she'd stood right there with a militant fire in her beautiful, intelligent eyes and said it right out loud like she really meant it.

Slowly, deliberately, he lowered his arm and set the bottle on the counter where the sun caught fire in the amber depths. He stood there a long time, feeling the warmth of a new day seep through the windowpanes into his skin.

He'd fought against feeling too much for a long time. Maybe too long, but somehow Karen had slipped under his guard and into that unprotected place where he still nourished a belief in himself and his worthiness to be loved.

She had the ability to heal him. She had the ability to hurt him so badly he might never be able to crawl back. He couldn't have one without the other.

A pressure built inside him, growing stronger, filling him. Lifting a callused hand, he rubbed at the worst of it, tucked up under his breastbone. Maybe the risk was too great. Or maybe he didn't have what it takes to change. Maybe he was reading her all wrong. Hell, a man with a concussion was bound to be a lousy judge.

Could he actually remake himself into a man she'd be proud to know? For a long time now he'd been so sure he'd protected himself too well, run from the pain too long, to change. And yet maybe with Kari he might find a way.

It wouldn't be easy. He knew himself well enough to have a damned good notion of the hell he could put her through while he struggled to put the past behind him. To learn how to trust again. To give her the love she claimed she wanted.

If she still loved him. If it wasn't too late.

An icy fear jolted through him, and he felt a clammy sweat bead on his flesh. No, he thought with a savage scowl. He could handle anything but that.

Teeth gritted, he upended the bottle and watched the numbing whiskey gurgle into the sink and down the drain. The bottle went into the trash.

First he would see if he could shave without cutting his own throat, and then he would make a beginning on the long climb back.

Seventeen

Karen loved the small, old-fashioned solarium tucked into the western end of the hospital's fourth floor, especially when the sun was cascading through the tall windows to make neat squares on the linoleum. Whenever possible, she stole a few minutes there alone to rest and quiet her nerves.

Since leaving the ranch—and Cassidy—two weeks ago, she'd come to the solarium often. So often that her co-workers always looked for her there first when they didn't want to bother with the paging service. Which was why she wasn't surprised to see Lindy show up late Friday afternoon, with briefcase in hand and a TGIF look in her rich brown eyes.

"Storing up energy for the big day?" Lindy asked as she slid onto the bench next to her.

Karen smiled. "I still can't believe my baby is turning nine tomorrow."

"Is she excited?"

"To the point that she's got my unflappable mother wearing a perpetually dazed expression and my stepfather-to-be swearing under his breath."

Lindy laughed. "You, of course, are impervious to all the fuss."

"Of course," Karen assured her solemnly as she brushed dust from the split-leaf philodendron in the nearby corner. "That's why I've spent the last two mornings making piñatas in the shape of horses and dogs. And one extremely fierce-looking bull of which I'm extremely proud, if I do say so myself."

"I'll be sure to look for it tomorrow."

Karen nodded, then drew in a deep breath and shifted her gaze to the mountains outlined above the city sprawling beneath them. "Billy called this morning before I left for work."

She could feel Lindy's attention sharpen. "How's he doing?" They both knew she meant Cassidy.

"The good news is he's not drinking. The bad news is that he loses his temper on an average of once an hour, and Billy's had to promise the men hefty bonuses to ride it out." She turned her head in time to see Lindy's sympathetic nod.

"Have you talked with him?"

"Once. He called Monday to tell me he'd be tied up with USDA inspectors most of the week and that it would be better if Vicki didn't come on Wednesday."

"And you immediately decided he wasn't telling the truth?"

"No, Cassidy never lies." She bit her lip and listened to a replay of the conversation in her mind, savoring each word as if they were rare gems. She smiled as she recalled the laugh she'd won from him when she recounted some of Vicki's more exalted plans for her birthday celebration—including a whole list of extravagant presents.

"Maybe I'm investing too much importance in a laugh," she said, as if her thoughts were clearly audible.

Lindy received that with her usual aplomb. "Scared?"

"Terrified." She took a shaky breath. "I know the next step has to be his. But I'm so afraid he won't be able to take it."

"He's had years to build up those walls. He's not going to tear them down overnight."

"No, but I'm only asking for him to move the first brick." Karen looked down at the toes of her sneakers. "How long can that take?"

"It takes as long as it takes," Lindy said, rising. "I know that's not the answer you wanted."

Karen took one last look toward the long stretch of purpling sky and wondered how long she could hold out. "Maybe a little gentle prodding is in order."

"Uh-oh."

Karen grinned, her mind made up. "I think I'll see if I can fit in a quick trip to the mall before Vicki and I drive out to the ranch tomorrow morning."

"What's at the mall?" Lindy asked as they walked toward the elevator.

Karen waited until the orderly pushing a patient in a wheelchair passed out of earshot before turning to say, "French lingerie."

Lindy lifted one delicate eyebrow. "Isn't that playing dirty?"

"Yes, but a girl can only wait so long for the man she loves to realize he loves her back. After that, it's time to use a little gentle persuasion."

Lindy shook her head as they reached the bank of elevators. "Sounds more like guerrilla warfare to me," she said, pushing the down button.

"All's fair," Karen said with a confidence she was far from feeling.

"Something tells me Cassidy Sloane doesn't have a chance," Lindy muttered as the elevator stopped at their floor and the doors slid open. As they stepped into the car, Karen could only pray that her friend was right.

It was setting up to be a perfect day for Vicki's birthday bash, Cassidy decided as he gazed at the puffy white clouds drifting lazily over the pasture where he'd been riding fence since sunup. He only hoped he didn't miss it on account of the black devil in horsehide limping along behind him.

Both horse and man were covered with red Colorado dust, and after a few miles of breathing the stuff, his mouth was bone-dry. He figured he'd walked a good year's worth of sole off his favorite boots, with the better part of a mile still stretching between him and home.

After sidestepping another gopher hole, he shifted his gaze to the clutch of low rock and timber buildings in the distance. By even the most optimistic reckoning he was a half hour from home. More if he wanted to make sure Lucifer wouldn't suffer any more than absolutely necessary.

Not that the cantankerous beast deserved special consideration, he grumbled to himself. In fact, he had half a mind to whack the ugly animal between his ears.

As if reading his thoughts, Lucifer snorted and tried to shake free of the bit. Without bothering to look behind him, Cassidy answered with a sharp jerk on the reins.

"Patience, you stubborn jackass." The contrary animal kept trying to bolt for the barn and his ration of hay. Not that Cassidy could blame the beast. He, himself, was hungry enough to chew his saddle cinch. Though it galled him to admit it, even to himself, he was also feeling profoundly guilty. Lucifer was hurting and it was his fault. His preoccupation with his own private demons had made him careless, which was out of character for a man who prided himself on heading off problems before they took hold.

This one had been so obvious a blind man could have seen it—unless that blind man was tangled up in thoughts of a dark-haired angel who kept telling him she loved him, no matter how hard he tried to push her away.

The gelding had been ground-tied near a stream Cassidy had been inspecting when a jackrabbit broke cover a few feet away, spooking the high-strung horse into bolting. By the time Cassidy had tracked him down, Lucifer had been lathered and lame, and Cassidy had been footsore and ready to kill.

Behind him, the black beast snorted another protest, causing Cassidy to glance over one dusty shoulder. "I have enough sins of my own to battle, so don't even think about blaming me for yours, you mangy bastard," he muttered with a disgusted scowl even as his attention was snagged by a distant streak of white arrowing along the access road.

"Damn," he muttered as he drew close enough to recognize Karen's Blazer rocketing down the lane toward the ranch house.

Fear, icy and far too familiar, shot through him before he battled it down. Didn't she know how fast accidents could happen? Or how fragile a life really was? Dammit, he knew exactly what kind of sickening damage a car could wreak on a human body.

He quickened his step, then checked to see if Lucifer could handle the faster speed. Satisfied that his horse was up to the pace, he returned his attention to the speeding Blazer.

He hadn't stopped thinking about her. At night, when he paced or worked or read instead of reaching for a bottle. At dawn, when he woke with his body engorged and throbbing and his mind filled with images of her lush body and welcoming eyes. At times when swearing and sweating weren't enough to drive away the acid taste of guilt.

He ached for her. Burned to hold her, even when he'd been talking himself out of going to her. When he was astride one of his horses, he longed to have her riding next to him, her head thrown back and her cheeks pink from the wind and her own inner joy. When he was in town on an errand, he scanned every female face looking for hers. He'd even parked outside her mother's house late one night and stared at her bedroom window, as heartsick as a tongue-tied teenager.

What he didn't do, couldn't do, was go to her and say the words he knew she was waiting to hear. Not until he was absolutely certain he meant them. The memory of the last time he'd spoken them was too raw, too vivid in his mind.

But God, he missed her.

Vicki saw her father first, walking toward them with an easy, loose-jointed stride that carried a quiet air of command. He was leading the devil's spawn that had nearly killed him. Though the gash in his temple had healed, the vivid red scar gave testimony to his narrow escape.

"Look, Mommy! Daddy's been riding Lucifer," Vicki exclaimed as she unsnapped her seat belt and reached for the door handle. As she did, Rags came streaking from the back of the house, barking furiously.

"After you say hello to Daddy, carry the box with the favors into the dining room, then come back and help me with the cake." Karen was amazed that she could speak so calmly when her heart was galloping so hard in her chest.

Cassidy had reached the paddock gate, close enough for Karen to see the dark scowl on his face as he called something to Billy, who was standing in the open doorway, a too-thin boy with sandy hair next to him.

Dora's nephew, Ryan, Karen registered after a puzzled moment. Billy had mentioned the boy during one of their frequent conversations. Ryan had taken to Cassidy immediately. But then, everyone did, although she doubted he noticed.

Vicki darted an impatient glance in the direction of her father as Rags raced halfway to the paddock before making a wide circle that brought him back to the Blazer. Tongue lolling, he leaned against Vicki's sturdy legs, waiting, while mother and daughter watched Cassidy lead the limping gelding toward the barn.

The conversation was predictably brief, punctuated on Billy's part by a terse nod now and then, on Cassidy's by a clearly evident impatience. Business concluded, Cassidy ruffled the boy's hair, slapped the horse on the rump and only then turned to walk toward her.

As he drew nearer, she heard the jangle of his spurs over the rustle of the wind in the aspens lining the driveway. His beat-up chaps were caked with almost as much dust as his boots, and his hat had become even more battered than she remembered.

He, himself, looked harried and worn, a man with too much on his mind and shadows of lost battles in his black eyes. As he drew closer, she saw that his jeans were looser than usual. He'd lost weight, a good ten or so pounds by her estimate.

"Hi, Daddy!" Vicki called as she ran toward him, her arms outstretched to fling herself at him. He caught her easily and swung her around as she babbled a mile a minute.

"Happy birthday, peanut," he said when she finally wound down.

"We're early 'cause Mommy wanted to make sure everything was ready before people start showing up."

"Guess four hours early should do it." He held her aloft

in a bear hug for a long moment before setting her on her feet. Only then did his gaze find Karen's. The impact was immediate and powerful. Sexual attraction flashed between them, as hot as ever, and she was suddenly breathless.

"Hello, Karen," he said quietly, but she thought she detected a rough burr of nervousness in his deep voice.

"Hi," she said, without bothering to conceal her pleasure at seeing him.

He took off his hat and brushed an arm over his grimy face, then ironed the flatness out of his unruly hair with impatient fingers. She realized she was staring, and cleared her throat. "Isn't it a beautiful day for a party?"

"Beautiful." His voice came out scratchy and much too harsh. She didn't seem to notice.

Vicki, on the other hand, looked from one parent to the other with a puzzled look. "Mommy and me went to the mall before we came and I got my very own bottle of perfume."

He shifted his gaze and lifted one eyebrow. "I hope you remembered what I told you about the bra."

Vicki gave him a disgusted look before her face brightened again. "Mommy bought herself a birthday present, too. Since she's the one who had me."

"She did, huh?" His gaze came back to hers, a little amused, a little tense. And filled with heat.

"Yeah, only it's not a surprise 'cause she had to buy it for herself."

He took a step closer, and she felt a hot shiver of anticipation shoot down her spine. "That doesn't seem right."

Karen had trouble breathing. He was intimidating and virile and earthy, his authority sitting easily on those big shoulders. With every rise and fall of that massive chest, every tilt of his head or shift of that wide, confident stance, he projected a natural sensuality that wrapped around her with the same thrilling impact as the touch of those wide, work-scarred hands.

"Uh, Vicki, why don't you take the favors inside now while Daddy and I discuss a few details," she said when she found her voice again.

"Okay, and then can I take Domi her carrot?"

"Yes, but try not to get straw in your hair, okay?"

Vicki grimaced as she spun toward the Blazer, with Rags at her heels.

"She's growing up," Karen said as they watched their daughter walk toward the back door, the bulky cardboard box filled with gaily wrapped party favors balanced carefully in front of her.

"Too fast," Cassidy said, a rueful look imprinted on his weather-battered features.

"But inevitably."

Cassidy thought he'd never seen his Kari looking more beautiful. Or more nervous. He took that as a good sign because to take it any other way was unacceptable.

He wanted to bury his hands in the shiny brown hair curling wildly around cheeks that were appealingly pink but concentrated on smoothing the brim of his hat just so with fingers that shook whenever they stilled.

"I, uh, thought we could set up the tables in the side yard, under the aspens. There's good shade there, and the house will keep off most of the dust."

"That's a good idea." She cleared her throat, and he thought it was the sexiest sound he'd ever heard. "I can hang the piñatas from the lower branches—unless you have time to help?"

He felt his stomach jerk. "I have time."

She nodded, her teeth worrying the inside of her lower lip. When he found himself doing the same thing, he damn near groaned in embarrassment.

"I should clean up first," he said, because that was the only coherent thought in his head.

"Don't bother on my account."

He shifted. "I smell like horse sh...dung."

Her mouth softened into the first real smile she'd given him since she arrived, and he allowed himself a cautious moment to hope.

"How are you doing?" she asked softly.

"Okay." He glanced down and concentrated on worrying his hat for a few seconds. "I'm not drinking."

"I know. Billy told me." She'd done her homework and learned that a person with a certain chemistry and a predisposition to alcoholism could become addicted after only a few heavy bouts of drinking, which is exactly what she suspected had happened with Cassidy.

Karen saw his shoulders tense and braced herself. When he simply nodded, she felt the awful band of uncertainty cinching her chest ease up a little. "Has it been rough?"

"Rough enough. I'm handling it." He lifted his gaze to hers. His eyes were still dark, still rimmed with burnished gold around the edges. There was wariness there, and a fierce intelligence that she suspected would push the IQ charts to the limit. And for an instant, tenderness so overpowering it stripped her bare.

"I'm doing what you asked me to, Kari. I'm trying."

Her lips parted in a shaky smile that tested his control more savagely than the craving for alcohol ever could. "I'm glad."

"I can't make any promises yet."

"All right."

He couldn't stand it. He had to touch her. "Kari."

Karen thought she'd never heard so much longing in one simple word. "Yes?" she whispered. The tenderness was back in his eyes, and along with it, a desire so strong it took her breath.

"You never said what you bought. In the mall," he amplified when she frowned.

She let her lips curve just a little. It was going to be okay. She knew it. She felt it. And she wanted to shout with happiness. But all her instincts told her that she had to let Cassidy find his own way in his own time. Still, it wouldn't hurt to give him a little nudge in the right direction. "A nightgown."

His eyes heated. "Yeah?"

"In case there might be an invitation thrown my way to spend the night." She gave him what she hoped was a sublimely innocent expression with just enough sass thrown in to get his thoughts moving in the right direction.

The heat in his eyes took on sizzling edges. "What color?"

"Black."

He swallowed hard. "Silk?" His voice had a strangled quality that made her hum inside.

"Some silk. Mostly lace."

His mouth twitched. "Don't say any more. I'd hate to embarrass both of us in front of the hands."

"Oh, please don't hesitate on my account."

He looked startled and just a little scared. "You said you wouldn't come to me until..." He broke off, his gaze boring into hers.

"I changed my mind."

Cassidy felt a door slam shut almost before he'd gotten used to having it open even a sliver. He'd come so close. So damned close to believing that she loved him in spite of all his emotional baggage. He should have known better.

Very slowly he straightened his shoulders. He would get through this, he realized with a grim certainty. And without diving back into a bottle. But it was going to be so damn hard—standing next to her at the important milestones of their daughter's life. Seeing her smile, smelling her perfume, hearing the music of her laugh. Knowing just how special she is. How beautiful inside and out.

And that she'd once been his.

Karen had been enjoying the play of emotion over his face, the first tentative softening of a playful smile, the crinkle of sexual amusement in his eyes. The first cautious attempt at trust. And her heart had begun to soar.

Then suddenly, in the literal blink of an eye, it was gone. Wiped clean. She felt a chill, a shiver of fear as he took his time resettling his hat, angling the brim so that it hid his eyes. And then it hit her. He'd misunderstood her meaning when she'd told her she'd changed her mind. He'd thought she was turning away from him, rejecting him. And why not? It was exactly what she would have expected if she'd lived as he'd had to live.

Pride fairly crackled from him as he turned his gaze toward the house.

She felt a rush of anger at the thoughtless parents who'd failed him, followed by a deep tenderness for a scarred, wounded man who'd made himself into the kind of son any parents would be proud to claim.

"Stop looking so impatient, and look at me."

That got his attention.

"What?"

"I swear, Cassidy Sloane, if you walk away from me while I'm still in the middle of seducing you, I'm going to strangle you with the aforementioned black nightie and then you'll never get to see how stunning it looks on me."

His head came up with a surge of power and outrage and his eyes snapped a savage challenge. "What the hell are you talking about?"

It wasn't fair, blackmailing him with French silk and sex, but she would worry about that later.

"At the moment, I'm referring to my scheme to entice you into bed as soon as we can decently send our guests on their way, including our daughter, by the way, who is going to be taken to the circus by her doting grandparents."

His gaze narrowed, but there was a mesmerizing glint flickering in the obsidian depths. "Scheme?" he repeated, as if testing the meaning.

"Well, more like a scenario. I brought extra whipped cream."

"Whipped cream?" He stared at her warily as if he was forty spaces behind her and racing to catch up.

"Hmm. All week I've had this almost irresistible urge for whipped cream." She took a step closer and lifted her hand toward his face. He jerked but stayed rooted, his strong legs braced squarely and his head high. "You have the most incredible mouth." Fighting a sudden attack of acute vulnerability herself, she gave in to an urge to trace that hard mouth with her fingertips.

"Haven't you ever wondered how skin would taste when it was covered with whipped cream?"

He made a strangled sound deep in his throat, and his hand shot up to manacle her wrists with hard, callused fingers.

"Are you trying to make me beg, Kari? Is that what this is all about?" His eyes glittered dangerously, but now that she saw him with different eyes, she was able to discern the terrible hunger buried beneath the white hot fury. The hunger of a caged prisoner who's been shut away in the dark for so many years he was afraid to trust the sunshine pouring through a hole blasted into the side of his cell.

"Cassidy, I am trying to seduce you, but you're being deliberately obtuse, and—"

"Obtuse?"

"Oh, hell," she muttered before fisting her hand in his hair to steady herself as she arched into him and covered his mouth with hers.

He stood like a statue for what seemed like forever, then he groaned and dragged her against his hard chest. His mouth turned hot and hungry, and his arms were velvet-covered steel. As she molded her body to his, she could almost feel prison walls crumbling as a hard shudder ran through him.

Long moments later, Cassidy tore his mouth from hers, pulled her arms from his neck and stood looking down at her. "Run that by me again," he demanded, every inch the powerful rancher. "Slowly this time."

Karen was giddy with happiness, which was playing hell with her vaunted detachment. "Which part? The black lace nightie or the whipped cream?"

His mouth twitched, but the taut lines of his face still radiated tension that was painful to see. "The part where you told me you changed your mind about loving me."

A warning bell set up a clamor in her mind, and she suspected he would have to accept her love in manageable bits, testing each one before he was ready for the next. "I said no such thing. Of course I love you. I was referring to that silly pronouncement I made about your having to come to me." She lifted her hand again, until her fingers were flat against his hard cheek. "I know you already love me, and since it's taking you an impossibly long time to realize it, I decided to help you."

His throat worked. "Just like that?"

"I can make it a lot rougher on you, if that would make you feel better."

"Rougher how?" he asked carefully. Warily.

"Well, in the lingerie store, they had this collection of imported...toys. And I remember watching you showing Billy how to use that old bullwhip you found in the loft. It was a hot day and you had your shirt off. I loved the way your muscles rippled, so—"

"God help me, you bought a whip?" He sounded outraged and adorably helpless. Lord but she was going to love teaching him to laugh.

"Just a little one, and the lashes are velvet. They came in a variety of colors, but according to my mother, black goes with everything."

He blinked. His eyes narrowed, then filled with something fierce and hot and intimate. And yet, there were still troubling shadows lurking in the depths.

"Is this the way it's going to be with us from now on, Kari? A series of one-night stands?"

Her happiness wobbled. "I'm not interested in an affair with you or anyone else," she said quietly.

"Then what's this about?"

"Commitment. Marriage." She managed a smile. "Starting over."

He drew a breath. "And medicine?"

"Is a part of me, just as the ranch is a part of you." She hesitated, then realized that the next few minutes would determine if she and Cassidy had a future together or not. "I've done a lot of thinking, Cass. About what's important and what's not. I want us to be together more than just about anything else I can think of. I can compromise and I can bend. Instead of private practice, I can join one of the managed care groups, where the hours are far more normal. Other than a rotating on-call schedule, I'd be home at night and most weekends."

"Would you be happy in that kind of situation? After all the hard work you've put in."

She nodded. "What would make me unhappy is giving up medicine entirely."

His gaze studied her, an unreadable expression in his golden brown eyes. "In other words, if I want you, I have to share your...love with your work?"

His voice was too quiet, too controlled. Her hopes plummeted. Why hadn't she waited? Why did she have to push him now, when he'd obviously been trying so hard to change?

"Yes, just as I accept your love of this ranch and the work you do."

He frowned, then dropped his gaze. "I've been a real ass, haven't I?"

"At times, yes."

His head shot up, and he gave her a startled look that almost instantly turned sheepish. "Guess this means you haven't completely given up on me, huh?"

She felt the fear gripping her heart loosen its hold. "Not a chance, cowboy."

Something stark and scary rose in his eyes. "I can't promise not to backslide."

"I can't promise not to yell at you if you do."

His shoulders rose and fell as he dragged in air. "But you won't walk out, right? Not even if I let you down sometimes?"

The insecurity radiating from him nearly broke her heart. "Trust me, Cassidy Sloane, if I haul all my belongings and a ton of Vicki's things all the way back here, I'm never leaving again."

His mouth slanted a little. "No matter what?"

"No matter what."

"Some folks might consider that a little crazy."

"Some folks don't know a good thing when they see one."

The smile started in the deepest darkness of his eyes. And then he grinned, a lopsided, boyishly irresistible, unabashed smile that curled her toes. "What am I going to do with you, Dr. Sloane?" he asked in a thick voice.

She smiled. "Love me?"

When his face stilled, and the smile drained from those

fathomless eyes, she felt a moment of stark panic. "Just a little to start with," she hastened to amend, keeping her tone light.

His jaw worked. "What the hell," he said gruffly. "Let's go for the whole thing."

He bent his head, wrapped those big arms around her and kissed her senseless. A long time later her husband lifted his mouth from hers. "I do, you know," he said in a husky voice. "Love you."

"And I love you."

She heard a sound then, a shout. A chorus of shouts as rowdy and raucous as the cheering around the corral on the day Cassidy and Lucifer had fought to a draw. Cassidy twisted around, braced for a fight. Deciding it was unseemly for a doctor to get involved in a brawl, Karen contented herself with peeking over his broad shoulder.

They had gathered quite a crowd. Every one of the hands, and Vicki, front and center next to her mother and Frank. Money was changing hands, and everyone was grinning.

"Oh, dear," she said, trying desperately not to laugh at the look on Cassidy's face. "Don't spoil their fun," she said, her lips twitching.

"What the hell, wife. If they want a show, let's give 'em one to remember." As he bent his head, Cassidy Sloane finally realized that, in spite of the ten years he'd lived on this place he loved so much, he was finally coming home.

*   *   *   *   *

continues with

YOU MUST REMEMBER THIS

by Marilyn Pappano
available June 1998

Here's an exciting preview...

You Must Remember This

June 6th

The emergency room was bustling, but the man walked past all the waiting patients to the broad hallway, where a harried clerk stopped him. "Can I help you?"

He looked blankly at her. Did he need help? The crack he'd taken had left him a little dazed, and the bright lights in the hall made the ache in his head throb. When he closed his eyes to block them, he swayed unsteadily. The woman took hold of his arm. "Sit down over here. Did you hit your head?"

He sank into the chair and realized how good it felt to sit. It had been a long walk from the banged-up car to the hospital. The clerk crouched in front of him, pen poised over clipboard. "What's your name?"

He opened his mouth, but nothing came out. *Nothing*. In an instant, panic surged through him. It was a simple question, the simplest question in the whole world. What was his name? It was...

Still nothing.

When he reached out, his hand trembled. When his fingers made contact with the clerk's hand, they wrapped tightly around it. She tried to pull free, but he didn't let go. Instead, he leaned closer, staring fearfully, desperately, into her face. "I don't know... I don't..."

Oh, God, he couldn't remember.

"Should I list him as John Doe?"

He lay on his back, only half listening to the conversation

of the medical staff around him. He had been poked and prodded, X-rayed and interrogated. His clothes had been searched for identification, but none was found. His wallet—if he'd had one—was gone. His driver's license was gone. His identity was gone.

On the up side, so was his headache.

"He doesn't look like a John to me. I think we should call him Martin—"

The other female voice joined in. "Smith. Perfect. He's a character on the soap opera we watch. He's tall, blond, blue-eyed—"

One of the women gave him a furtive glance, then lowered her voice. "A hunk."

That was good, wasn't it? It meant he didn't look half as bad as he felt—and he felt pretty damn bad. He was scared.

Finally, the doctor spoke to him. "Do you want to be Martin Smith?"

No. He wanted to be— He wanted to be whoever the hell he really was. But he could be someone he wasn't. He knew how to do that. So he nodded. Sooner or later, he would find out who he was.

Wouldn't he?

"All right, Mr. Smith. You can get up now. We're just about finished."

He sat up on the examination table so that he was facing the mirror. He combed his fingers through his hair, then touched his face. The mirror image did the same.

He was looking at himself.

He was looking at a stranger.

"Mr. Smith? Will you come with us?"

If the police officer hadn't spoken the name practically in his ear, he wouldn't have responded. How quickly he'd forgotten the soap opera hunk. Forgetting could be a fatal error, one he rarely made.

As he left the waiting room with the two officers, he smiled the faintest of smiles. This time, he'd forgotten the biggest, most important, most vital thing of all.

He'd forgotten himself.

The Following April

Juliet Crandall sat at her computer, her attention about fifty feet away, she estimated, at a table in the library's reference section. The man seated there was called Martin Smith, but no one knew who he really was, he least of all. He was a regular at the library, poring over anything that might jog his memory. Though Juliet had been in town only a few weeks, she'd learned from library gossip that he'd been searching for ten months for some clue to his identity, and for ten months, he'd come up empty-handed. The police had taken his fingerprints, but they'd gotten a not-on-file response. So he wasn't a cop or a criminal. Just an average citizen, like a few hundred million other people in the country.

Not. Martin Smith, whoever he was, was definitely not like other ordinary, everyday citizens. He was the stuff fantasies—hers at least—were made of. Broad-shouldered, lean-hipped and long-legged. Carelessly tossed blond hair and eyes of stunning blue that actors and models paid money to achieve with contacts. Skin of creamy gold, as if he'd just finished a month on a tropical beach, instead of a winter of snow and ice in the Rocky Mountains. He was enough to distract even the most dedicated computer archivist from her work.

"Excuse me."

For a moment, Juliet didn't respond to the quiet interruption. When she finally looked up, she wished she hadn't. Her face grew warm, her mouth went dry, and her fingers went limp on the keyboard.

"I'm Martin Smith." His mouth twisted in what might have been meant as a smile but was actually a grimace. Her palm was probably sweaty, but it would be too noticeable if she took the time to wipe it on her dress so she shook the hand he offered, then quickly drew back.

Without waiting for an invitation—one she never would have thought of offering—he sat in the only chair in the room. "I don't know if you've heard about me, but the woman who used to have your job said you were good with computers. Can you help me?''

Not ten minutes ago, she'd wondered why he'd never sought her help. Now that he had, she wished he hadn't. Helping him meant spending time with him, and while that was certainly an appealing prospect on one level…on another, it was terrifying. She didn't do well one-on-one, especially with someone as handsome, intense and fantasy-quality male as Martin Smith. *But there was no way Juliet could not help him. And there was no way she could stop her heart from doing the funny things it did when he smiled. But if she discovered who Martin Smith really was…would she have enough time to make him discover her?*

The World's Most Eligible Bachelors are about to be named! And Silhouette Books brings them to you in an all-new, original series....

World's Most
Eligible Bachelors

Twelve of the sexiest, most sought-after men share every intimate detail of their lives in twelve never-before-published novels by the genre's top authors.

Don't miss these unforgettable stories by:

Dixie Browning

Marie Ferrarella

Jackie Merritt

Tracy Sinclair

BJ James

RACHEL LEE   Suzanne Carey

Gina Wilkins

VICTORIA PADE

MAGGIE SHAYNE   *Anne McAllister*

Susan Mallery

Look for one new book each month in the **World's Most Eligible Bachelors** series beginning September 1998 from Silhouette Books.

V™ *Silhouette*®

Available at your favorite retail outlet.

Take 2 bestselling love stories FREE

Plus get a FREE surprise gift!

Special Limited-Time Offer

Mail to Silhouette Reader Service™

3010 Walden Avenue
P.O. Box 1867
Buffalo, N.Y. 14240-1867

YES! Please send me 2 free Silhouette Intimate Moments® novels and my free surprise gift. Then send me 6 brand-new novels every month, which I will receive months before they appear in bookstores. Bill me at the low price of $3.57 each plus 25¢ delivery and applicable sales tax, if any.* That's the complete price, and a saving of over 10% off the cover prices—quite a bargain! I understand that accepting the books and gift places me under no obligation ever to buy any books. I can always return a shipment and cancel at any time. Even if I never buy another book from Silhouette, the 2 free books and the surprise gift are mine to keep forever.

245 SEN CH7Y

Name	(PLEASE PRINT)	
Address	Apt. No.	
City	State	Zip

This offer is limited to one order per household and not valid to present Silhouette Intimate Moments® subscribers. *Terms and prices are subject to change without notice. Sales tax applicable in N.Y.

UIM-98

©1990 Harlequin Enterprises Limited

Sizzling, Sexy, Sun-drenched...

SUMMER SENSATIONS

Three short stories by *New York Times* bestselling authors will heat up your summer!

LINDA HOWARD
LINDA LAEL MILLER
HEATHER GRAHAM POZZESSERE

Experience the passion today!

Available at your favorite retail outlet.

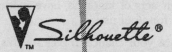

Silhouette®

Look us up on-line at: http://www.romance.net

PSUNSEN

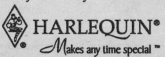

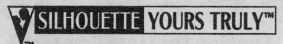

When tomorrow is uncertain, the only sure thing is love... **36 HOURS**

If you missed any 36 Hours titles, then order now and discover how, for the residents of Grand Springs, Colorado, the storm-induced blackout was just the *beginning!*

#65006	**LIGHTNING STRIKES** by Mary Lynn Baxter	$4.50 U.S.☐ $4.99 CAN.☐
#65007	**STRANGE BEDFELLOWS** by Kasey Michaels	$4.50 U.S.☐ $4.99 CAN.☐
#65008	**OOH BABY, BABY** by Diana Whitney	$4.50 U.S.☐ $4.99 CAN.☐
#65009	**FOR HER EYES ONLY** by Sharon Sala	$4.50 U.S.☐ $4.99 CAN.☐
#65010	**CINDERELLA STORY** by Elizabeth August	$4.50 U.S.☐ $4.99 CAN.☐
#65011	**FATHER AND CHILD REUNION** by Christine Flynn	$4.50 U.S.☐ $4.99 CAN.☐
#65012	**THE RANCHER AND THE RUNAWAY BRIDE** by Susan Mallery	$4.50 U.S.☐ $4.99 CAN.☐
#65013	**MARRIAGE BY CONTRACT** by Sandra Steffen	$4.50 U.S.☐ $4.99 CAN.☐
#65014	**PARTNERS IN CRIME** by Alicia Scott	$4.50 U.S.☐ $4.99 CAN.☐
#65015	**NINE MONTHS** by Beverly Barton	$4.50 U.S.☐ $4.99 CAN.☐

(quantities may be limited on some titles)

TOTAL AMOUNT	$
POSTAGE & HANDLING	$
($1.00 for one book, 50¢ for each additional)	
APPLICABLE TAXES*	$ _____
TOTAL PAYABLE	$ _____
(check or money order—please do not send cash)	

To order, complete this form and send it, along with a check or money order for the total above, payable to Silhouette Books, to: **In the U.S.**: 3010 Walden Avenue, P.O. Box 9077, Buffalo, NY 14269-9077; **In Canada**: P.O. Box 636, Fort Erie, Ontario, L2A 5X3.

Name: _____

Address: _____ City: _____

State/Prov.: _____ Zip/Postal Code: _____

*New York residents remit applicable sales taxes.
 Canadian residents remit applicable GST and provincial taxes.

Silhouette®

Look us up on-line at: http://www.romance.net

36BACK10

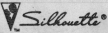